MW01222225

Abraham Lincoln, a Novel Life

Abraham Lincoln, a Novel Life

BY

TONY WOLK

Ooligan Press
Portland State University
Portland, Oregon

Illustrations by Jessica Wolk-Stanley

Ooligan Press
Center for Excellence in Writing
Department of English
Portland State University
P.O. Box 751
Portland, OR 97207-0751

Library of Congress Cataloging-in-Publication Data

Wolk, Tony, 1935-
Abraham Lincoln, a novel life / Tony Wolk.
p. cm.
Includes bibliographical references.
ISBN 1-932010-00-9
1. Lincoln, Abraham, 1809-1865--Fiction. 2. Presidents--United
States--Fiction. 3. Evanston (Ill.)--Fiction. 4. Time
travel--Fiction. I. Title.
PS3623.O59 A27 2004
813'.6--dc22
2003026912

Printed in the United States of America

For Libby Solomon,
friend and fellow writer

Contents

Foreword

I CAME TO Abraham Lincoln by chance, twice. The first time in a frenzy back in 1953 when I needed an informal picture of myself for my high school yearbook and at the last moment opened a nearby American history text, flipped to a photograph of a beardless Lincoln in three-quarter profile, and said, "Here!"

Curious. A photograph of Lincoln that looks nothing like I did then. But now, looking at that image of Lincoln I see myself—the same eyebrows, lips, mouth, dark hair, pensive expression. Since then we've both gone on to grow beards, pass for wise. We relish the same pithy utterances: *If you can't be honest as a lawyer, be honest in some other profession.*

Forty years later I returned to Abraham Lincoln, chancing on a time-worn volume on a shelf of books across a room at Portland State University. Curiosity took me by the hand and led me to the book: *The Complete Works of Abraham Lincoln*, Volume X, edited by John Hay and John Nicolay, Lincoln's two young secretaries when he took office in 1861. The edition was from 1894, my father's birth year.

The *Works* proper begins with a brief "Note to Secretary Stanton" from February 8, 1864. And last is a short telegram dated February 4, 1865, in Lincoln's hand, written at the Telegraph Office of the War Department, a short stroll from the Executive Mansion:

> *Officer in command at Johnson's Island, Ohio:*
> *Parole Lieutenant John A. Stephens, prisoner of war, to report*

to me in person, and send him to me. It is in persuance of an
arrangement I made yesterday with his uncle, Hon. A. H.
Stephens. Acknowledge receipt.

A. Lincoln

On that fateful day, I scanned the volume, and I was swept away by a mental portrait of a president who tends to his daily business with his own eyes and hands. Who writes a "cordial thanks" to Harvey Williams by way of John F. Griggs for the "fine specimen of the Mackinaw Trout," or composes a speech to deliver in Baltimore at the Sanitary Fair (the forerunner of the Red Cross), noting how the "sheep and the wolf are not agreed upon a definition of the word *liberty*, . . . especially as the sheep was a black one." That same speech tells of a "painful rumor—true, I fear . . . of the massacre by the rebel forces at Fort Pillow, in the west end of Tennessee, on the Mississippi River, of some three hundred colored soldiers and white officers, who had just been overpowered by their assailants." A footnote adds that "President Lincoln did not use any retaliatory measures." Ten days later he jots a telegram to his wife, presently in New York, asking her to "tell Tad the goats and father are very well, especially the goats." All this in the midst of a cataclysmic war.

I didn't guess that day that I had taken the first steps along a road that brings me to this moment ten years later, writing a foreword to my novel, *Abraham Lincoln, a Novel Life*. I knew nothing that day of the context of the telegram to the commanding officer at Johnson's Island. I didn't know it was the sole fruit of the Hampton Roads Peace Conference that Lincoln had returned from the day before. I had never heard of A[lexander] H. Stephens, the Vice-President of the Confederacy and an old friend of Lincoln's from his single term in office in Congress in the 1840s.

It's as though a sudden tide from the mid–nineteenth century had carried me far out to sea, and by the time I made it back to shore I was transformed. Had I met the Sirens and become one with them? I hope so. What I do know is that I found myself transporting Abraham Lincoln from that moment in early February, having just penned that telegram to Johnson's Island, to Easter weekend, 1955.

I found myself with Abraham Lincoln on Howard Street on the North Side of Chicago as he is dislodged from time, bewildered, but ever resourceful. He finds a copper coin that bears his image and puts it in his pocket. And so the story unfolds, for writer and for reader.

That's one version of the launching of my story. Another involves a 1950s pulp science fiction magazine called *Imagination*, sitting atop that same volume of Lincoln's *Works*. And from that proximity, the man sprung to life, like Athena from the head of Zeus—if you'll pardon a grandiose simile.

I found as I read biographies by the dozen what Abraham Lincoln was like, or seemed to be like, to writers such as Ida Tarbell, Emil Ludwig, Oscar Lewis, Stephen Oates, James McPherson, and on and on. By rights, Lincoln should have been a psychic wreck, given the catastrophic war he had hoped to avert, the death of his beloved son Willie, his wife Mary's depression. Lord Charnwood, whose *Abraham Lincoln* I read only after my own story was told, captures the spirit of Lincoln as I was coming to regard him: "The time of his severest trial cannot have been the saddest time of Lincoln's life. It must have been a cause not of added depression but of added strength."

Not that I understood (or pretend to understand) whose life was in my hands. I had stumbled into the White House in February of 1865. To paraphrase Hamlet, *the interim was mine*. And so I wrote for Abraham Lincoln a day outside the life we know—Easter Sunday, 1955. What we came to that day, Lincoln and I, surprised us both. And the day ending, there were more surprises, the kind of surprises every writer faces, narrowing choices, closing doors, finding ways through, recovering balance, writing on, till a last word writes itself, and you find yourself sitting there, pensive, your hands pressed together, fingers to your lips, in wonder at the journey just ended.

TONY WOLK
Portland, Oregon
July 2003

GUIDERIUS   Peace, peace, see further: he eyes us not, forbear;
            Creatures may be alike: were't he, I am sure
            He would have spoke to us.
BELARIUS   But we see him dead.

WILLIAM SHAKESPEARE
Cymbeline

If we believe in him, all is well.

JORGE LUIS BORGES
This Craft of Verse

◆ I ◆

History

10 April 1955

IT WAS WELL PAST midnight. He stood on the sidewalk, facing north. Far ahead lay Canada and the Pole. More of a walk than he had in mind when insomnia roused him from his bed. Considerably to the west, the Father of Waters ran south, the great Mississippi. Lake Michigan was just a few blocks to the east. He pictured the lake, a dark expanse, immense. It was so easy to forget that the lake had a northern flow, then on to the other lakes (Huron, Erie, Ontario), the St. Lawrence, and finally the Atlantic. All of which situated him in the middle, in the thick of things. He was reminded of the twin poles, where the next step allows for but one direction: either all south or all north.

He turned, heading back toward the center of town and the hotel. He got into his stride, but what was his hurry? The Orrington was hardly more than half a mile. He shortened his stride, slowed his pace. The houses, what he could make of them under the street-lights, were not as surprising as the neatly paved streets and side-walks. Prosperous times. He hadn't thought to return to Illinois, not this soon, if ever. And where was Mary? Far off in muddy Washington City?

Mary hated his dreams, his premonitions. No, she hated the telling. He should never have told her he had dreamed of his death: the President upon the bier, yet himself watching all the commotion, the wailing. "The President has been killed by an assassin," they said.

Would he return to those dreams, to that life? He imagined himself saying, *But Mary, this was not a dream. It was not a dream.*

Though that's exactly what he had thought at first: another dream. But the firmness of the ground, the totality of landscape, the wearing on of time, the very wondering whether it was a dream, all had led him to the opposite conclusion: it was real. Suddenly, there he was, on Howard Street, reeling, as if he were perched on the edge of a cliff, peering over. And when he'd recovered his balance he was standing before a cobbler's window, the gold letters arcing across the glass:

J. BROWNE

SHOEMAKER

Then wandering along the brightly lit street, ducking into a tavern and watching a few minutes' worth of what they termed a television, and finally the long walk up to Evanston. Don't ask why he chose north. As time wore on, the clearer it all was. Yet it was so like a dream. Deep inside he knew that before long it would end and he would return. But first he had to come to the end. As with so many other moments of his life, he would let time tell its strange and surprising story. Again Mary came to mind. She would like their television; it would while away the time, take her mind from the woe.

Up ahead was the hotel, a tall shadow amid lesser ones, and the end of his midnight ramble. It wasn't much more than an hour ago that he had come awake in the darkness of the hotel room, trying to make sense of the steps that had led to his lying on a bed in the next century. He had dressed, descended, said "Can't sleep" to the night clerk, and gone investigating. This present, he realized, no longer seemed so far beyond his own time. The rows of automobiles parked on both sides of the street were becoming commonplace, as were the electric streetlights, and the wires strung overhead, for still more electricity, and for their telephones. A telephone would be handy on a stormy night—no need to walk over to the War Department to read dispatches. He had yet to see an airplane, just a picture in a magazine entitled *Life*. A good title, he thought, if broad. A magazine with a date, 1955.

It's not that he knew with a certainty that this interlude would come to an end. And maybe "end" wasn't the right word. Like a dream this—this interruption, this journey, this lesson—it was all middle, without a frame. He had found himself here; he would find himself back. There were no doorways. It was like a river flowing. Perhaps in his own time there had been no disruption, no one wondering where he had wandered off to. He had a picture in his mind of everyone frozen, a whole host of folk in mid-stride, yawning, or scratching, or halfway through a gesture. Aleck Stephens, Nicolay and John Hay, and Stanton, even Lee, sword by his side, and Traveller, saddled and alert. All caught in a web, suspended in time.

There was another picture, which he hated the thought of, where the clock had never stopped. Where everything he had ever known was gone, was dead. Where only the newborn could be alive today, and in her nineties. He had never had a daughter. His sons were gone, all gone. He closed his eyes to clear away the image of gray stones in a cemetery, weathered, canted, overgrown with weeds. Forgotten.

Such a quiet time of night.

He needed to get on back. As it was, he never got enough sleep. He should watch out that he didn't get caught short. Folks back home would observe how fatigued the President looked and think they knew the reason.

Yes, sleep, as though time and its hours were ordinary. Tonight should be easy enough, but what about tomorrow? What if he were still left to his own devices? There should be ways to raise a little money, and he had never shirked an honest day's work. In his mind he started a list:

Item: *Antique currency from wallet and pocketful of odd change. Value to collectors: upward of $20.*
Item: *Penknife of former president of the United States. Problem: difficulty of proof. Value: questionable.*
Item: *Signature of said president, on document of your choice. Problem: authentic ink and paper. Value: doubtful.*

All told, slim pickings. He had hoped for richer fare. What a fool. Why did it have to be himself, Abraham Lincoln, marooned in this situation? Let Greeley or Sumner—the Harvard boys—go traveling. Let them have the exercise of staying afloat with nothing but their wits to sustain them. Greeley, though, would have his share of problems—what would he do without the buttress of his mighty *New York Tribune* to shore him up? No, not the sturdiest fellow when it came to standing on his own two feet without a preconception to guide him. Mr. Horace had known that a country boy from Illinois would be in over his flaggy ears within half a day, flamboozled by the city-slickers. That was how Greeley saw him, pants too short, coat too tight, handy in the fields and a blockhead indoors. A rube. One step up from a Plugugly.

The hotel. He stepped into the quarter-circle of the rotating door, traversed the 180 degrees, and entered the lobby of the Orrington. The night clerk looked up from his magazine, nodded, and returned to his reading.

He entered an open elevator and pushed the button for the seventh floor. Back home New York already had an elevator or two, and after the war they would be everywhere. Progress. The elevator doors closed. The door to his room opened, then closed. He set the key on the dresser alongside the penny from Howard Street. He had picked the coin up from the curb, and when he turned it over he saw a portrait of himself. An artifact. He could imagine himself back at the Executive Mansion, bleary-eyed, presenting his coin to John Hay. And the story unfolding. Lord knows what it would do to Mr. Stanton.

He took up the coin. The likeness was a fair one. 1955. Brand new. An infant, not even a toddler. He put it in his pocket. No reason it shouldn't make the traverse home, when the time came. Hadn't all else come the other direction?

Enough cogitating. He should try to get back to sleep. His jacket he hung in the closet; he folded his pants across the seat of the chair, hung his shirt and tie over the back, removed his shoes and stockings, attended to necessity, then turned back the linens and stretched out his long, weary shanks. It felt good, the blood circulating, gravity turned sideways.

He lay there, eyes closed. Daylight was a couple of hours away. He had yet to see the sun in this new world. When he had arrived it was barely evening. Maybe that would be the charm, a sunrise. And like the button that triggered the elevator doors, the ascent of one orb, and the descent of the other behind its dark horizon, would catapult Abraham Lincoln back to his native time.

He didn't much like the waiting. It invited passivity, caution. General McClellan wouldn't mind it. He could use the time to plan, to devise strategy, to parade his soldiers in starched uniforms, to order more supplies. Anything but go forward.

Lincoln rolled onto his side, one arm under the cool pillow. He didn't like the waiting. He needed to think over the evening, but not tonight. It was time to sleep, to dream.

LINCOLN GLANCED ONE MORE TIME at the menu. "I'll have the flapjacks, a double order while you're at it." It was a different waitress from last night when he had ordered the Hamburg steak. She had already poured him a cup of coffee. "And sausages," he added.

"Anything else?" she asked. "Juice or melon?"

"Juice," he said. "Orange juice. Large, if you please." Since the war, oranges had been scarce, a rare treat to take along on hospital visits. The waitress nodded, noted his request on her pad, then headed for the kitchen.

He had the restaurant nearly to himself. A couple of men sat with their coffee, absorbed with their newspapers. It was fairly early, just after seven o'clock according to the big round clock on the wall. It was a clear day, and the sun was on its way across the heavens. He remembered thinking as he fell asleep that quite possibly he would wake up in his own bed and then he wouldn't be sure whether or not it had been a dream. But waking into this other present he had to laugh at how forgetful the mind is. He hadn't begun this journey in his sleep. He had been sitting at his desk, working on a proposal to Congress that would bring all hostilities to a halt on or before the first day of April next. In exchange for abandoning their resistance to the national authority and extinguishing their peculiar institution of slavery, the Rebel States would be paid what amounted to the costs of propagating the war for two hundred days, or four hundred million dollars, to be distributed pro rata on their respective slave populations. He was to present the proposal for peace to his Cabinet come evening. They would do their best to scotch it. He knew that like the palm of his hand. Still, he must try. To that moment he assumed he would return, himself at his desk, pen in hand. And so, when he had dressed, he made sure the copper penny was in his pocket, the coin with his face on its own face. To take home as proof. It would be enough. The magazine, *Life*, he could leave behind, wouldn't want to tote that everywhere. Of course he could have stuffed his pockets with a dozen oddments from this leap forward: the postcard with the picture of the hotel from the desk drawer, the small cake of Ivory soap wrapped in two sheets of paper, any page from a newspaper, matches, which didn't appear to come in boxes anymore, the paper napkin lying across his knees.

Pretty soon he would have to put his mind to devising a scheme for getting through the day. It might truly come down to selling his money. Such a funny notion, and very un-tycoonish. It seemed so long ago that young Hay had thought of him as the "Tycoon." When things were just heating up, none of them foreseeing the arduous road ahead. *Had we foreseen the slaughter, who would have ventured ahead?* he wondered. Better to live in the shadow of the present. War is monstrous enough as is, but to walk through that blighted wood by choice—

"More coffee?" The steaming glass pitcher was poised for his answer.

"Please. Sorry there," he said. "Guess I was in another world," and with a nod and a smile she was on her way.

So strange to have left that dark world behind, knowing that so much of the country lies smoldering, Sherman still on the march, the wounds still fresh, and blood still flowing. Yet for the moment he was on a distant shore; he had crossed the river of time.

His platter of flapjacks arrived. He was alive and hungry. He spread butter between the pancakes, poured a spiral of maple syrup on top, picked up his knife and fork and cut himself a golden, steaming wedge. Strange how his appetite had come alive in this new world.

HE HADN'T REALIZED IT WAS Easter Sunday. Folk were in their Easter best, though it was hard to judge where best started and stopped here. He smiled and nodded at the friendly salutation of "Fine Easter morning." Back in his time, Easter was two months away. He surveyed his own clothing—passable, thanks most of all to this new-fangled jacket built on the model of John Hay's. At home he lacked the courage to wear it outdoors for fear of being laughed at.

He couldn't regret the choice to walk along the lake after breakfast. He had been up here a few years ago, the year he was elected. The university was in its infancy, a couple of buildings with trees surrounding them, and all the students were men. Now women too were welcome in the halls of learning. He had liked that, the equality. If he were young, he would have loved the chance to study at such a university, in peace and quiet. He could do it now, as long as they'd let him stay at the hotel. But no, before long, they'd be asking questions. He'd soon need a place to live, assuming they didn't come for him, his escort back to the past. He pictured half a dozen shadowy men, who, out of nowhere, would surround him, and whisk him back into the other world of gaslights, horses, buggies—and a bleeding nation. But it wouldn't happen that way; he didn't expect any warning, a chance to say farewell, to choose.

He looked across the lake. With the sun low and the breeze catching the tips of the waves, it looked like tiny candles sparkling. It was nearly ten o'clock. Despite its being a holiday, a few students were out and about, books in hand. Several were milling about the entrance to a large brick building—in the windows he could see shelf after shelf of books. The library.

What if he went inside and looked himself up? Found out why he was on the penny, why the automobiles said "Land of Lincoln" on their number plaques, found out what had happened—found out what was going to happen? And could he change it?

You've never lived in ignorance before, he said to himself. *And no reason to now.* He turned his back to the shimmering lake and headed for the large brass doors. A man who reminded him of Nicolay (though no one had a beard and only a few had mustaches anymore) held the door open for him. "Good morning," they said to each other. Lincoln stood there, not going in—preferred not to be served, to be waited on. He wanted to be like everyone else. But this man didn't know he was the president; and he wasn't, not now. "Thank you," Lincoln said finally, leading the way inside.

The man nodded. He was stoop-shouldered, with sandy-colored hair and thick glasses. "Easter morning, and here we are at the library," he said.

"And the lords have arisen and gone forth to their books," Lincoln intoned. "Pardon the sacrilege, friend."

The man smiled, his eyes alight. "Sam Holmberg, English Department," he said, holding out his hand.

Lincoln took it, gave it a shake. "John Thomas," he said, surprising himself. An old joke, but no sign of anything untoward in Holmberg's eyes. "Department of Bad Taste, if you're looking for a tag."

"It's all one to me," said Holmberg. "A poor and pitiful lot we are, not worth the defense, to paraphrase Sidney. In a word, I'm no Christian."

"Can't say that I'm much of a churchman myself. It may be the long sitting I don't much cotton to. I'd sooner be up and about, traveling the circuit with my law partners. Or paying a visit to the printed page." Sure as sure, he was going to get himself in a peck of trouble by talking too much in this world.

Holmberg nodded thoughtfully. "Me, I'm at a hateful stage of my work," he said, his hand taking in the shelves of books and the cases of small file drawers. "All the people who say Shakespeare wasn't Shakespeare. Can you imagine? But I can't ignore it. It goes with the territory."

"You're working on Shakespeare?" Lincoln asked.

"Yes, a book on his biographers; and alas, that includes the host who say he wasn't himself. It goes back to a crazy lady named Bacon,

Delia Bacon, who thought she was a descendent of Francis Bacon, and it wasn't enough for her that Bacon wrote what he wrote. In her twisted mind, Shakespeare hadn't had the requisite training—Oxford. And his blood wasn't historic enough. She wanted to dig Shakespeare out of his grave, was sure there'd be letters about the true author of *Hamlet* and the *King Henries*."

"Never would've occurred to me, that a man wouldn't be himself. Though I've met with that prejudice more than once or thrice in my day. Folks take me lightly with this western accent—to their chagrin I might add. And Mr. Frederick Douglass is welcome at my house any day of the week."

Again Holmberg from English nodded. "Frederick Douglass," he said. "I'd welcome him myself," and then silence fell between them.

"Well," said Lincoln, "I'll let you get on with your demonstration that we are who we are. Which is precisely what I'm here for"—he couldn't keep his words from leading him on. "Somewhere, among this ocean of volumes, they're telling my story, and I would like to know what it tells. It's been a pleasure, Professor Holmberg," and this time it was Lincoln extending his hand.

WHERE SHOULD HE BEGIN? The nudge that had brought him this far was flagging. Had ever a person faced such a choice? He closed his eyes and willed his legs to take a step forward, and then another. His destination was the small-drawered oak filing cabinets in the middle of the room. He exhaled deeply and opened his eyes. *Damn fool*, he said to himself. *How do you get yourself in these situations? Stanton wouldn't hesitate for a moment. After all, who's to say that what meets the eye will in truth meet the eye when push comes to shove?*

That's what it was, that's what was troubling him. Not that his death was waiting for him on a small printed card or in the pages of a book. We all have to die, and he had sent so many to their deaths, for a cause. A noble and vital cause. But that a path had been laid out for him, and that his footsteps were already upon it, down to the last. He feared that the very freedom he had given up peace of mind for was not to be his. That he had no choice but to fulfill destiny.

He could die tomorrow, or next week, or a year or ten years from now. Every morning of his life he had faced that uncertainty. He would have jumped at the chance to trade his life for Willie's. Who wouldn't step before the bullet to save his child? But no bullet offers such a choice. And so we go on, and behind us lies the memory of a happier day that we were too ignorant to savor. We take the good for granted until the door closes with us on the wrong side, and all we have are memories.

HE STOOD BEFORE THE BANK of drawers. Each drawer had a label, "D–DesCamp," "Frank–Friedman," "Jameson–Jones." Ah, authors, alphabetical. The next bank bore the label "Subject Index." All right. He was getting closer. The L's, his name. He slid the drawer open.

He heard himself exhale, like a wind sifting through trees. The drawer was filled with cards describing books about himself. He didn't begin at the beginning. He looked at one and then another, front, back, and middle. *Lincoln and Greeley* by Harlan Hoyt Horner, a recent book, just two years old. He could understand why someone would write that book. Horace Greeley was so outspoken, so critical. *Was*. As though Greeley weren't alive, wasn't breathing at this very moment in New York City, still talking peace, urging conciliation with the South. Well, he'd found the solution to that. When Greeley wanted him to appoint an ambassador to meet with the representatives from the South at Niagara Falls, he had appointed Greeley himself and sent along John Hay to keep an eye on things. He had prescribed two simple conditions: the abandonment of slavery and the integrity of the Union. Greeley discovered what it's like to wrestle with the Devil and was never quite the same thorn in his side thereafter.

A card from further on:

```
Tarbell, Ida Minerva. 1857–1944. 1917. 901 p.
The Life of Abraham Lincoln, drawn from original
sources and containing many speeches, letters, and
telegrams hitherto unpublished, and illustrated
with many reproductions from original paintings,
photographs, et cetera. New ed., with new matter, by
Ida M. Tarbell.
New York. The Macmillan company, 1917. 2 v.
```

Strange. Here Miss Ida M. Tarbell is dead now for eleven years, though she lived a good long life, eighty-seven years. And back home Miss Ida is an eight-year-old child.

He took up another:

```
The Life of Abraham Lincoln. (Motion picture) Thomas A.
Edison, Inc. 1915.
Cast: Frank McGlynn.
Summary: Presents highlights from the life of Abraham
Lincoln, beginning with his years in the Senate and
ending with his death at Ford's Theater.
```

Ford's Theater? His death at Ford's Theater? He shuddered. It's one thing to know you'll die. No one but a fool would believe otherwise. Better if it said "Springfield, in his bed." Ford's Theater. Well, why not Ford's Theater? God knows he spent enough time there. At least he might be watching Shakespeare. Damned if he'd give up the theater. Whoever would avoid his fate will surely run headlong into it. And what was this about the Senate? It was the House where he'd served his one term, not the Senate. If it was wrong on one count, what about the other? *No, you don't get off that easy.* And Thomas A. Edison? The name was familiar. "Tom, sir. My name's Tom Edison." Selling newspapers on the train? No, not newspapers, campaign pictures. A boy about twelve, Willie's age. It was possible. Wouldn't Matthew Brady love to see pictures in motion! He had already spoken of the possibility.

How much did he want to know? And did he want to discover it here, on these little white cards?

```
Nicolay, John George. 1832-1901
Abraham Lincoln; a history by John G. Nicolay and
John Hay.
New York, The Century Co. 1914. 10 v.
```

He did the arithmetic. Sixty-nine years. A fair shake. Still, when he went back, it would be troublesome knowledge. And ten volumes! Of course he had said all right the morning the two Johns had come to him with the idea of a project to record a presidency as never before. And indeed they proved to be indefatigable collectors.

He was playing with fire, and he knew it. Fool. This building was crammed to the gills with everything between now and then. If he had come here before the war began and read of deaths by the million, would he have let it begin? Would he have found the strength had he known how long the parade of death would continue?

He should walk out of this cave of the Sibyls. Walk right out. McClellan would. But not Grant. And neither would he.

On a small slip of paper he jotted down the numbers that went with Nicolay's history and closed the drawer.

HE WAS DIRECTED INTO the "stacks," as the young woman called them, shelf after shelf of books, hundreds and thousands of them. The numbering system took only a moment to sort out. There were charts directing you to the appropriate level and area. He understood from the drawer of cards, devoted almost entirely to himself, that he would be—that he was—the subject of endless scrutiny. Some of that he could fathom. His presidency had brought the country to its second crossroads. Washington had safely led it past the first, and it looked like it would weather this, the second.

He knew what Lee would say if he were here before him now:

I never did believe in the institution of slavery. In my heart I have always been for the Union. I do not believe in war as a solution to our affairs of state. I have gained nothing and lost all in its propagation. My wife must provide for herself until I can find some gainful means of employment. As a soldier I am finished.

Lee was one man he would never understand. No, not so. The adage "Blood is thicker than water" has its application in Lee. The mind knows and the heart feels. The condition of citizenship is a mental fabrication. Look around in the morning as you rise from your bed, do you see citizens? No, you see wife and child. Is she a slave, the woman who lights the fire, who cooks your breakfast, who launders your clothes? No. She is Betsy or Jane or Old Sarah. And though you know slavery is an evil, and though you have given freedom to Betsy, Jane, and Sarah, you do not wish for others to render like service for all the Betsys, Janes, and Sarahs. You would say you have never been an oppressor; and I would counter, *Oppression is not a matter of politics; it is a fault in the soul.* So Lee, the man of conscience, the lover of peace, the kind husband, was also the man who defended treason, who devoted his life to war, and who made the words *brother* and *enemy* synonymous. Or could the root simply be that Robert E. Lee was no citizen of the United States of America? That he was, above all, a Virginian.

The light was poor. You would think this harnessing of electricity would lend comfort to the eye. Oh, there was enough to see by, but such a dismal scene. The light in the prisons must be like this, utilitarian and no more. Every book, it seemed, bore his name. *Lincoln, Lincoln, Lincoln. Lincoln, a Life. Lincoln and the Civil War: Diaries and Letters of John Hay.* Yes, he knew John was keeping a diary. It had occurred to him to keep one himself, but there was no time. Besides, what would he have put in it? Events of the day, frustration with his generals? What Willie said at breakfast?

He crouched down before a row of fat brown volumes—*Abraham Lincoln: A History.* He counted to ten. How could it take ten of them to tell the story of his life? Such scrutiny. And there were Miss Ida Tarbell's two volumes, bound in a pale red.

His hand reached for the first volume. Opening it was like jumping into an icy river. He turned to the title page. *The Life of Abraham Lincoln,* a "New Edition with New Matter" published in "MCMXVII." Nineteen hundred and seventeen. Staring at the heavy black letters were two Lincolns: himself and a bust of himself. He doubted the day would ever come that he'd accept that bearded fool as himself. No, Abraham Lincoln is clean-shaven, youthful, with a spring in his step. A picture makes you weigh a ton, a bearded ton. He thumbed through the first few pages, preface and more preface. His eyes skimmed along. In 1894 the editors of *McClure's Magazine* began collecting reminiscences of his contemporaries "as were then living." Soon they had a Lincoln Bureau set up in their editorial rooms. Come 1895 Miss Ida was writing articles for the magazine, and by September of 1899 she had written his life. The Preface, together with the "Preface to the New Edition," went on and on. He spotted a new word for his vocabulary, "Lincolniana." God, what a mess of syllables for the tongue to twist through. Page xxi launched a new paragraph:

> It is quite clear that he was not afraid of the people mis-understanding him when he exercised powers, however unusual, that he thought essential to the single aim he had in view—the saving of the Union.

Is that what it was? He couldn't recollect. A single aim, as if there was but one arrow in his quiver.

He turned pages. Familiar names flitted by. Vallandigham, his ar-rest: the spirit of the Constitution that sets aside the letter in time of rebellion—the drug that is good medicine for the sick is poison to the healthy. Hardin, "a new letter written to him in 1845" when the nomination to Congress was in dispute. Mary's cousin, trying to weasel an extra term for himself. Waste of everyone's energy there. And then a year later he's killed in Mexico. Who can look ahead? Well, he had an answer to that one. Himself. To a degree. Here he was ahead, but what lay ahead?

Lincoln glanced to his left. It was the Shakespeare man, Holm-berg, emerging from the floor below, a book in each hand. "Find what you're looking for?" Lincoln asked.

Holmberg nodded. "It's not so much what I'm looking for as what I'm hoping not to find. I want the story to be straight and simple, so I can get on with it. These people are like one of those animals you have to kill to make them let go. What is it, a wolverine?"

"Could be," said Lincoln. "Never faced up to a wolverine, and never hope to. I shot a wild turkey once, through a crack in the wall, and that was it for me with big game."

Holmberg nodded. Wild turkey was evidently not in his domain. "How about you?" he asked, gesturing toward the shelves.

"I suppose I'm like you," Lincoln said. "A good deal I know al-ready. It's what I don't know that worries me. I'm of a mind to aban-don the chase and let the fox have his day." And having uttered those words, he realized he had come to a decision. Later, maybe, he'd accept the challenge of these shelves. He'd stood here long enough. He let the covers close on Miss Ida's rendition and reshelved the book.

Holmberg, a couple of yards away, craned his neck to see what book it was. "Tarbell wrote a life of Lincoln?" He nodded at his own question. Lincoln wondered just how familiar his face was here in the next century, given the penny and all. But there was no way any sane man would ask if he were Abraham Lincoln. *Lincoln's dead as a doornail, and don't you forget it!* Someone might notice a resemblance, and if anyone said anything, he could nod sagely, and allow how it was a quirk of nature that he'd been cultivating over the years.

Holmberg was still cogitating about what to say next. Best to let him work on it. "Interesting," he said finally. "I know about her book on the history of Standard Oil. Read about it in high school history. I suppose it figures you don't write just one book—I'm a case in point there. I never did study much American history in college. College is a funny place. You survey the distant and the long ago, but the here and now is of no consequence."

"It is the ground we walk on," said Lincoln, "and not the greater part of wisdom to ignore. You used the word *survey*, and in my youth I did my fair share of that trade, surveyor, like Washington. Three dollars a day, and fifty cents for the map. It taught me how to use my eyes. But for now my eyes want the light of day."

Together they headed out of the stacks and back to the library proper. Folk were in greater evidence now, especially young folk. It was hard not to stare at the expanse of leg on these young ladies. But they were just going about their business, with arms full of tablets and books, and certainly not thinking about what effect a well-turned ankle would have on an old codger like himself. *Oh my*, he thought. *Here it goes.* One of them, just come around the bend, was staring directly at him, her breath held, and her finger raised like she was testing for the wind. She was wearing short pants. His impulse was to cover his eyes, like when you happened upon girls bathing. Lord knows what customs had come to. Holmberg, with his thick glasses and preoccupied manner, noticed nothing. Time to move on.

Too late. "Excuse me," she said and then faltered. He was used to this failure of the will. When they got up close, and his height told on them, they'd grind to a halt.

"Let me guess," he said. "I remind you of your Uncle Joseph from Philadelphia."

She shook her head and smiled, her face bursting into bloom like a blown rose. A good thing humor transcends the times. "No," she said, "and besides, Uncle Joseph's moved to Boston."

"I should have guessed," he said. Clara Harris. Yes, she put him in mind of Clara Harris, Henry Rathbone's fiancée, a face clear and bright, with no evident sign of the bitter war that cast its shadow upon the rest of us.

Holmberg was looking at them quizzically as though they were conversing in an alien tongue.

"Just discussing a mutual acquaintance," Lincoln explained. "Or the absence of one. It's what every conversation comes to, sooner or later. Or so Harry of the West used to say. Clay, I mean."

"Well," said the latter-day Clara, "I hope you enjoy your stay in sunny Evanston. So long for now. My best to Mary."

"So long," Lincoln echoed to the departing figure.

"That," said Holmberg, "reminded me of the opening of a scene from Shakespeare, where the characters follow each other easily but the audience is half in the lurch. *Lear*'s a good example."

"Yes," said Lincoln, "the odd talk about Gloucester's bastard son."

They were at the door now where they had first met. "My pleasure, Mr. Thomas," and Holmberg was gone.

Lincoln paused a few steps from the door. It was like he was on holiday, though the only holidays he had lately were at the front. He and Mary had talked of a trip to Europe when the dust settled, but it would be a good four years before his term ended. Wishful talking. Uncle Joseph's niece from Boston—had she penetrated the lack of disguise? *My best to Mary.* Lincoln smiled. How could it be a comfort, being here? Yet somehow it was. He'd better make the most of it.

THE PATH RAN ALONGSIDE the lake. There were a few benches, some stone, some wood. A couple bore brass plaques, Gift of the Class of

1923, that sort of thing. He took a seat. Any moment now he might be whisked back home. He realized he didn't want that, not yet, even though there was nothing for him here. He belonged here as much as on the moon.

Yet the number plaques on the automobiles did proclaim it to be his: "Land of Lincoln" they said. And what was to stop him from coming right out and saying who he was? Why had that not occurred to him? Why must it be a secret?

Common sense gave the answer to that question. Take him for a lunatic, they would. But fun to imagine:

> HIMSELF [An itinerant, going door to door, in tatters and patches, hat in hand] *Howdy, Ma'am. I am Abraham Lincoln. I have come out of my time and into yours.*
>
> MRS. CHELTNAM [A motherly woman, in apron, with dishcloth in hand, and no short pants. Tessie, in pigtails, is peeking out from behind her skirts] *How do, Mr. Lincoln. There's wood needs chopping by the side of the house—*

No, he'd got it wrong. He was knocking on a door from the wrong end of time—from boyhood days—and he was the lad standing beside Mother. He had loved those times. Men on the grub line passing through. They'd do the chores. Then as they drank their milk and ate their plate of beans, they'd tell stories.

There was one day a wagon broke down nearby, a family with two girls. While the men were mending things, the women cooked in the kitchen. They spent the night, and the woman had books and read them stories aloud, the first he'd ever heard. Stories of gods and goddesses, and heroes and beautiful ladies, soldiers with swords, and the old king with the fifty sons. Troy. He'd learned what the story was years later. Back then it had sounded like it was just a few years back, but far away. It was the dark-haired girl he'd taken a shine to— Penny, they called her—not the blonde who chattered and whined and never was still. He had written a story in his head, where he took old Moses, his father's horse, and followed their wagon till he caught up, and they were surprised to see him, but kind. He persuaded Penny to elope with him, and he put her on the horse and together they started off through the woods, and they rode a couple of hours till around sundown they came to a broken-down wagon and men repairing the axle. They were back where they had started from just a few hours before, and the mother scolded the daughter for riding off without saying anything. The next day they tried the same thing, and again the horse went in a circle. This time they concluded they ought not to elope, and they did the right thing, and stayed until he had persuaded the father to give his daughter to him. He had always meant to write out that story, about true love and the horse that knew what was honorable. He had started to once, but concluded there wasn't enough of a story there to fill a jar. But that dark-haired girl did mark the beginning of dreams of love.

A dog was sniffing at his cuffs, a black Labrador with a gray muzzle. "Howdy, Dog." He scratched under its chin. "What's it like living in these times? Does a dog still lead a dog's life?" The dog looked up at him, seemed to say "Yes."

"Glad to hear it," Lincoln said. "Suppose you don't recognize me, do you? The fellow with his face on the coin, used to be your president. Well, not exactly yours. You live somewhere nearby, or you just grubbing? Spite of your dark hair, I'll not try to whisk you off to be my true love." The tail stopped wagging. Hang-dog look. "Didn't mean to disappoint you now. Doesn't mean you can't be my friend. A friend's best dog is his man." Lincoln chuckled. He always liked the looks of confusion on a face as they tried to integrate that sentence back into sense. Stanton especially. Looking as if someone had set him backwards on a donkey.

"Rusty!" said a voice from nearby. "You leave that man alone."

Lincoln looked up. It was a youthful woman, wearing a skirt, thank the Lord. She was bare-headed, with long dark hair woven into a braid. She smiled apologetically. He smiled back and said nothing.

"Sorry," said the woman. "She gets out ahead of me and next thing I know she's found a friend, willy-nilly." Rusty meanwhile had assumed a middling expression, waiting to see which way the wind was blowing.

"Rusty?" Lincoln asked. "That's her name? Well, why not? I once knew a goat called Kitty, but don't get me started telling stories."

The woman bent down and patted the dog, ignoring the story of the goat called Kitty. "My daughter," she said, "picked the name when Rusty was a puppy. We tried to explain that Rusty was a color like red is." The woman smiled at the futility of trying to persuade a child about the meaning of a word. "And now I wouldn't know what to do if her name was anything else." The woman fell silent, looking at the ground. In her right hand was a leash loosely coiled. Suddenly she was crying, quiet tears, which she caught at the corner of her eye with a fingertip.

He stood, and touched her arm. "I'm sorry."

"I just never know when it's going to catch me," she said. "My daughter, Emily, and her dad were killed, in a plane crash. It's not like it was yesterday, but some moments that's what it feels like, yesterday."

"I know," said Lincoln, the image of Willie rising before his eyes, not Willie at the last, but just Willie sitting there at breakfast with a bowl of porridge and a storybook, not even looking up when his father happened by. The fragility of life. He didn't take it for granted. Mary wouldn't come to the funeral, refused to go out for what seemed like months afterward. He had no choice. It was almost as if Mary had died too. He was no comfort to her, nor she to him. He tried to imagine what a plane crash would be like and realized he was picturing the tumble and tangle of railway cars scattered along the tracks.

"It was a DC-3," the woman said. "The kind they say never crash. Not one of these giant four-engine planes they have now. In Bryce Canyon, so it was over in a hurry." She paused. "So Easter's a hard day for me." She was dabbing at her eyes with a handkerchief, her breathing composed again. "I suppose at twelve the lure of colored eggs and the Easter Bunny would have faded, but I can't silence my imagination. So I thought I'd take Rusty for a walk. That was some awful storm night before last, wasn't it?" She gestured toward the branches scattered about, which he hadn't noticed.

Just how, he wondered, could he explain his transition from then to now? That he hadn't arrived till the day after the storm. Not that he had plans to account for his presence here. But suppose he did tell the truth? Would he declare it a pure mystery and warn her not to be surprised if suddenly he were to disappear? Well, he hoped he wouldn't be plucked back in the middle of a conversation like this. He'd spend the rest of his days pondering the shock he'd left behind.

Might there be a chance he would have some control over his return? That thought hadn't occurred to him till now. He'd been seeing himself like an oak leaf in a tempest, with no will of its own. But what if there needed to be a sign from himself? This was like a holiday, after all, with time off from all responsibility. The leaf come to rest on a branch halfway down, until it decides to give itself back to the winds. "I don't know," he said gently, remembering now her question about the storm.

The woman nodded thoughtfully.

"If you're planning to walk on a pace," he heard himself say, "would you mind if a visitor kept you company, partway at least?"

"Of course not," she said, and she extended her hand. "Joan Matcham."

"Pleased to meet you, Mrs. Matcham"—and as he was saying this—his hand already meeting hers—it was too late, and he didn't know how to go on. "Abraham Lincoln," he said. "And would you do me a small favor?" The words were spilling out in a rush, and God only knew where they'd land. "I know I've said who I am, and I know who I can't help but look like, but before you jump to any conclusions, will you grant me the courtesy to hear me out?"

Stunned silence.

"Rusty, what about you?" he asked. Silence again, but to judge from the tail, not without a ray of hope.

"Yes," said Joan Matcham softly, equivocally, then "All right" in a firmer voice. "Go on. I'm listening."

"Might I explain as we walk? You still wish to walk?"

"Yes," once more, an all-purpose yes, with a measure of self-control.

"Thank you," he said.

"Though something tells me—"

"Don't heed it," he interrupted, and with a slight shrug she acquiesced. She'd made her decision, and it looked like she'd stick with it. He'd better make it good while he had the chance.

With Rusty in the vanguard they headed north up the path. "I will be forthright," he said. "I didn't mean just now to give my name. I was caught up in the moment. I may be a slow-witted man, but I know possible from impossible as well as the next person. So thank you for listening, for not taking flight, you and Rusty." His words were pouring out like molasses. "Inexplicably," he went on, "I find myself beyond my own time and into this present. I have no inkling of what brought me here. There's no cause why you should hear me out or why I should so wish to account for my presence, other than that I am in the habit of finishing what I start. I will be satisfied if you don't bolt headlong like a scared rabbit." Which she didn't—her pace matched his, stride for stride.

He risked a moment's silence. The path, he noted, was paved, and they had it to themselves. He remembered his visit to Robert at Phillips Exeter—that was right after the Cooper Union speech—word had gotten around, and the curious had lined up along the way to see the strange Westerner. Robert, having failed fifteen of sixteen subjects on the entrance examination for Harvard, was hard upon a course of study to remedy the difference. Meanwhile, he was done with Harvard and, against Mary's wishes, was with Grant. "Sorry," he said. "For a moment there I got to thinking about my son Robert. He's at General Grant's headquarters now—or was. My mind, really it's as if it's in two places at once."

"I'm listening," she said. "Though I can't imagine where your tale is heading."

"Then we're in the same boat," he said. "My story has brought me to this path, this moment. I can go back a trace and fill in two or three bits, but beyond that I have no clear vision. I am like a tree uprooted and hoping for the best."

She looked at him quizzically. "May I ask a question? You say you've been taken from your time and shifted to this one. Well, just how long would you say you've been here?"

"It's not what you're thinking. It was just last evening that I—I'm searching for the right verb." He hesitated. "That I came. Arrived. There, how's that?"

She said nothing—what could she say to such a story? Her face tilted his way. "You do look the image, you know, of Abraham Lincoln." She continued walking, her hands working the coil of the leash. He could see her mulling over troublesome questions. Right now he didn't want any questions about Mary, better to keep that in the shadows. God forbid that Mary should find out he had been conversing with a woman, unescorted. "I was wondering," he said, "since I know so little about the current state of affairs, if you wouldn't mind filling me in." There, safe territory.

"The current state of affairs? You mean politically?" Another sideways glance. "Historically? You're asking me for a survey of the world over the past hundred years?" She looked amused. A step in the right direction.

"Not hundred," he said. "The last few, maybe the last ten years."

"The last ten years," she echoed. "A lot can happen in ten years, earthquakes, volcanic eruptions. You want the last ten years' worth?"

He nodded. He couldn't expect any better, not from anyone this side of sanity.

"All right," she said. "I can do that. It's April. Ten years ago, in April, we were still at war, in Europe and in Asia, though it was nearly over. You really don't know?"

He shook his head. Her question didn't leave much room for choice.

"Well, Hitler was still alive. And the bomb hadn't been dropped."

"Hitler, and the bomb not dropped," he repeated.

"Yes, Hitler and the bomb. You want me to tell you about Hitler and the bomb, as if you know nothing?"

"Yes, please," though he didn't want it to be a game. "As if I know nothing," he said.

She took a deep breath. "Hitler, Adolf Hitler, was a demon. No. He was a person, like me, like you, I suppose. I don't pretend to understand who he was. He came to power in Germany after the First World War, 1914 to 1918. I know dates. Germany had been defeated by the Allies, France and England and other countries. And by the United States, which came upon the scene later. I had an uncle who went over there before we joined the Allies, fought with the Canadians. They called it 'The War to End All Wars.' They spent years defending a few miles of no-man's land, the trenches going a little this way, a little the other. It ended with an armistice. But anger got the better of the Allies, anger over the horror we said was their fault. The best-laid plans, you know. Then came bad times for the Germans. And in bad times, there's a vacuum. The Communists offered one answer. I haven't mentioned the Bolsheviks. You asked only for the last ten years."

"It's okay to fill in," he said. Up ahead Rusty had found a bush to investigate.

"Okay. The Nazis—that was Hitler's party—offered a safer choice than the Communists. For the majority. They told the people it was safe to hate the Jews. Millions of Jews. I'm no expert here. My answers are probably too simple. I don't know facts, the tiny facts. I don't know how the butcher's wife in Munich felt, or the manure salesman in Frankfurt; I don't know how angry they got when the hospital didn't have an answer for why the baby wouldn't stop crying in the night. And how that grew to a vague fury, so when the time came to vote, they found themselves seeing hope in Hitler, and later were willing to take up arms against—oh my—you'll have to forgive me and Shakespeare. I was about to say 'arms against a sea of troubles.'"

"You're pardoned. I have the same disease—his words edging into mine. You mentioned the bomb. I hesitate to ask, but what bomb?" He needed to know. One reason for his own war was to demonstrate to the civilized nations of the world the virtue of democracy and the futility of war. The war to end all wars. A bitter phrase.

"It's one of the wonders of an airplane," she said through gritted teeth, "that not only can they carry passengers, and the mail, and

37

vaccines to save children in remote villages, but also missiles, torpe-does, and bombs."

"You mean they drop bombs from airplanes? Yes, of course. I'm sorry. I was thinking of a bomb as a shell delivered by a mortar. I had no idea." But already he could picture a torrent of these bombs, raining from the sky. Unlike a balloon, a plane could ignore the untoward wind and go wherever it pleased. Anywhere. Over Vicks-burg. Over Washington. God! How much easier to be simple, like Rusty, to rely on your teeth. There'd be less war if we had to have our enemies square in our jaws. If we had to taste death. He had asked the wrong question after all, he realized. Seeking to avoid the thicket, he had found the bramble.

She turned his way. They had slowed and then stopped. "The story of the bomb can wait," she said.

He nodded. "It's worse than I can imagine, isn't it?" He was pic-turing the disaster with the Petersburg mine, but now aboveground, and engulfing a whole city, a Philadelphia, a Boston.

"There's so much else to tell," she said. "Not all of it ugly. I am not responsible for the history of warfare in this century, and won't be. Another war has just ended, in Korea. But we didn't call it a war, not officially. Congress didn't declare it. They referred to it as a 'conflict.' For three years we fought a conflict but not a war. The Chinese and ourselves."

"It's unending," he said. "I see the picture. You needn't tell me more."

"Thank you," she said. Then, her face angled his way, "You said you got here last night?"

"I said I came here last evening, not long after suppertime."

She nodded. The path had ended at a chain of one-story buildings facing the campus. "Fraternity houses," she said. "Where the boys live. And that's the gym, Patten Gymnasium. This marks the north end of the campus. I usually circle back from here."

"It puts me in mind of the Wigwam. Don't suppose that's still around."

"I don't know. The Wigwam?"

"It's where we held the Republican convention that put me on the ticket. It was built for the occasion, at the corner of Market and Lake. Lots of hoopla, so they told me. I was in Springfield, behind the scenes."

"I think it must be gone. If it was around, by now it'd be a museum, what with all its history."

"Yes," he said, "so I would guess," though he hadn't. Rusty meanwhile had continued on to the sidewalk and was looking up and down the avenue.

"Heading back, Rusty," Joan Matcham called out, and Rusty turned to the right, trotting along the sidewalk between a row of automobiles and the backside of the fraternity houses.

Lincoln glanced up toward the main north–south street, Sheridan. Earlier he had happened on Sherman. Probably there was a Grant too. This one was—he squinted at the criss-cross street sign. Wouldn't you know! And not named for his cousin Levi, the sometime governor of Massachusetts.

Lunch with Mr. Lincoln

10 April 1955

Joan Matcham followed Rusty down the sidewalk toward the lake. The man who called himself Abraham Lincoln was behind her. Out of the corner of her eye she spotted him trying to make out the street sign at Sheridan. "Sheridan" would be easy enough to read, facing as it was this way. But "Lincoln" was at an angle. Maybe he could make it out, the street named after himself.

What if he was a charlatan—but that didn't ring true. A madman? But there was nothing mad about this man, unless it were the whole man, a perfect madness. He seemed such a kind man, so gentle. "Rusty," she called. The dog was taking her good old time. She couldn't hear his footsteps behind her. He was a quiet man. If she turned around, she'd see him, wouldn't she? This could be a figment of her imagination, but she knew it wasn't. When you're dreaming you might not know whether it's a dream or not. But the same wasn't true when you're wide awake, at least not for her, practical Joan.

She didn't turn. She was alongside the last fraternity house, Acacia. She liked that it was named after a tree and not the stupid mystery of the Greek letters. If it wasn't a dream, then who was he? Tom Matcham would see him as a madman, no better than the people who call themselves Napoleon and walk around with their right hands tucked between their shirt buttons. That's what Tom Matcham would see: the obvious. Best to avoid him, however good his intentions to his brother's widow, however sound his financial advice.

Why hadn't she recognized him at once?

He fell in step alongside her. Where were they heading? She couldn't picture the moment when she'd say, "Well, it's been nice meeting you," and turn on her heel to join the rest of humanity that live free of phantoms.

"I've been thinking," he said.

"So have I."

"Doesn't surprise me. Probably on the same track. What I was thinking was that I should offer up some proof about who I am." At that he smiled. "As I said, I didn't mean to reveal my identity. No one seems to recognize me, and I could have continued on in my present state of blissful ordinariness. I mean, if we were to be whisked off to another planet a million miles away, of course no one would know either one of us. And then if a stranger said, 'Hello, my name is Lady Macbeth,' well, we'd both say our hellos and our names. What am I trying to say?"

"I'm not sure. Maybe that you don't know quite what to say, that you're not responsible. Something like that?" She hesitated to say much more. He was trying to get a grip on reality, and she couldn't bring herself to say just how upset he would be if he really were Abraham Lincoln, launched out of his era into this one. Yet he didn't seem all that upset. Certainly, he looked like Lincoln, the beard and the bushy eyebrows, the deep-set eyes, the Lincoln on the face of the five-dollar bill—though his jacket didn't match any photos she'd ever seen. Still.

"Responsible," he said thoughtfully.

Rusty was looking over her shoulder at them; they weren't keeping up the usual pace.

"I know what I was about to say," he said. "That I didn't intend to make you a part of this affair. That I'm sorry. But it seems I've caught you up in my wake. I assure you it was purely an accident."

"It's all right," she said. "I understand. It is true I was wondering about the ways I might be deceived, but nothing seems hypothetical about you."

"Glad to hear you say that, for that's precisely how I think of myself. Unhypothetical. And what do I mean by saying that I have made you a part of this affair? I take that back. You're as free as a bird on the wing."

With those words he came to a dead halt alongside her. He had given her a cue.

Now what? She would have to decide one way or the other. Here was her chance to turn the clock back to sanity. Wasn't she the expert on keeping life disentangled? It wouldn't take much: that she needed to be getting home, that she'd been out longer than she'd expected. Keeping her tone of voice matter of fact. That it had been nice meeting him, and *have a pleasant visit here in the twentieth century*. But there he stood, arms at his sides, as patient as an oak. "No," she said, "what would I do if the situations were reversed? I'd hope you wouldn't leave me in the lurch." She'd made her choice, though it felt more like the choice made her.

He nodded. "No, I wouldn't do that. You are a generous woman, Mrs. Matcham. I would like to invite you to join me for lunch, but I reckon few establishments would have provisions for Rusty here."

"Well, thank you. Rusty and I were heading back home. You're welcome to join us." She'd taken the leap. "And yes, lunchtime isn't far off. You said you got here around suppertime?" It struck her again how hard it was to believe she was having this conversation.

"Yes, last night," he said. "Around suppertime. Though when I left, in my own time it was morning. I've managed surprisingly well. I spent the night at a hotel, the Orrington, and no questions came up. They booked me in and let me dine. Can't say how long that will last. Besides I have no way of paying the debt. Maybe they can post an 'Abraham Lincoln Slept Here' sign, as though I were George Washington. I do see problems up ahead, though that's nothing new—I've been unfit for what life has sent my way as long as I can remember."

"And yet here you are," she said, "with an invitation to lunch."

"You've got me there," he said with a smile. She'd never pictured Lincoln smiling. "Guess I'll just count my blessings," he went on. "But just now, thinking ahead, I was picturing myself at home, in

Washington, knowing what I now know. And I wonder just how much I am meant to see of this next century."

"I don't know," she said, though the question wasn't particularly addressed to her. Just how much did he know, not about now, but about his own life, his own death?

Ahead was the library and the bench he had been sitting on. They were coming full circle. Passersby paid no special attention to this tall stranger. Were they just oblivious, or had a spell been woven? Once again she looked sideways at him—he was intent on his own thoughts. Without a doubt this was the living, breathing, walking, talking Abraham Lincoln, not an apparition. He was nearly as recognizable as Eisenhower or FDR.

His eyes caught hers—gray eyes—and he gave a half smile. "You're wondering what to do with me, aren't you?" he asked. "How to explain me to a neighbor or a friend. Ordinarily, I take the direct route, without preamble. 'Mary, this is Kate Chase.' Kate Chase is my wife's nemesis. But, I don't think you'll want to give anyone the advantage of the name that goes with this grim visage. As I did with you. You can see the damage from that one slip of the tongue. So you had best have a ready word and a quick tongue. Let's see. How about Abrams, Alfred Abrams? It's not a familiar name hereabouts, is it?"

"No," she said, "not at all."

"Well good. That's settled easily enough."

"Should I ask who Alfred Abrams is?"

"I am Alfred Abrams. What a foolish question."

He had spoken with such a straight face that for a second it seemed the house of cards they were living in came tumbling down. She wasn't with Abraham Lincoln after all; she was with this stranger named Abrams. Then the smile reappeared and the illusion was shattered. "Yes," she said, "of course, a foolish question. Alfred Abrams is who he says he is. Not, by the way, that I expect to meet a host of friends this Easter morning."

"And I must be from out of town. Have you traveled in the world?"

"Yes," she said. "I've traveled. It's what was recommended for me after the crash, and it gave me sufficient time to realize that what I didn't want to do was forget. It was enough to dampen anyone's spirits. So I came home halfway through my trip."

"Where did you go, if you don't mind my asking?"

"Well, it was supposed to be a Mediterranean cruise and then a tour of Europe. I bypassed Europe."

"Yes, I'd say you got bad advice. When the pain is not so fresh, then it might work. I've always wanted to do a bit of traveling, mind you, and without politics along for the ride. These last few months the notion's been moving forward from the back of my mind. I am rambling on. Sorry."

"It's all right," she said. "Maybe someday I'll find myself in Europe." But it was Abraham Lincoln she was picturing, crossing the Atlantic, and not alone. He and Mary Todd Lincoln and a host of wardrobe trunks, and then a tour of the capitals, receptions in Paris, Berlin, Rome, London. And their sons—she couldn't remember much about his family and was wary of asking. Not that she needed to, not now. She must be careful what she said. Was it her place to warn him?

She glanced at her watch. It was a little after eleven o'clock. An hour ago she and Rusty had set out. Pity Robert wasn't here. He was the one who loved history. Robert had brought Plutarch along on their honeymoon. And worse, had found time to read it. She took a deep breath. What a waste; others were more worthy; she wasn't the best candidate to cross paths with Abraham Lincoln. She was only Joan. And *Only Joan* was best left to her own devices.

"Some of these buildings look pretty old," Lincoln said.

"I guess," she said. "Victorian even. You know Victoria ruled up into the twentieth century, by a year or so. Till 1901, I think. They had a Golden Jubilee in the 1880s."

"Long reign," he said. "Two terms'll be more than enough for me, if I last that long."

She let that go by. He had been looking at University Hall, an ugly old building if ever there was one. There was no one style of architecture here. They built whatever was current as the need arose. "Up ahead," she said pointing, "is Fisk Hall, where the Medill School of

Journalism is. I live a block and a half across from the campus. We'd better stop so I can get Rusty's leash back on."

Rusty, who knew the routine, had already stopped up ahead. "Come on, girl." Joan half kneeled and snapped the leash onto the dog's collar.

Lincoln stood alongside them. "You said Medill, for the journalism building?"

"Yes, why?" she asked, now leaning against Rusty's pull toward home.

"Must be Joseph Medill. *The Tribune* still going?"

"Oh yes, it's an institution. A very Republican newspaper. Ask me and I'll tell you about the '48 election."

"I know a cue when I hear one, and I'd be glad to spell you with that leash on the eager beaver."

She slipped the loop from her hand to his. Now Lincoln was a half step ahead, already answering Rusty's call, his arm taut. "You can cross when there's a break in the traffic."

He nodded. Holding Rusty back from the street, he looked left and right. One car then another went by; when the way was clear, he let Rusty drag him across Sheridan. "Well," he said, "guess I managed that all right. Funny thing, but I keep thinking that these automobiles would mow you down without a second thought. Not like a horse that will give pause. But I guess the drivers pay close attention. Do they often crash into each other?"

She smiled. "Yes and no, hardly ever. They do get wayward at times, though it's rare. I haven't been in an auto accident since forever—ten or twelve years at least. But they say airplanes are safer." She couldn't keep from adding that, dammit. And once again, like a tight fist, there was that knot just behind her breastbone. She caught her breath. "Left here on Hinman," she said, "then a block to my place."

"Okay," he said. "You were going to tell me about that '48 election."

"Right. Let's see. The Republican was Thomas Dewey, governor of New York, and everybody was so sure he'd win. And Harry Truman, a piano-and-card-playing ex-haberdasher from Missouri—he'd served out the last few years of Franklin Delano Roosevelt's fourth term—"

"Fourth term?" Lincoln was shaking his head in wonder. "Might as well go back to the days of King George!"

"Well, there's a constitutional amendment now," she said. "Two's the limit. It was wartime though, we were in Europe already, and Roosevelt wanted to carry on. Or we wanted him to. Both. He had taken us through the Depression. Plus, he promised peace."

"Who would promise war? Except for Davis. And Polk. I take it back. You're better off promising war. Maybe that's what a vote for me signified for many a voter. I was a blood-thirsty monster who'd force your daughter to marry a Negro. What choice did you have but to stand with your back to the barn door, pitchfork in hand?"

"I can't imagine the North caving in to the South, and that old world still with us. Our word for it is 'ante-bellum,' which is supposed to summon up a picture of a quiet plantation, a white-columned house, harmonious singing in the cotton fields, and the watchful eye of a kindly master. No one reads *Uncle Tom's Cabin* any more."

"You have though?"

"Yes."

"And you do not consider yourself a typical woman?"

What should she say to that? He was smiling. She had forgotten he was a lawyer. "All right. Some people must read it, but we read it as a window into another era and not because we believe the issue is still with us. And no one, I think, would call herself typical. No one is quite like her neighbor, no one lives at the center. That's my house, with the picket fence and the green shutters."

"Aha! The promised land. Home, Rusty."

She had to run to catch up. A strange man. Morose one moment, enthusiastic the next. Lincoln stood to the side as she unlocked the door and opened it. This wasn't going to be easy, she realized. He was standing there on the porch like a statue of Abraham Lincoln. God knows what he was thinking. For that matter, what was she thinking? Of going inside, of getting lunch together. He was waiting for an invitation. "We can leave Rusty outside—I latched the gate. Come on in."

"Right," he said, bending over to undo the leash. And then he was inside and the door was shut.

"Kitchen's this way."

"Sorry if I'm a bit absorbed," he said. "It really is another world for me, you know. A hotel room is as much like a house as an onion is like a salad. And a library is no domicile either, except to its books."

"It's okay. I'm sure I wouldn't know my way around your world." She opened the refrigerator then paused, her hand on the handle. "This refrigerator, half the time I still think of this as the icebox. Words are slow to change sometimes. And now it turns water into ice. Don't ask me how that works."

"Handy," he said, peering inside. "Electricity for everything."

She nodded. "Let's see—I've got tuna fish, cottage cheese, eggs. I could fix a cheese omelette."

"Fine. I grew up on eggs. Mind if I have one of these apples?"

"Sure, help yourself."

Simple enough. He stood there crunching away as she got together her ingredients and the frying pan. "What would you like to drink? I think I'll have tea, and there's coffee. And milk too."

"Milk's fine. You know this kitchen is a wonder. Mind if I explore?"

"No, of course not. I don't think you can get in any trouble. The stove's electric." He was already wandering around, opening and closing the refrigerator, hunched over and squinting at the Waring blender, then standing by her shoulder at the stove as the burner came on and reddened and the butter melted. She could hear his breathing. "There's bread in the breadbox behind you," she said. "I like toast with my eggs."

"So do I. I suppose you have an electric toast machine too?"

"Yes, it's called a toaster; they're automatic."

"Like automobiles, except for the riders. This is the toaster." Not a question.

"You just drop the bread in the slots and push down on the black bar."

"It's already sliced."

"Yes," she said. "There's an old expression, 'The best thing since sliced bread.' Though it's pretty recent when I think about it." She tilted the pan to let the liquid egg flow around the sides, then tested to see if it was sticking—almost done. "You want to hand me a couple of those plates in the cupboard?"

"Does it matter what color?"

"No, any's fine."

He set the dishes on the table, and she gave him half, herself half. She buttered the toast and poured his milk.

"Fit for a king," he said. It sounded like a well-rehearsed joke, but he nodded appreciatively at the first bite. "It'll be a pity to leave this behind."

"The omelette?"

"Well, the omelette too. Though I intend to take it down to the bare plate—I seem to have picked up a boy's appetite in this century. No, I mean this peaceful country—from what I've seen, with an exception here and there." He took another bite. "When I think about it," he said, "it just about unsettles my stomach that at any moment I may be whisked away, back to wartime and slaughter. Though something tells me I have a bit of time."

"You don't want to go back?" Such an innocent question.

He shook his head. "No, it's not that. I have to go back. It's my whole life. My sons and Mary are there, and my work. The storm isn't over, far from it." He resumed eating.

She stole a glance at him. He was intent on eating. The face bespoke a thoughtful man. She couldn't picture him angry, though that would say something for her lack of imagination. It was hard to know which was the greater mystery, his being here or her being so calm about it.

WHEN SHE HAD FINISHED her last bite of toast, Lincoln asked to be excused for a moment. She refilled her cup from the teapot, then added a bit of sugar. She stared idly across the table where Lincoln had been sitting, the chair still askew from his pushing it aside as he stood up. Her gaze extended beyond the kitchen and down the hallway, past the bathroom door, and into the living room.

When he returned she drank the last of her tea. "Give me a few minutes and I'll be through here. Feel free to look around." She cleared the table, ran hot water in the omelette pan, set it aside. She took her time doing the dishes, washing them with a bit of soap, setting them in the rack. A sparrow lighted on the lilac by the window, glanced her way, and then was off.

She backed up a few steps and saw Abraham Lincoln sitting in the rocker by the fireplace, his big hands folded across his lap, his chin against his chest. His eyes were closed. Maybe he was accustomed to afternoon naps. She had heard that he was a homely man and awkward, but she had seen none of that. What she did see was foremost a person who was tall, who was gentle, who was kind. She should let him sleep. She was in no hurry, she realized, to rejoin him. Perhaps he felt the same way. But for different reasons. What had they talked about? She couldn't remember. Oh, that's right, she had filled him in about World War II, the shorthand version. And she was going to tell him about the atomic bomb, but didn't get there. And then what? She had invited him to lunch but couldn't remember how that had happened. It was like picking up hitchhikers, which she never did. A spur-of-the-moment thing, but she wasn't a spur-of-the-moment person.

Now he was dozing in Robert's rocker. He was staying at the Orrington, had a room there, until—until what? He'd probably be all right there for another couple of days. No one would ask questions so long as he minded his business. April wouldn't be their busy season. She could show him around town, give him the grand tour: the Outer Drive, the Loop, the Prudential Building, Marshall Field's, a walk along Michigan Avenue and all the elegant shops. Then they would drive home. Did she want to cook another meal? Or perhaps a movie and a tasteful bite afterward? When had she last seen a movie? A year ago maybe. Marlon Brando, *On the Waterfront*. She wondered what was playing at the Granada. She didn't much like the downtown theaters—so impersonal, and you had to wonder where all those people had come from. At the Granada, at least there were students.

The rocker creaked ever so slightly then settled again. She could picture going to a movie with him. First they would have dinner at one of the little restaurants along Howard Street. And after the movie—

Already it was too late. So swift? Fragments too slight to measure. Noticing them only now, a flood of images. His long arms reaching for the dishes from the shelf. His hand brushing hers as Rusty's leash passed from one to the other. The silence as he sat at the table eating. His eyes. His easy voice. Whatever they did with their afternoon and evening, how could she take him back to his hotel, to risk never seeing him again? What if her hand were on his and the time were to come for the change, for the return? Would his touch draw her back? Would hers keep him here? Oh, how ordinary to see a man, this man, in the next room, so wrapped in his thoughts.

Another sparrow, perhaps the same one. Who can tell the difference? Sparrows. *This woman is madder than a hatter*, they're chattering. She didn't want him to go. She wanted Abraham Lincoln to stay with her. There was such a pure quality about him, and such a natural and easy way of walking, of standing still, just being himself. It occurred to her that this wasn't the real Abraham Lincoln. This was an Abraham Lincoln without a care in the world, Careless Abe. She looked down. The omelette pan was clean, had been clean a dozen times over. The house had three bedrooms. She'd been meaning to call up the university and put her name in for a foreign student but never got around to it. How far afield should she lead him? Where would they be in a day, two days, a week? Or longer? And what fool would go back so John Wilkes Booth could shoot you in the head while you were sitting beside your wife watching a play? When did he say it was that he made the leap? He had been president a good while, that was obvious. He looked like the Lincoln who was the president, not a younger Lincoln. Was it before his re-election? After? Yes, after, and the war nearly over. Not much time left.

She was crying. She watched a tear drop into the sink, then wiped her cheek with her knuckle. She'd maintained her independence so well these last years. Kept her life going. Talk about screwing up and setting your sights on the impossible! Well, things weren't that far along. But oh, she could do with having this man by her side through the night.

◆ III ◆

South

10 April 1955

L INCOLN GLANCED TO HIS LEFT. It seemed so easy for Joan
Matcham, and no doubt it was. Second nature, like riding
a horse. Her touch was so light, one hand on the wheel to
direct the automobile as it sped its way south.

Half the time he was holding his breath. If this was how it felt
to ride in a car, what would it be like to fly in an airplane? He had
confessed to her that he didn't have the vocabulary to go with the
times. So she had been naming the components for this vehicle; the
three pedals—gas, brake, and clutch; the steering wheel; the ignition (she laughed aloud when he asked if there was a fire inside the
car, though he was only joking); the hood; the engine. Many words
were altogether the same: streets and avenues and lanes. This highway was six lanes wide, with an ingenious system for changing the
numbers of lanes at "rush hour," so that at times it was two, or three,
or four lanes, either way.

They were heading into Chicago, though he couldn't tell where
Evanston stopped and Chicago started. It was her idea to take him
on a tour. "Wouldn't you like to see what a modern city looks like?"
Her voice had an uneasy edge. No surprise there. He tried to imagine what it was like for her. He could have used her resilience under
fire a few years earlier, back when McClellan was forever calling for
reinforcements for the confrontation with Lee.

Yes, he would like to see Chicago, he had replied, though just sitting there in her parlor with nothing to do was a gift beyond imagination. Not having to think ahead to the Cabinet meeting and the entire host of Secretaries stroking their beards and pointing out that however earnest his desire to effect peace was, there was such a thing as too much conciliation; that Congress in its present temper would certainly disapprove. Not to mention that Alexander Stephens and the others at the Peace Conference made it clear the South didn't fully understand that the show was up and the time had come to put their house back in order. Jefferson Davis was an unyielding man, that was certain.

He willed himself to relax. Back home he would have ample opportunity to worry this down to the nubbin. "Will these buildings never end?" he asked. "Are people living in every one of them, stacked up like sardines in a tin?"

"Yes," said Joan Matcham, "every building is occupied, and almost every apartment. Sardines? Yes, some, further on, especially on the South Side. The chain of buildings doesn't end till you reach Indiana, not that we're going that far. Millions of us live in Chicago. Only New York and Los Angeles are larger."

"Los Angeles! In California?"

"Yes."

"I know Los Angeles as a Spanish mission, not a city."

"I suppose," she said. "I've never been to California, but I do know that after the Great Depression people moved west by the millions."

"Great Depression?"

"Yes, the 30s. Banks failing, men out of work, bread and soup lines blocks long. Ten years of drought, the soil blowing away, Okies—Oklahomans—piling their belongings in the back of a run-down Model-T and heading west to the land of golden opportunity. I should give you Steinbeck's *The Grapes of Wrath* to read. It took the war in Europe to bring the Depression to an end."

"Wars," he said. "Their futility and their utility. You wonder which step moves us forward and which is retrograde. You know, it wasn't ten years ago in my time that all this"—he gestured with a sweep of his hand at the fleeting landscape—"was no more than grassy marsh, the houses on stilts, the sidewalks on piles."

"I may have known that," she said, glancing sideways at him, briefly, steadily, before her eyes returned to the road.

Dark eyebrows, he thought, *dark eyes*. "Yes," he said, not sure what to say.

And with her right hand she touched his knee gently, just her fingertips, then her palm, a long moment, before returning to the two-handed work of steering.

"It's just me," he said. "I am here. It's no dream, not for you, not for me. All these cars, no two alike." He wished he could say, *And you, your hair, your eyes*. "I was about to say," he said, his words shifting, "that in another ninety years, there's no telling what the eye will declare commonplace." His breathing became even again. "And thanks to what disaster? A translunar cataclysm, spaceships—I love that word."

"You know about spaceships?"

"From a little magazine at the hotel—they haven't landed yet, have they?"

"Not yet, but it won't be long, I suppose. There are movies about them. I want to take you to a movie, but not one of those. I hope there's time."

"So do I," he said. "I have a choice?"

"Yes, by the dozen. I brought the movie page from the newspaper. *Gone with the Wind* is showing, but it's very long." She paused, glancing his way.

He could see her measuring her words. "So how long is long? Longer than a play?"

"No," she said. "Well, maybe. About three hours. Ordinarily we go to movies in the evening. Or I do, when I go, which isn't very often these days. I rarely even come downtown. I don't much like the crowds. Luckily this is Sunday." She pointed off to the right. "I'll park up ahead, on Michigan Avenue. Then we can walk."

"Good," he said. "I look forward to being ashore. You realize that as I view the days, I have just spent the better part of a day on the *River Queen* voyaging from Fortress Monroe on the James, then overnight up the Chesapeake Bay, and finally back up the Potomac. From one perspective, that was just yesterday."

The car had come to a stop at one of the signals, its red light lit. She looked his way. "I keep forgetting," she said, "what time is for you. Or nearly so."

She drove on. "There's a parking space. You don't mind walking, do you?"

"Not a bit. As I said, I've done too little lately."

The car crossed the intersection, then pulled close to the curb. She switched off the ignition with her key and gathered up her purse. "The other way with the door handle, then push that silver button to lock the door."

He stepped from the car onto the sidewalk and waited for her to come around. Folk were passing by, and no recognition. No one here would greet his wife tonight with, "Guess who I saw?" Usually it was the reverse, with all eyes on him. And double the number when a lady was by his side. Mary would find reason to be annoyed with Joan Matcham—she would criticize her height, or call her a beanpole. No, he didn't mind one whit that no one would report how fine he looked accompanied by this tall woman with the thick braid.

They walked several blocks in silence. She was letting him drink it all in. Never had he seen so much glass. Immense panes of it. He had to remind himself to look through it. And behind, jewelers, clothiers, furriers, furnishings of every sort. Folk who called themselves travel agents, their offices adorned with photographs of old London and its Houses of Parliament, the canals of Venice, pagodas in China, the Pyramids, the Matterhorn, models of airplanes. One was just passing overhead, the sound of its engines catching his ear. It had the look of a turkey buzzard, lazy but persistent. He studied it as it shrank into the distance and was gone. "What must we look like from so high up?" he wondered. "Like ants? Less than ants. Shadows of ants."

"I don't think you see anyone from so high up. Maybe if it was a parade. You can see cars rolling along the highway. But mostly you see the land, farms laid out in squares, forests, meandering rivers. Not people." She paused. "You know," she went on after a moment, "I've been thinking. What if, like you, I were thrust a hundred years ahead of my time? What would surprise me, leave me speechless? Weekend trips to the moon, undersea hotels, summers in Antarctica, robots everywhere and us with time on our hands? The plague of 2040? One government the whole world over? Or no government, anarchy, for good or for ill?"

They walked another block in silence. Then Joan looked at him squarely and said, "You know, if you shaved your beard and wore a blazer maybe, and loafers, no one would give you a second glance, if you know what I mean. Not that anyone is noticing who you are anyway."

"Actually there was a young woman in the library who was about to say something."

"What happened?"

"I forestalled her with a bit of a joke, and moved on. And before I forget, what's a robot?"

"A machine in the form of a human, an intelligent machine. I think the word comes from the Czech word for 'worker.'"

"Blazer, loafers?"

"There's one, the dark blue jacket with the brass buttons. Loafers are off-duty shoes, without laces."

"Lessons in the twentieth century, home delivered. Shall we cross?"

"Yes," she said, "though I am in no hurry to arrive. It's odd. I don't feel I am quite myself right now."

"I know what you mean," he said. "I'm not at all myself either. I should be frightened, or put off, or wary. But I'm not, Mrs. Matcham."

"Good," she said with a smile as they crossed the street. A brass plaque above the doorway of a marble edifice caught his eye, Lincoln Savings & Loan. *Why Lincoln over and over again?* he thought. *Why not Polk or Jackson? Why always Lincoln?*

HIS EYE TOOK IN A SOLDIER in a gaudy uniform, much like poor Ellsworth and his regiment of New York firemen dressed as Zouaves. The paintings covering the walls were of children. Ellsworth little more than a child himself. War had turned out to be no game, and they all knew better now than to call attention to one's gaudy self. This museum, he thought, was an apt choice for the afternoon. An entire building where time has come to a stop: the Chicago Art Institute. Still, it was difficult not to think about concurrency, to wonder where Lee is, where Grant, where Sherman and Joe Johnston. The war lurked in the background, and it seeped to the foreground of his mind. For so many years—forever it seemed—he had been going over to the War Department to see what was new on the Potomac or the Genesee. So strange that now there was nothing he needed to know.

To his left Joan stood enraptured before an enormous painting, longer than he was tall, of folk in their Sunday best with parasols, in a wood by a lake. The picture was done entirely in pricks of the paintbrush upon the canvas, pricks by the million. He smiled.

"What?" she asked.

"Nothing," he said. "When did you say this Frenchman painted his picture? I've seen nothing like it before."

"The 1870s I'd guess. Let's see," and she stepped closer to the massive canvas. "It says 1884–1886. I think it's a recent acquisition. I don't know how I could have missed it."

"It's odd," he said. "All these strokes bringing time to a halt. I used to know a painter, Francis Carpenter. He did nothing like this, though. He spent quite some time at the Executive Mansion assembling our portraits to represent the first reading of the Emancipation Proclamation. He finished just last August. I wonder where the painting is now. Catching dust probably. Like myself." A sneeze was coming on, and he faced into the skylight and let it roar. Eyes flashed in his direction then turned away again. Joan looked at him inquiringly. "It's all right," he said. "Just the air, a little dusty I guess."

"We should be on our way anyhow. That way we'll have plenty of time to get a bite to eat before the movie starts at seven." She was waiting for his assent.

"Sure," he said. "You're the general. This way?"

She took one last look at the canvas, then caught up to him. They passed silently through the corridors and were back outside. The whole afternoon had been like this; as though they were holding their breath, were going through the motions until they came to the crossroads of midnight.

"I HAVE TO WONDER," Joan was saying, "whether any of this will go back with you."

Lincoln set his pastrami sandwich back on his plate. He had never been any good at talking and eating at the same time. At that moment he'd been back in Washington, with Mary standing across the room, her arms folded tight as a knot. "Any of what?" he asked.

Joan's fork was poised over her potato salad. She took a deep breath. "This. Everything here. Everything about now. I wonder whether you'll remember this. Whether your life back in your own time will be exactly the same, as if you had never been here. And I wonder too: if you don't remember it, will I?" She stopped suddenly, like a horse pulling up short.

He knew what she was thinking, it was obvious enough. She didn't want him to go; she didn't want to lose the memory of him. He couldn't remember a woman thinking of him so intensely, and without irritation. She had been looking him straight in the eye, and now she looked away and took a half-hearted bite of her salad. All afternoon they'd avoided this subject, their talk centering on this fact and that: how tall the tallest building was; whether Rembrandt was Dutch or Flemish; whether tomatoes were poisonous; where drinking water came from; whether the farmers had disappeared along with their horses. Her sudden blurt of questions had skidded their toying with words off to the side.

He agreed that he too would hate not to remember, not just for the loss of what was forgotten, but also for the knowing—the knowing now—that his memory later—or rather earlier—would be false. Maybe he could put something in his pocket to remind himself to remember. He already had the copper penny with his profile. Perhaps a note with the name *Joan Matcham* in his wallet? Or the single word *television*?

"I bear no guarantees," he said. "I would like to think, to be certain even, that what is, is, and will be eternally. Or at least until I die. Nor can I imagine forgetting. I don't forget much. I wish I could make promises," he continued. "I could promise that we'll go to a movie this evening, and most certainly the promise would be safe, would be fulfilled. But I cannot promise to go with you ten years hence, on a Sunday in early April. That would be tempting fate. Not that I'm a fatalist."

"I know," she said. Then abruptly she changed the subject. "I love these pickles, don't you?"

"Yes. I wonder if the Jews I know have pickles like these at home."

"Most likely they're too good to be a recent invention. Do you know many Jews?"

"Some. There are a few lately that haven't done their people any great service, trading between the lines. Exceptions, like most everyone. Just a week or two ago I found a young Jewish boy, from Pittsburgh, outside my office. He was ill—the fever was bright in his eyes. He wanted a furlough and believed that if he could just see the president, every wish would come true. He looked so young, too young to be a soldier for the North. The Southerners are oh so young right now. He had lied about his age in order to enlist. Because of me, he said. His name was Rosenthal."

"What did you do?"

"Wrote a note and sent him to see Secretary Stanton."

"What kind of note?"

"A short note; a few words go a long way with Mr. Stanton. One reason I carry this little book wherever I go. Mind if I borrow that pen of yours? I'll show you how the magic works." As she nodded her assent, he realized with a start what was so familiar about her. She fit to a tee his picture of Kate in *Henry V*—maybe a few years further on, and with her hair already graying, and edgy, wary of this hero conqueror who says he's just a farmer. He'd better write out that note. He turned a couple of pages and came to a blank sheet, and wrote it out, then looked it over once. "Here."

She took it in her hand, scowled at it. "Secretary of War, please see this Pittsburgh boy. He is very—"

"Young," Lincoln supplied.

"Young, and I shall be satisfied with whatever you do with him." She looked up from the note, suddenly serious.

"What is it?" he asked.

She looked stunned. "It's your signature," she said. "And that's all the note needs to say? You must know Stanton very well."

"In some ways, yes. We work well together."

"I wish you could write a note like that for me." She was smiling now.

"And what is your wish?" He could play this game.

The smile intensified. "Maybe you could just sign your name and let me fill in the rest."

He shook his finger. "I'm afraid it doesn't work quite that way. Mr. Stanton is a cautious man."

"And what if this turned out not to be in Mr. Stanton's area?"

"My note must go somewhere."

"Yes," she said. "Well, perhaps I'll save the note for later. But the Pittsburgh boy, did he get his furlough?"

"I expect so. I'd like to think of him as coming back into health, his childhood sweetheart sitting by his side, holding his hand, and after the war, they marry, and years later, their great-grandchildren, now in Pittsburgh."

"Tell me again," Joan said, her voice suddenly brittle, "where you were—or what time it was—when you came into this world, this time."

He set his sandwich down. "I'm not sure I said exactly. I think I said I'd been on board the *River Queen*—that would've been the day before, Friday, and I'd come back to Washington early yesterday, Saturday morning. That evening I reported to my Cabinet on the Peace Conference at Hampton Roads—nothing had come of it beyond my agreeing to parole the nephew of Alexander Stephens. Stephens the uncle was in Congress with me back in '47, and now he's the Vice President of the Confederate States. He was one of the three peace commissioners at Hampton Roads. I like Aleck Stephens. He's a tiny man, and he was all bundled up in scarves and an overcoat that hung below his ankles. When he emerged from all that, it was the littlest ear from the biggest shuck you ever saw. His is about the only story worth telling from that conference, but I had to go, to show my willingness to let the war end. When I asked Stephens if I could do anything for him, he said his nephew, a lieutenant, was in prison at Johnson's Island on Lake Erie. I may be setting the scene more than necessary."

"Not at all."

He continued. "Then, waking the next morning, Sunday, I returned to the idea of compensated emancipation that I had put forward at Hampton Roads. What if instead of spending millions to bring the war to a close, we were to compensate the several states with slave populations for the emancipation of those slaves? The cost of war for two hundred days amounts to four hundred million dollars. My condition is that all resistance to the national authority must cease by the first day of April. There are more pieces to it, but those are the principal elements. I would—rather, I will—present it to the Cabinet when it gathers—I could say, tonight, Sunday evening. Though I know Mr. Seward stands in opposition to it. I had just written out the proposal when I got shunted onto this track. I don't know if all that tells you much."

She was watching him thoughtfully. "Somewhat," she said. "Some people make a study of the Civil War. I can't even tell you much about the last war, not much beyond Pearl Harbor, when the Japanese bombed Hawaii. But I don't remember what happened next. It was Robert who kept the past in order for us."

"Yes, we forget," he said. "But today is the fifth of February, in eighteen hundred and sixty-five, a Sunday." He looked to see what that specificity told her.

She nodded, searching for the right words. "And the war?" she asked finally.

"About over, I hope. Grant has Lee pinned down. Savannah is ours. The Southerners wish it were over but are afraid to give in, Jefferson Davis most of all. You know those names?"

"Yes."

"Should I tell you more? I've been re-elected. My inauguration is one month away."

Again she nodded, as though this were sufficient. He wouldn't press her as to why she was asking. He returned to his sandwich, and she to her soup. Each knew part of what the other was thinking, and was willing to let it go. Or at least try, for now.

✦ IV ✦

The Theater

10 April 1955

S HE STROKED HER FOREHEAD, a habit, as though she were
prone to headaches. Her fingers felt oily. She wished she had
phrased the question differently. "Was there anything else you
wanted?" she had asked, thinking of nothing but dessert, but the
words said more. It was as if their words were in a hot oven, rising,
carrying more than the usual burden. She grimaced. As though she
wanted *No* for an answer. They were in no great hurry.

"No," he said swallowing, "I've had plenty, thank you. Three big
meals in one day is a lot for me."

He seemed so matter-of-fact. It was her impatience speaking. It
was a month until his inauguration; Lee was yet to come to Appomattox. Must be early '65. He would be killed just after Lee surrendered. Meanwhile he's enjoying pickles and mustard, as though
he doesn't have a care in the world. "Excuse me a moment," she
said, sliding out of the booth. She followed the arrow to the Ladies'
Room. She closed and locked the door, then stood there. If she
could start the day over, she'd go the other direction with Rusty, and
by now she'd be home with a book, carefree. What did he expect
from her? He was like the stray cat that shows up on your doorstep,
and you make the mistake of giving it a dish of milk.

She shuddered. She caught sight of her reflection in the mirror
above the washstand. *Fool*, it said. *Better hustle your bustle back out
there, and pronto. No matter how you figure, this man doesn't have
much time.* "I know," she said aloud. "I just don't want to get hurt."

And how much longer could she go on chitchatting with Abraham Lincoln? With the man whose signature she had recognized, "A. Lincoln," the two capital letters joined with a loop, a totally legible signature, almost like a schoolchild's. It was a jarring moment, snagging her doubt, her wariness, and rattling her bones. And he had seen it, had seen the game turn to no game, and they had gone back to a land of make-believe, as though life were nothing but a lark, two children side by side at the beach with bucket and shovel. The doorknob rattled. "Just a minute," she called out softly.

"Sorry, hon," called the voice from the other side.

Joan took another look at herself. No one but herself. She flushed the toilet, as though she had used it, smoothed her skirt, and opened the door. It was their waitress, a florid woman, maybe her own age, with dyed blonde hair. She rolled her eyes at Joan, and Joan nodded, acknowledging the message, whatever it meant. Kindred spirits.

Of course he was still sitting there, his spectacles perched on his nose, menu in hand, reading. She stood alongside the table and said, "We might as well be going." She picked up the check from beside his plate and crossed over to the cashier. She handed across a ten, waited for her change, left a tip on the table, let him hold the door for her as they left.

"Has something gone wrong?" he asked. It was nearly dark, and no one else was on the sidewalk. "You've already done more than was necessary."

She turned his way. "Is that what you want. To be set free?"

He recoiled as if she had struck him. "No," he said. "I just want to be sure you don't feel obliged. I just want you to know—"

"Know what?"

"That you don't have to put up with me. I'm sorry I'm having such a hard time with words. I do, unless I get to rehearse. But I haven't had time for that, so I'm kind of raw. I don't mean to tie you down, but I don't want you to walk off either. Or send me off to see Secretary Stanton."

She looked up at him and had a fleeting impulse to rise on tiptoe and kiss his lips. She'd never kissed a man with a beard. She hadn't kissed many men. "I too am out of my element," she said, "and I'm tripping over my own feet left and right. Sounds so stupid, what I just said. What other feet do I have?"

"Only ones I see are those two. Can I say that I hope you'll give me the pleasure of your company a while longer?"

"Yes, you can, and yes, I will."

"Good," he said. "Which way?"

"It depends," she said, "whether we walk or not. If we walk, then we have to walk back. I'd say drive."

"Drive it is then," he said. "I'd offer my arm, but I don't see much of that here."

"You're right. People sometimes hold hands, but that's a bit more intimate, I think, than a gentleman giving a lady his arm." They stopped for the light. "Of course parents and their young children do it. It's one of those things we learn not to do as we grow up."

"I could pretend to be your son," he said with a wry smile. "I am a newborn, if you think about it."

"Which makes me old enough to be your grandmother, thank you kindly. And here's my car." She unlocked his door, then circled round to her side. It came easily enough, the man's role—paying the bill, the chauffeuring, deciding whether to walk or drive, to do this or that, stay here or there.

"Tell me again about this movie we're going to see. You say it's like a story?"

"Yes. It's a story with pictures, but the pictures are continuous. What it really is, is a machine that shows a succession of photographs, each one almost exactly like the next, with just a tiny difference, and to the eye it's like a river flowing smoothly along. I guess it doesn't take all that many pictures to fool the eye."

"Hmmn," he said. "Sounds like a glorified magic lantern. Or even like those little geegaws for children, where you spin something like a disk, one side maybe with a horse, its legs outstretched, the other side with the legs tucked in, and seen together the horse is galloping."

"Yes. I had one of those when I was a teenager, on a charm bracelet. Anyway, they project the images on the screen, up front. Like a theater. This one's from a story by John Steinbeck, the same man who wrote about the Great Depression. I haven't read the book."

"I don't suppose every movie retells a book?"

"No, and maybe it's better if they don't try to. There's always so much more to the story in a book. I wish *Casablanca* was showing, my favorite movie. I don't think it's from a book."

His door clicked open and swung shut, locked. She locked her own door and joined him on the sidewalk.

"*East of Eden*," he said, pointing to the marquee. "You haven't seen it, have you?"

"No."

"But you know who these actors are: James Dean, Julie Harris, Raymond Massey?"

"Yes, they're the draw. James Dean is our current *enfant terrible*. Julie Harris is the plain and sensitive type. Raymond Massey is a character actor, a generation older." She bit her tongue. It would have been so easy to go on: What he's famous for is having played you.

Two couples were in line, and Joan recognized the older, the Silvermans, Beth and Ira. They had a cabin at Lake Geneva, where she and Robert used to vacation. She handed Lincoln a five-dollar bill, gesturing toward the ticket booth.

As Lincoln stepped forward to the cashier, Beth Silverman turned their way.

"Why, Joan Matcham!" she said. "It is you, isn't it? Haven't seen you in an age."

"Yes," said Joan. "It's me." This wasn't going to be easy. "How have you been, and how are your little girls? Not so little any more?" Lincoln turned their way. "This is a friend of mine," she said before Beth could say anything. "Alfred Abrams. Alfred, Beth Silverman. Robert and I used to rent a place up by Lake Geneva, where the Silvermans have a cottage."

"Pleased to make your acquaintance," said Lincoln with a slight bow. "Beautiful country thereabouts. I was up there years ago, before it was built up. No time for that nowadays of course." Tickets in hand, he was moving toward the glass doors, elbowing aside easy conversation.

"Well," said Beth. "Hope you enjoy the film. I'd love to see you again, Joan. Give me a call. We're in the book. Nice meeting you, Mr. Abrams," and with that she joined her party, already inside.

Lincoln handed the usher the tickets, then leaned close. "Handsome devil on that five-dollar note."

"I'm sure," she said. "What's his name? Abrams?"

"Could be. Without my spectacles, I couldn't be positive. You did that well, by the way, with Mrs. Silverman, as if you had been rehearsing."

"Partly," she said, "but I've also gotten pretty good at forestalling small talk when it's inconvenient. Looks like the theater's not at all crowded tonight."

"Quite right," he said. "We can sit anywhere we please?"

"Yes, just so it's not right up front."

"Well then," he said, leading the way down the aisle. About a third of the way along he stopped. "Far enough?"

"Perfect," she said, taking the second seat in to leave room for his legs to stretch. Immediately the lights dimmed and the curtains swept across the stage. "VistaVision Visits Norway" declared the screen. "They call this a short subject," she said. "It won't last too long. This new wide-screen technique is all the rage, and here they make the most of it."

"Amazing," whispered Lincoln, who sat leaning forward and staring raptly as the credits flowed across the landscape. "No wonder you wanted me to see one of these. I had an idea of what this would be, but my, the idea falls a mile short of the thing itself. It's like the camera is soaring in mid-air—"

She was airborne, her eyes shut, her shoulders pressed against the seat. She felt a hand on her wrist. His.

Three deep breaths. She hadn't guessed what the scene was leading up to, and now it was all too clear, even with her eyes closed—the camera airborne and hurtling deep into one of Norway's ragged fjords. She willed her eyes open. The camera had come out of its sharp dive.

He was looking at her closely.

"It's okay." Her breathing was returning to normal. "It caught me by surprise too. One moment they were just beautiful mountains, and suddenly the camera was diving toward the water and sweeping along the fjord and you felt as if the wings were about to scrape. But I also knew you were here, that we were in a theater, and I couldn't die in a plane crash in a theater."

"No," he said softly. "You couldn't. Though I think that I am going to die in a theater."

"You do?"

"Yes," he said, his voice low. "This morning in the college library I read a few sentences on a small card saying that a man named Edison would make a motion picture of my life, from my early years in Washington to my death in Ford's Theater. Sooner or later every one of us must die, and why not in a theater? Who says it must it be on a battlefield? Or in bed? Of course I could avoid Ford's Theater like the plague, but there's no cheating death. Hamlet has words for it, doesn't he? The fine line between now and later."

She said nothing. His voice had come to the end of his soliloquy, and as in a soliloquy, he had spoken his inner thoughts. He had seen what must read like a prophecy, and had been mulling it over all day, wrestling to give it meaning. What would it be like to know the place of your death? And she who knew the fuller story of how he would die, hadn't given a moment's thought as to what a theater would represent in the life of Abraham Lincoln.

Now on screen, it was Mr. Magoo's turn. As usual, he and Waldo were out for a Sunday drive, and Magoo nine-tenths blind would—thanks to the good grace of the Lord—survive to see another day.

Lincoln was beyond restraint, shaking and guffawing, helpless as a newborn baby. He didn't catch his breath until Waldo was safe and sound and the indignant and righteous Magoo had said what needed saying to the stunned policemen. "I'm sorry," Lincoln said. "You should have given me notice."

"Had I known," she said. "Here." And she handed him a handkerchief.

He dabbed at his cheeks and returned it to her. "Thank you."

"Sure. I think you can relax now," she said. "Once the film starts there shouldn't be any big surprises. After that we shouldn't be talking, even whispering."

"I understand. I will exercise firm control."

Joan returned her eyes to the screen, and there he was, his young majesty, James Dean, tiptoeing through the shadows like Puck, wary but urgent, drawing closer and closer to a clapboard house. He certainly was intense, you had to say that for him. Tormented. She glanced to her right. Lincoln's eyes were riveted to the screen.

She settled back, willing her shoulders to relax. The story unfolded; she tried to give it her full attention. But it was hard to give oneself up to theater, however worthy, while brushing arms with Abraham Lincoln and wondering what the rest of the evening could hold.

♦ V ♦

Dessert at the Hebrew National

10 April 1955

ABRAHAM LINCOLN STRETCHED his legs, crossed them at the ankles, and flexed his toes. *How long will it last?* he wondered. A time and place where no war was raging, where people's lives were their own and no one was called upon to be a hero, to rally to the bugle's call. A place and time where Mary was finally at peace, where the ghost of Willie had given up its grip. For that was the burr that Mary couldn't shake. An impossible task, to cancel memory, to shake off the full-blown pictures in our minds of ones we have loved, still love, cannot help loving: Willie and his pony; young Willie scowling as he puzzles out the words on a page one by one; or Willie abed, his breathing labored. And the echo of that stentorian breath in Mary's own stifled sobs was the burr he lived with.

The door marked "Women" opened and Joan appeared, her eyes darting anxiously left and right, until she spotted him. *We are both displaced,* he thought. He had drawn her from her comfortable niche, as surely as the turtle from its shell. He was standing now, offering his arm. "Where to?" he wanted to say, but dared not.

They passed through the lobby, where a few dozen people were filing in for another showing of the film. And just this side of the glass door stood Beth Silverman, a fur scarf about her neck, four silver martens linked together, the teeth of one fixed on the rump of the next, like elephants on parade. "Oh, Joan, there you are. I was hoping we'd see you. And Mr. Abrams. We were going to get a bite after the show—wasn't James Dean wonderful? Lester and Thelma had to go, the baby-sitter, you know. But Ira loves his cheesecake, I tell you. You'll join us, won't you?" An expectant pause.

Joan's eyes edged his way momentarily. He knew what she was thinking: that the story of this Mr. Abrams was thinner than a robin's blue eggshell. The slightest probe and it would shatter, and out would spill Abraham Lincoln. Excuses rushed through his mind (train to catch, appointment with an old friend, sick and about to vomit), but he feared giving expression to them on the off chance he might have to live with the answer.

Finally a slightly apologetic smile materialized on Joan's face. "Oh Beth, you know we'd love to, any other time, but—" And then silence, rigid silence.

Oh my, thought Lincoln. So soon the well's run dry, the storehouse of words empty.

"No *buts* allowed," said Beth Silverman. "And here's Ira." She gestured toward a long black automobile just stopping in front. "The Hebrew National, on Howard Street. You know it." A statement and not a question.

"Yes," said Joan, her smile thinner than when it started.

"We'll see you in a few minutes," Lincoln said to the departing figure.

"Sorry about that," Joan said after Beth was gone. "I just couldn't think what to say. I drew a blank. We don't have to go."

"It's all right. And I'm afraid we do. We both gave our assent. And it shouldn't be too bad, should it?"

"No," she said. "It's just—" And again words failed her.

"I know," he said. "You don't want time to fritter away. None of us do; we never do. But it doesn't work that way. We all intend more, but along comes a child with a runny nose or a 'Watch me,' or a weeping widow waits in the hallway, and we mark our place, close the book, and hope for the best. So we'll go. She wants to see you, I'd say. Or doesn't want to be alone with Ira. She knows something you don't. Or it is something you know but have discounted."

"So, we'd better go," she said, holding the door for him.

69

"Tell me again how you know her? At Lake Geneva where you had nearby cabins?" The sidewalk was empty as they walked to the car.

"Yes," she said, "that's the story. They owned their cabin, and we rented ours. The children got along, so the adults followed suit, at least Beth and I did. And there were mutual friends. The sort of thing where you say you'll have to look each other up when you go back to town, and you mean to. But—"

"Nothing comes of it."

"Yes. And then—then the bubble bursts, and you forget it ever existed. Even the children forget." She hesitated, then said tentatively, "You have an older son, don't you?"

"I have two sons, Robert and Tad. Robert's with Grant, though Mary fought me tooth and nail on that one. And Tad is with us." The car was just ahead.

It was strange. As in the moving picture he had just seen, he could imagine folk in a darkened theater watching General Grant at his folding table, writing a note, and the young captain there to carry the message to the telegraph, dark-haired Robert Lincoln. He pictured campfires across the river, tents pitched in shadow, a soldier laughing, a voice in the night; dawn soon to come, and the battle to resume. Then the note sent, the campfires long out, the voices stilled, and Grant long gone. And himself with his face on the penny. And the five-dollar note. He stood aside as Joan unlocked the door.

"Thank you," he said, and he watched her circle the automobile, unlock her door, and slide in. In some ways she reminded him of Kate Chase, though now she was Mrs. William Sprague. It wasn't elegance they shared, for the elegant stand out, like speech that calls attention to itself. Aptness was a better word for it. Aptness in gesture, stance, and expression, all managed without art, or the appearance of art. Lincoln slid into his seat and folded his hands across his stomach.

"You're a considerate man," she said. "Are you always so generous with your time, with yourself?"

He shrugged. "I don't know. That's not something one chooses or avoids. And remember, I'm off duty. Mr. Nobody."

She laughed at that and started up the engine. "The Hebrew National's not far from where we had dinner. It's known for its desserts."

"Good. Nothing wrong with a sweet now and then. Actually, an apple does the trick for me as often as not. Many is the time when John Hay and I take a few minutes off, looking out the window, munching away. John is one of my secretaries, the younger one, a good lad and a fine set of extra eyes when I need them. Though Mary and he are like fire and ice, or is it oil and water? The latter, I guess—they don't mix, yet both survive the encounter."

"And I guess we'll survive ours," said Joan. "I mean the encounter with Beth and Ira," she added.

"I wondered there for a moment. Thought you meant the happenstance of you and me."

"Well, yes," she said. "At first I meant the one and then I thought of the other."

"Well," he said, "I expect we'll survive both. Though now the literal sense of survival and the narrow margins of our lives occur to me. I hadn't thought of the possibility of an accident here in this time and the consequences it would bring about back home. I didn't just disappear did I—the history books don't record that, do they? Here today, gone tomorrow?"

"No," she said. "You didn't."

"Good. Drive carefully nevertheless. No sense fooling with fate."

THEY PARKED DIRECTLY IN FRONT of the restaurant. "There they are," he said.

"Okay, here we go, Mr. Abrams. But I'll call you Alfred, and you must call me Joan."

"I'll do my best."

The Silvermans were sitting at a table near the front with silverware, glasses of water, and tea cups upside down on their saucers. "Ira, Alfred Abrams; Alfred, Ira Silverman. You've already met Beth."

"Howdy," said Lincoln, shaking hands with Ira and taking a seat beside Joan. Silverman, he noted, was aptly named, his hair silvery from temple to temple, his eyes silvery gray, even a silvery mustache thatching his pursed lips.

"Ira was just saying that James Dean gives him a pain in the stomach. What did you think?"

Beth's question was directed to neither of them and to both of them. It was a challenge, really, and a jab in the ribs at her silent partner. "Well," said Lincoln, "the young man gave a good performance as an estranged son to a righteous father. And once the wash is out and drying, he does prove an able son. Small joke there, Cain and Abel, you know."

Beth Silverman was staring strangely at him, as though she hadn't expected a considered opinion so swiftly.

"I liked him too," said Joan. "He's awfully young," she went on, "but you can't blame that on him. It's his brother who comes across as dull, if you ask me. Steinbeck must want us to be thinking about Genesis, and of course our choice is Abel, but Cain certainly is the more interesting. There'd be no story without Cain. You haven't ordered yet, have you?"

"Not yet," said Beth, and Ira shook his head.

A red-haired waitress with even brighter red lips appeared with menus and a pot of steaming coffee. A pitcher of cream was already on the table. "Evening," she said, righting their cups and filling them one by one. "You folks want a minute to decide?"

"Please," said Joan.

Lincoln glanced over the list: desserts galore, but an apple was all he wanted.

The waitress reappeared.

"My husband will have the chocolate cheesecake, and I'll have the custard," said Beth.

"One of the brownies will do for me," said Joan.

His turn. "An apple for me, good and crisp, thanks."

"It'll just be a minute," said the waitress, smiling her own apple-red smile as she headed for the kitchen.

Beth Silverman took a deep breath. "I have heard a little about you, Joan, since Lake Geneva, and I've thought about you more than once." The warmth of the wife distinguished her from her silvery husband, who may as well have been a mute.

"Thank you," said Joan. "Life does go on. I'm busy enough. And you?"

Beth Silverman shrugged. Lincoln had the sense that there would be more of an answer if he and Ira were out of earshot. "Alfred, you're not from the area, are you?"

"What makes you think not?"

"Your manner, your accent, knowing Joan."

"Knowing me?" said Joan. "In what way?"

"Oh, how you're not someone who finds the easy way easiest. Wasn't Robert from Maine, an island off the coast?"

"He was, though we met here, in Chicago, not on the high seas."

"And myself," said Lincoln, "I do, and I don't, hail from hereabouts. From Springfield, but it's been a while."

"Springfield, my ass!" interjected Ira, rising to the fore. Not a mute after all.

"All right then," Lincoln came back, "not Springfield. Would you prefer Oregon? Say I was the governor, but that's been a while. And presently I'm on tour."

"Right! You and the Philharmonic. So where's your magic wand?"

"Ira," warned Beth, "don't say another word if you want to enjoy that cheesecake." And then turning toward them she said, "Ira's got the stomach of a baby. Some days, he has nothing but custards and tapioca and oatmeal." It was hard to picture such a mean-spirited man satisfied with a bowl of oatmeal.

"What was that?" said Ira.

"What was what?" said his wife, with heavy emphasis on the "what."

Just in time, the waitress appeared, as if on cue, laden with desserts. Ira snared his right away, and while the others were still being served, began to devour it. The irascible turned gluttonous. It was hard to picture this man as a parent. In hard times, his children would starve unless they were cut from the same gobbling cloth as their father.

"So bring me up to date on your children," Joan said to Beth, her thoughts perhaps on the same track as his.

"They're fine. Elinore's fourteen and Naomi's turning twelve. She's a swimmer. I think if we pushed it, she could make the Olympics. But we won't. She has a life to lead."

"That's funny," said Joan. "I remember her refusing to go near the water. She was afraid of the minnows nibbling her toes."

"You have a good memory. That's right; she was used to the pool at the club. I'd forgotten about that."

The conversation drifted on, Beth and Joan exchanging stories. Ira was safe for the time being with his wedge of cheesecake, though it was fast diminishing. How Joan managed it so equanimously Lincoln couldn't fathom. Maybe time does heal, and he knew it did, but he couldn't forget those first weeks and months after Willie died, locking himself in Willie's room, grieving for his son. And for himself, and for his entire nation. If he could count on staying here, in these modern times, he'd want to meet the children—no, the grandchildren—of Robert and Tad, and hold their fragile bodies in his arms. With a start he realized he was giving rein to the gloom of his old hypochondria. The hypo.

He looked up. It took a second to get his bearings. He'd forgotten where he was, forgotten that he was among strangers, that the war was over, that the victors were dust, that bombs now fell from the sky, that the man across the table had taken an instant dislike to him, that he and Joan Matcham would say goodbye to Beth and angry Ira and climb into Joan's automobile and sit side by side, the panel lights glowing, the engine humming, the lights from other vehicles bearing down on them, then tearing by. Their voices, he realized, were like the rumble of distant thunder. He could hardly hear what they were saying. Beth was turned toward Ira, who pulled his wallet from his pants pocket, and Joan was saying they shouldn't, but Beth insisted and Joan had no choice but to give in. He wanted to say thank you, and maybe he did, but he couldn't hear himself any better than he could hear the others. He paused at the doorway and looked back inside, to fix the memory of this other world, the red-haired, red-lipped waitress squeezed into her white uniform, the burnished steel and thick glass of the display case jammed with jars of pickles and olives, rounds of cheeses, and slabs of cold meat, and the middle-aged Jewish man at the cash register with a smile as warm as the noonday sun. Lincoln turned back to the street and managed a nod in the direction of the Silvermans.

"Poor woman," Joan said. "Poor woman."

◆ VI ◆

North

10 April 1955

T HEY WERE HEADING NORTH AGAIN. Joan had chosen a
roundabout way. She didn't want to arrive, didn't want the
destination to be fixed, didn't want to put a period to the sentence. She should think of something to say; she could even say
the old reliable "I don't quite know what to say," but she didn't. It
was dark now, no street lights, not even tail lights of parked cars
reflecting.

She glanced at the dashboard. When she drove alone, which was
almost always, she'd turn on the radio and let it chatter away, an
outward voice to keep the inward voices at bay. The car hadn't had
a radio when she first began to drive, which was a year or so after it
happened. "It"—also known as "the crash," and never thought of
as an accident. Tom said radios were a distraction. But distractions
could be a plus. Often enough she was also driving away the melancholy.

She should give him a radio to take back to his time. A portable.
With a special dial for tuning in to the future. Did he even know
what a radio was?

She felt as if a spell had been cast. It had descended at the Hebrew
National when they had parted from the Silvermans. Ira was such
a strange man. At the sight of her companion he had practically
snarled. Had he recognized Lincoln? She shook her head. No, but
he must have recognized some element that put him at bay, backed
him up against the wall, contradicted who he was, the face he put

forward. She tried to remember what he did for a living. She remembered thinking there was something shady about it. This man was no schoolteacher, no judge, no servant dedicated to the good of the community. No Abraham Lincoln.

"Stop! Stop the car!"

It took her a second to place the voice, his.

"Stop the car," he repeated firmly.

She did, pulling to the edge of the road, one foot still on the clutch, the other on the brake, the engine idling. She had no notion where they were, other than west of Sheridan. Lincoln opened his door and out he went. Not a word said. *What was it? Was this it? The end? Just like that?* She sat there, rooted. It wasn't time for the spell to end, the witching hour twenty minutes away. It wasn't fair. Who was he and what was he doing here in her life?

"Damn," she said and opened her door, then reached back to turn off the engine. She walked around the front of the car, then back up the road where the shoulder narrowed, yielding to the concrete railing of a small bridge. She could barely make out shapes, see where her feet were taking her. But what city? It didn't feel like anyplace she'd ever been before, neither Chicago nor Evanston. In between. In daylight she'd know, wouldn't she? Yes. She couldn't tell what the bridge bridged. A stream or maybe a stream only when the rains fell. Just a gully now. There were ferns at the gravelly edge of the road where the bank slipped away.

"Hello," she called into the well of darkness, her voice half-hearted. She took a deep breath. "HELLO," this time challenging the silence.

"Watch out," his voice came from below. "There's a car down here, rolled off the road."

"A car?" She could hear him tromping about now. "I'll get a flash-light."

She was back in a moment. The beam of the flashlight picked out a glint of metal and glass, not all that far down, but well below the level of the road. She made her way over rocks, through bracken and bushes. The car was on its side tilted against a tree, the two wheels on the driver's side off the ground. She shone the light where Lincoln was maneuvering.

"There's someone inside," he said.

"Be careful," Joan called.

Lincoln was struggling with the driver's door. Good thing he was tall. No danger of the car falling back, propped like it was against the tree trunk. He got the door open and with a grating of metal forced it further.

From inside came a groan. It was a woman.

"You shouldn't move her," Joan said. A rule of the road, though any accident she'd ever come across had people milling about and holding handkerchiefs to their heads.

"It's going to be all right," Lincoln said to the person inside. "Can you tell me if you're hurt?" Joan stood tiptoe on a bit of a hillock to see inside. He was holding the woman's hand now. She wasn't behind the wheel but had slid to her right.

"I'm okay," she said faintly.

Lincoln turned to Joan. "I think she's all right," he said. He turned back. "Do you think you can move my way a bit?"

"Yes," she said, and she twisted her shoulders so Lincoln could draw her over and help her get down.

"Why Beth, it's you! It's us. It's Joan."

"Joan," Beth said, puzzled.

"Yes, Joan Matcham." She couldn't think of Lincoln's other name. "Where's Ira?"

"He's not in the car," Beth said, her voice flat and the words spaced out. "Is he?"

"There's no one in the car," Lincoln said. "We better get you up to the road." He led her by the hand, guiding her along. She seemed able enough to walk, but moved woodenly as though she had no will of her own. When they reached the car, Joan opened the rear door and Beth got in on her own. Joan switched on the dome light and looked Beth over. "I don't see any injuries," she said. "Was Ira driving, Beth?"

She shook her head sideways. "No. I was. Suddenly I lost sight of the road, and, and—I don't know. I must have swerved. And then I don't remember. Next thing I know you were there, with—it's Alfred, isn't it?"

"Yes," said Lincoln. Then, "Can I have that light for a minute?"

Joan handed him the flashlight, and back he went—to look for Ira, she guessed. She turned back to Beth. There was a knot above her right eye, but no blood. "Beth, what were you doing around here? Is this on your way?"

"What do you mean?"

"Do you and Ira live nearby? Ira was with you, wasn't he?"

"No," Beth said. "No. He told me to go along myself. His office isn't far from Howard. He said he'd take a cab home. It wasn't the best evening in the world, and something about your friend sent him round the bend."

"Well, let me tell Alfred to come back. We thought maybe Ira had been thrown from the car and was down there."

"No," said Beth.

"I'll be right back," Joan told her. Below, she could see the cone of light, busy searching. "Alfred," she called. "Beth says she was alone. See if you can find her purse, then come on up."

"All right," he called back.

In a minute he was working his way up to the road.

"She was alone?" he asked. "Where was her husband?"

"She said he went to his office. Sounds like they had some kind of fight. We need to get her home."

THE SILVERMAN HOUSE WAS set back from the road—it would be easy to miss it altogether. Joan drove along the gravel driveway and stopped by the entrance. A porch light was on as well as several inside. It had been less than a ten-minute drive from the accident; there shouldn't be any problem finding the wrecked car tomorrow. Lincoln helped Beth out of the car, and together they walked her up the stairs to a wide front porch. Beth inserted her key and the door swung open.

"Thanks so much," Beth was saying. "I'll be all right now. Helen, our maid, is upstairs. She can handle anything. I don't know what I would have done without you. What if I'd been hurt?"

"Thank God you're all right," Joan said. "That's the important thing. Tomorrow you should check with your doctor. And your car's just down this road, two or three miles. I'll check with you in the morning."

Beth thought about that for a moment, then shook her head. "You don't have to. I can manage."

Joan shrugged. She'd call anyway, she decided.

"Night Abraham, night miss," said an odd and shrill voice.

It was a parrot in an old brass-wire cage, perched solemnly on its swing. All three turned toward it. "I didn't know you had a parrot," Joan said.

"That's Trinidad. He's been in the family forever. He was my grandfather's, if you can believe it. Weren't you, Trinidad?"

"Knows his stuff, knows what's up," said the bird.

Lincoln stepped right up to the cage and hooked a finger inside. "How do, Polly," he said. "It's been many a day since I've seen one of these bright fellows. There was one back in Kentucky, knew everybody by name the moment they walked into the store. You'd swear it was smarter than we were by half a day."

"Half a day, half a dollar," said Trinidad.

"See what I mean?" said Lincoln, now crouching down and eye to eye with the green bird.

"*Fa*ther," it said, stressing the first syllable as though just now recognizing its parent.

"Son," said the crouching man. Then he straightened up and placed his hands on his belly, as though he had just risen from the dinner table. "Not an everyday encounter, that's for sure." He stepped toward the door, a palpable sign it was time to go.

"Fast friends," Beth said. "Trinidad doesn't usually open up to strangers."

"Stranger than some, but not others," said Lincoln with a wry smile. "But we'd best be on our way, and give this woman a good night's rest. Good night, old Polly."

"Good night, old trooper," the parrot said.

YOU'RE CERTAINLY GOOD AT PARROT-TALK," Joan said. Once more, they were on their way to Evanston, this time no detours.

"Nothing special there," he said. "It's just the more they've been talked to, the more they talk, like any other creature that talks. Which could be the problem with the husband, Ira. Too little talk when he was a young one. Like the chicken that overeats and bursts its buckles."

"There really is such a thing as that?" she asked.

"No," he said. "It's just an expression, a shortcut."

"And the parrot calling you Abraham?"

"Hard to tell. Could be what it says whenever it sees a man with a beard."

"Which I'll bet would have been some time ago," Joan said. "The day of the beard is long since gone."

"Yes, I've seen nary a one. I've come to like a beard. My Secretary of the Navy, Mr. Gideon Welles, has the woolliest one you ever did see. It puts the grizzly in its place. They call him Old Man Welles. Not his friends though, and no one to his face. He reminds them, I think, of illustrations of the patriarchs from the good book." He patted his chin. "Actually, this here beard is still new to my face. During the campaign a little girl from New York wrote and said growing a beard might help me get elected, sallow cheeks and all, so I gave it a try."

"Really? It's funny to think that a little girl was responsible for how we imagine you years later."

"It's the God's truth. Grace Bedell is her name. And what a delight it is, not to worry about a shave. You women don't know your good fortune."

"Lucky us."

He leaned forward. "Is that Evanston, all lit up?"

"That's it." They were approaching the business district, with Dempster just a couple of blocks ahead. "I have a question," she said. But how to phrase it so the answer came out right? She took the plunge: "I could take you back to the Orrington Hotel—that's where you spent last night, right?"

"Uh-huh." Flat assent, non-committal.

"Or we could go to my house. It's not so late, and then—" And there her sentence died.

"I'd say it's later than you think." Lincoln was looking straight ahead, choosing his words deliberately. "I know the proper choice back home. But I don't see that I have a rulebook for what's proper under the current circumstances. That's my situation. You're in a different spot, with wagging tongues to contend with."

"If it's up to me, the tongues can wag."

"It is up to you. And I will be honest. In spite of its modern conveniences, that hotel does not work like a lodestone for these old bones. Lately I've learned to go my own way and do the worrying after. There's but one life we lead."

"Yes," she said. "One life." She heard her breath whistling softly from her lips. The audibility of relief. "I have a spare bedroom, you know."

"So I had concluded."

Joan smiled at the thought of this man, this impossible man, so blithely sharing the front seat of her friendly old Dodge, sitting there like Aristotle, performing deductions upon the number of bedrooms in her house. Well, not an irrelevant inquiry.

She turned left on Church and right on Hinman and parked in front of the house. Rusty greeted them at the gate, her tail wagging as Lincoln patted her on the shoulder. "Come on, Rusty," Joan said, holding the screen door open, letting the dog inside.

She closed the door. Lincoln stood there, left hand in his pocket, the other scratching at the side of his head. "I may not have been clear," he said, "but I would appreciate the opportunity to spend the night here. Folk at the hotel may have to put up with Bad Debt Billy one night's worth, but I'd as soon spare them the second."

"Of course," she said. "Of course. And if it's worrying you, there are ways to pay the bill—"

"Thank you, but it's not that heavy on my conscience. They'll get more than their money's worth if they use my visit as a testimonial. Course, there'd be some explaining to do. I did sign their guest register, you know."

She laughed. "I hadn't stopped to picture you going through their routine."

"Well, I did. The old autograph itself. Even wrote out an address for my law office in Springfield."

Lincoln said this with obvious delight. Well, goodbye to the myth of Honest Abe, walking miles with a few pennies in change. She had turned the lamp on in the living room. "Would you like a sip of Kahlua? It's an after-dinner drink, syrupy and coffee flavored. I sometimes have a glass at night."

He nodded. "I would, though I am virtually a teetotaler." He followed her to the kitchen, where she poured them each a small glass.

She handed the drink to him. "To your health," she said, raising her glass. As his matched hers, the image she had been avoiding all day long came to mind: a broad avenue, with windows draped in black and mourners grieving.

"The living room's more comfortable," she said, and she led the way back. Again Lincoln chose the rocking chair by the fireplace. It had been Robert's from before their wedding, and she seldom sat there nowadays—she didn't like the image of the spinster rocking like Whistler's mother.

"Are you going to sit?" he asked.

"Yes, I was just thinking." Deliberately, she sat on the couch.

"Delicious," said Lincoln. "Even with a trace of alcohol." And then, "You do know I don't know how much time I have. I mean here. It could happen any moment. Getting here didn't involve a choice on my part, and there may be none for the return journey. I'm certain there will be a journey home—I think I said that already." He thought a moment and went on. "It wasn't mere whim that delivered me here. I don't think it will be whimsy that undoes this excursion."

"Undoes?" she said.

"Bad choice of words. I meant no more than the return, not the undoing of this day and night and whatever follows. This is a part of my life, even if no one at home will ever know of it. I assume this will be the case, for I do not intend to share it, not even with John Hay."

"Thank you," she said.

There he sat, Abraham Lincoln, the father of our country. No, that was Washington; this the Great Emancipator. She had to remind herself it truly was Abraham Lincoln, when half the time he was anybody, nobody but his ordinary self. At the same time, well, she knew it wasn't a dream, knew not to pinch herself. She let her eyes take him in. Did he seem old for his years? She tried to remember exactly how old he was—in his fifties? Early or late? He didn't particularly look like photos of himself, but sometimes cameras lie. With those old cameras, she knew, you had to sit very still. No presto-chango, click open and click shut like now. And the tweed jacket made a difference. She remembered the shock of his smile—was it just this morning? It seemed like a century ago. Verb tenses were tricky.

"You said you have a family at home," she ventured.

"Yes, I do. My sons and my wife." Saying that he shut his eyes, and like a ripple of wind in a wheat field, a shudder ran the length of him. He opened his eyes and took a deep breath. "I do hope I don't make a habit of this time-jumping. To be alive, and to know your son is dead, all your sons. It violates the order of the generations. It doesn't console me that my son's sons, or daughters, have taken their place. I don't know them, for all that they are flesh of my flesh."

She nodded. "You haven't mentioned Mary."

"No, I haven't. You know her name. Do you know the names of all our wives?"

Oh my, a tender spot. She shrugged. "George and Martha Custis. Dolly and James Madison. You and Mary Todd. Your names have come down to us. Eleanor Roosevelt. I met her once and shook her hand, but that's different, my own time."

"I'm sorry," he said. "I didn't mean to snap. I've gotten used to folk knowing better than to ask me about my wife. She is the mother to my children and has given her all. And I think she has very little left to give. The women especially have had to learn the lessons of war. I'm learning to be more careful, to take very little for granted. If I am in the field and the troops are all in a line and waiting for their Commander-in-Chief to ride by—well, it's all right if I make sure the review is done with my general by my side, but not my general's young and pithy wife. A war does not make the home life any easier. I hope Mary will find peace when I am gone."

It was a long speech, and it had come to an end. He sat there gently rocking, his long arms on the arms of the chair. Talking of Mary had drawn him inward. He was with her now, weighing their life together. An image sharpened in Joan's mind: a figure in a white toga, suspending a balance, like Dame Justice. Poised on one side were the Lincolns, husband and wife, and on the other, herself and himself, the two of them standing, awkward, averted, shy. Which way would the scales tip? He had made one choice when he decided to come home with her. But he had pictured two bedrooms. Or had he? He was a man after all. And she was a woman.

"I want to tell you a little about myself," she said.

He blinked, the reverie broken. "Yes," he said. "Please do."

"I've told you about the deaths of my husband and my daughter, Emily. The airplane crash in Utah. What I haven't told you was how Robert and I were that last year or so."

He nodded, watching her intently.

"It wasn't good. If it weren't for Emily, I don't think we would have stayed together. I had become a person who drove him crazy. Not crazy like insane, but the small things I did, like using the wrong knife, or the way I cooked eggs, or did the laundry, or turned down the corner of a page to mark my place in a book, such minuscule things, but they weren't small in his eyes. Neither of us wanted the touch of the other. Once we had. So he took to reading late at night. Then it became simpler for him to sleep in the guest room."

"Not the life that was meant to be," said Lincoln, shaking his head.

"I haven't talked about this before. With anyone. When he was killed everyone pictured how his death would affect me. And I let them think what they would. My grief was complete anyway. What difference did it make? But it does make a difference." She stopped. She couldn't put it into words, or didn't want to risk saying it aloud. She didn't mind that Robert had died. It was nothing like Emily dying, a bright light going out, a blinding, searing pain. His death was like a death you read about in the paper; you're sorry for it, but you go about your business.

"Abraham Lincoln," she said, pressing on, her words urgent. "I am afraid that if I let you go to the next room, go to sleep there, I will never see you again. I don't know the rules of your being here, but I don't want to let you out of my sight. I want you to sleep with me tonight, to hold me in your arms." There, she had said it, and the world had not come crashing down on her head.

He was nodding thoughtfully. She couldn't decipher his expression, but she saw his chest rise with a deep breath.

"When we were at dinner," he said, "you asked me what I was doing when I was pulled from my time into yours. And I told you the story of the proposal I was preparing for Congress to end the war. I told you what I was doing, but I did not tell all. You were trying to fix a moment in time, I know that."

"Yes," she said, knowing this was the preamble to a confession.

"I would like to tell you as best I can what was going through my mind as I worked on that proposal. History will judge me by what I have done or what I have failed to do. What I think in the privacy of my mind will not enter into that judgment. I know some will see me as a monster and others as a saint. One I hope I am not, and the other I cannot be. I am an ordinary man in extraordinary times."

He paused, and Joan sat silent, her eyes fixed on his, eyes so gray, so lucid.

"My thinking that morning," he continued, "to put it broadly, was that I had been doing things as best I could and that I deserved better. I was thinking that conditions should be privileged for me, that I should have a better than fair shake at the game board. Thinking this, I felt myself growing remote, as though I were faltering from my steadfast self. We work to preserve the image of who we are or how we wish to be perceived. I had relaxed my guard and realized my true colors: the colors of a thief, a scoundrel, a gourmand, a coward, an arrogant knave. A Falstaff in the eyes of Prince Hal, and in that a reflection of Hal himself. I had been a good son to a father who had not earned such a son. I had married Mary as I promised I would. I was a faithful husband. I had lost and grieved for two sons. I did not scheme for advancement. When I engaged Senator Douglas in debate, I had undertaken a hopeless task for the good of mankind. I was a man of peace, yet I had spent almost my entire presidency as a general of generals. All this I thought and more."

He shook his head sadly. "I had earned my reward, and where was it? Here I was, once again turning the other cheek, forgiving the unforgivable. I would save lives of North and South alike. I would love my fellow man, even traitor Lee and stiff-necked old Senator Davis. Jefferson Davis. Like the worst of the Republicans, I could have taken satisfaction in vengeance. For the death of Elmer Ellsworth, who was like a son to me. For Edward Baker, killed at Ball's Bluff, and William McCullough, and Mary's brothers David and Alec. And so many others. All this I was thinking and more as I wrote word upon word of my plan to bring the war to a close. However poisoned my heart, my words were without malice. I look back and see myself wishing for a sign that I was meritorious, and deserving, and worthy. The acknowledgment that I had risen above and beyond frail clay. That I was no Falstaff. Then, suddenly, I was reeling on Howard Street in the twentieth century."

He rose and took two long strides toward her. "And now I have been invited to share your bed. Does it make any sense to me? To you? These words, my thoughts, are like a flight of crows at the sound of a gunshot, scattering in all directions at once. But I don't need to think, because I know what I feel. You asked what drew me to this time and place?" He shrugged. "I can't say. Perhaps it was you or perhaps it was some need within me, or both, or neither, I cannot say. But I am here, and you ask, Joan Matcham, will I sleep with you and hold you in my arms? Yes, Joan, I will. Yes."

◆ VII ◆

Sailing On

10 April 1955

ABRAHAM LINCOLN LAY ON HIS SIDE beside Joan. She had lit a candle, and its pale orange flickers cast shadows in the corners of the bedroom. The fingertips of his left hand were just catching the moment along her side where firm shoulder turns to soft and yielding breast. "I wonder," he said, "I can't keep from wondering. I keep thinking that time is its ordinary self, is flowing the way it should, with the minutes coming along one by one, and I'm still there. Here is there, now is then. This is my time, not yours. Maybe John Hay has news for me. He'll poke his head in, most likely for nothing more than to lay eyes on the Boss, the Tyrant, the Old Man. They have a devil of a time deciding what to call me."

"I know the feeling."

"You can call me anything, even Abe. I'm nobody's president, not here."

"Abe," she said softly, a test.

"The war," he went on, "it's less pressing now. Things are winding down. The South grows desperate. Some staunch soul from Virginia or Maryland will take it upon himself—" He stopped. Not when he was here, with Joan, in candlelight.

Gently she patted his cheek. They lay beneath a sheet and a light-weight blanket.

"It's me, you know," he said.

"Yes, I know, and I guess it's natural, a beard. It feels natural."

"Well," he said, "it is. It's very hard work not to have one."

"I'm sure." She moved slightly onto her side, so that her knees touched his.

He was in a woman's world now, not just because it was her bed and her house, but because this act of love, done in darkness or by candlelight, seemed more of the woman than the man. He couldn't read her thoughts. It was Joan who had found the words that brought them together. He would have waited forever. The hands of the clock would have gone round and the earth would have gone round and the sun would have come up and still he'd be in the rocking chair. Now she was content to say a word or two and let the silence flow around them. He couldn't remember moments like this with Mary, such quiet moments. He pictured Mary in her black dress with the pearls, and her bosom for all the world to raise its eyebrows at. All but himself. She didn't let him close anymore, spent more and more time with Elizabeth Keckley. They were like sisters shut away in a world of their own.

"Is there no one"—Joan's voice—"that you would tell about us, at home?"

"No one," he said. "My close friends are back in Illinois, Dave Davis, the others. But even so, what would I say? 'Guess what, boys?' There were plenty of stories like that when we rode the circuit—not mine, theirs. I suppose I might have wished I had stories. But mostly they were just fabrications, and not as good as fishing stories. What about you?"

"Me?"

"You. Will you tell a friend? Your sister?"

"No, I live too closed a life. And I have no sister. Besides, how could I make a story like this come alive? Would you believe this story?"

"No, not without tangible proof. And what would that be? A photograph of us together? No, I suppose even that could be falsified. Convincing a third party would be difficult. And you? In a week or a month, or later down the line, how will you know it was real?"

"You mean know this from a dream?" She was on her elbow, looking closely at him.

"I guess that's what I meant," he said. He knew he could never forget Joan by candlelight.

She was shaking her head and smiling. "This could never be a dream," she said. "A lot of it I could have dreamed, but not this, not you in bed, with me. I may not remember it perfectly, like I remember Harrisburg is the capital of Pennsylvania, but I won't forget. My body knows. The Shadow knows. That's from a radio program, *The Shadow*. It's supposed to be scary, about an invisible man, and it always has that line, 'The Shadow knows.' "

It was her joke, not his. Jokes often worked that way, privately. Quirky moments rising to the surface, odd associations that never quite translate to the other person. They take you back to another time and place, drop you down the well of memory, if just for a moment. And he could guess what a radio program was, from the days before television.

Joan was letting him be once more. What were their last words? They had been talking about his presence and the persistence of memory. That she knew it could not be a dream, not eerie like *The Shadow* was supposed to be. *Just what is it like?* he wondered. In many ways it was no different. He was the same man he had always been, but the landscape had changed. And soon it would change back. The time for return was coming ripe. Grant and Lee would be facing each other once more. He hadn't asked a single question about the ending, hadn't looked at the book that surely must call itself *A History of the Civil War*. It would tell of the last days, of stubborn Lee's refusal to admit defeat. There had been a time when Lee had seemed a Goliath, a Goliath in gray, with gold braid, and a saber, with his boots rooted upon the bloody earth, and that damn horse of his, Traveller. Lee, a Goliath who blocked out the sun and shadowed all our days. But lately, ever since Gettysburg, Lee had returned, bit by bit, to his own size, and presently he was so much less. It was David now who stood tall, his eyes steady, looking down at the field with its toy cannons, and the soldiers in gray, each month a year younger—boys, not soldiers. A David who saw the end as clear as clear could be, and wondered when they would be allowed to call it a day. Word was, Lee himself was sick and tired of it. But Davis would keep it going till he was clamped in irons and shut in a guarded room. It was better than he deserved. Many a day it was hard not to side with those who wanted to punish the rebels for the brink and beyond they had led us to. But remember, it's all one ship, and one sea, and one storm, and one crew. In his mind's eye he saw the other story, two ships, their sails in tatters, the brasses worn and dull, paint chipping, a story of two ships from the same shipyard, with one breath in their keels and now two breaths in the sails, each growing smaller in the other's eyes, one sailing north, the other south. The story Davis envisioned. Well, he wouldn't let it happen, thank you kindly.

"Tomorrow's Monday," he heard Joan say.

Would he be here on her tomorrow? He could be back in the heart of a day where young Lieutenant Stephens, nephew of Alexander Stephens, would receive word at Johnson's Island that he was paroled and should report to the White House. A day with Mary out and about, then her reception in the evening. Back to a day when loving was gone from his life.

"You know," Joan said, "I'm such a creature of habit, especially lately, that immediately after I wash the dinner dishes I go upstairs and set the alarm for morning. So I don't forget. But here we are on a Sunday night, up till all hours, out to a movie, and then to the Hebrew National, two gadabouts. And then—"

"And then?"

"Well, you know." She sighed. "Oh, Abe," she said and put her arms around him, gripping him fiercely.

"I understand," he said, not really knowing what to say. He patted the small of her back at its graceful curve. "You were thinking, weren't you, that you hadn't set your clock to start the week off on schedule. It's strange, for both of us. We have our lives and our routines. Then I walked into your life, though it was you and Rusty walking into mine. Two lives coming together. That's no new thing on the face of the earth. But the *how* has been different, hasn't it?"

"Yes," she said, relaxing her tight hold. "Different. And, you know, I've also been thinking about that, the difference, but I'm not sure I can put it into words."

"Go ahead, try."

"It's silly, but maybe it's something like this: this is one day in your life, sandwiched between the beginning and end. When you go back, the day will have happened, and you'll have it in your memory, and you will carry it with you to the end. And then, years later, my time will come. Dwight Eisenhower will be elected, and a couple of years later you'll come along and sit on that bench by the lake. The trouble is, that while this day will happen again for you, my time will be long gone."

"Oh my," he said. "Let me think about that a minute. It sounds right, the way you say it. Once I'm back, today, this day, is still to happen. So say it does. But your part can't be over and done with. It has to be you every time. It's never Catherine the Great, or the lady next door; it has to be you with me this day, this night."

"Then it's a different me, one whose life has been exactly the same as mine up to that moment. But it won't be the me who's here. And you won't have any memory of this because it will be new again; none of this will have happened. It won't be the you who carries the memory of now. And we'll come up to this moment and this conversation and—oh my God!"

"What?" he asked.

"What if we're not the first Abe and Joan?"

"Lordy be!" And he couldn't keep from laughing.

"What's so funny?"

"I'm sorry," he said. "You must pardon me. You really must."

"I must?"

"Yes," he said. "You must." His hand, he noticed, was on her hip. He had an urge to kiss her breast one more time. "It's one of my rules," he went on, "the rules of law that pertain to the sexes, male and female, in moments of intimacy, that when one calls for a pardon, the other is bound to provide it. That's the law, and you must abide."

"Perhaps," she said. "But you yourself admit you're just an ordinary citizen here and now. It may be your law, but your law is not the law of the land. Still, this once I will accede. You carry a certain historical weight, you know."

"I suppose I do; I suppose I do."

"So now tell me what's so funny."

"What I was thinking about was the wonderful absurdity of you and me forever here and forever renewed. Or maybe it'll be like a drawing, where first there's the preliminary sketch, then the artist goes back at it. I've watched Carpenter at the White House. He did the whole Cabinet, me included. Spent six months with us, imagine! Gradually more and more of the image emerges, till pretty soon it's done. Cooked. Maybe the first time we didn't think this at all. Maybe we added it later, the third or fourth time, this whole chain of foolish Abrahams and sweet Joans."

"Sweet," she said. "It's such a funny word. We hardly use it nowadays, at least directly. We may refer to someone as sweet, but to say someone is sweet to her face, that's rare."

"Well, you are sweet, and considerate, and generous. I could go on. Kind, and loving. I've been thinking of one other thing that's strange. It concerns Mary—I keep thinking of her. I'm sorry."

"It's okay," Joan said.

"I was thinking of the night of the reception when Willie took sick. Washington had never before seen the likes of that evening, the White House gloriously redone in spite of my penny-pinching. It was to have been the night when Mary showed Washington what stuff we were made of. Instead we took turns by Willie's bedside. I can't tell you what a light Willie was in our lives. Ever since that night Mary has been a different person. Not that I am the same, but I've gone on. I had to. And now, there's a gulf, an abyss, that each day grows. Sometimes I can reach across, but so rarely nowadays. Mary chooses the past, wants to find Willie. Calls in Spiritualists and asks me to come along. Willie needs both of us to answer the call. That's what they tell her. And so, the vine of affection that is rooted between us could not choose but branch. And so it has."

"Oh." Silence.

"Or wither."

She held him close. He heard her exhale. "It's natural, I suppose," she said. "I haven't given much thought to the flesh lately myself."

"Two of us then, two fish lost in the same waters. I'm glad I found you, or you found me. And the other thing, about our different selves. I don't think it matters. It all comes down to the moment, to now."

"I know," she said. "I know."

I know, he heard, weariness coming on him unawares, *I know*, echoing through the dark forest of his mind as he drifted off to sleep, his eyelids sealed, weighted, and a ways off a boat with the two of them, sailing, getting smaller. And blue water, blue sky, and sunlight.

◆ VIII ◆

The Ninth Moon

10 April 1955

JOAN LAY THERE, DROWSY. They were on their backs, side by side, thigh to thigh. She let her hand rest on his leg, gently. She opened her eyes and looked at this man beside her. His left hand rested on the coverlet. She traced his other arm with her fingertips to where his hand lay against his belly. The covers at the end of the bed were like distant mountain peaks, rising sharp against the dark sky. The feet of Abraham Lincoln. Was there any way to hold him here? She shook her head. No.

Later, if she wanted to, she could track things down, see where, or when, he had come from. He had mentioned meeting with the peace commissioners from the South, on a riverboat. And two Cabinet meetings, the second tonight, tonight in his world, a Sunday. The end of the war was near at hand. Her own memory of the events as told in the history books was fuzzy. Sherman marching through Georgia, Lee surrendering to Grant at Appomattox, the war all but ended. Within days, a week more or less, John Wilkes Booth would undo this life, his life. Why should it happen? She should wake him, warn him, "Don't go to the theater," or "Have Booth arrested." He had told her he would die at Ford's Theater. He had already decided nothing would change the course of his life. What would she do in his place? One thing, she wouldn't put Emily on that damn plane, to hell with Providence and the fall of the sparrow. But how do you turn fate aside? Or is it always being turned aside? Every step a road

94

not taken. Who knows, maybe now it wouldn't happen. Lincoln not the same Lincoln. But there was no alteration that she could see. Nothing had shimmered in her own time, like a gyroscope careening into a baseboard and ricocheting off in a new direction. Would any alteration wait upon his return? And the headlines would read:

BOOTH ARRESTED
IN ASSASSINATION ATTEMPT
PRESIDENT LINCOLN
SAFE AND SOUND

Of course already there was an alteration, however slight. Another inside story. This man within her, his coming. And not for all the blessed gold in the wide wide world would she ever give it back. Let the universe be unbalanced for all eternity. And what if—oh God— like Emily, conceived on the Fourth of July of 1942, with Lieutenant Matcham home for a single evening, one train in from New York, the other bound for California, and husband and wife ensconced at the Palmer House, making a baby. And like the moon she'll wax, and go on waxing, moon after moon, and never wane, not till the ninth moon.

Did he have to go? Yes, she knew the answer was yes. She couldn't keep him here in her time. The impulse was to grab his arm. They won't take him while he's awake, will they? There'll be no tug of war, will there? *No,* she thought, *they'll sneak up on you when no one's looking and nab you, take you back to goddamn John Wilkes Booth.* She reached for his hand, and no hand was there. Gone, he was gone. Already gone.

◆ IX ◆

Choosing Sides

5 February 1865

Abraham Lincoln stood at the window, hands in pockets. He'd gone to sleep in one century and come awake in another. Thirty-five years from now, as the century turns, folk across the face of the whole planet will do that and think it ordinary.

Why had he been singled out? No answer. Would he rather he had not been chosen? Or that he not remember? Here he did have an answer. No, he wouldn't wish it otherwise, but that wish was not a simple one. He had failed Mary in so many ways over the years. Notions of child-rearing, his absent-mindedness, the time spent away from home while on the circuit, his plainness, his dreams, his thousand bad jokes. And now he had this added burden of guilt.

Upstairs Mary was still asleep, deep under the covers, curled up like a child. The longer she slept, the less of the day she had to face. "What?" he said, not turning his head, staring out the window at nothingness. From deep within he knew that John Hay had spoken, had said, "Look." He knew that John was at the small desk engaged in some project this Sunday morning. If it wasn't a book, or his diary, or filing correspondence, or writing a letter to the elder John, John Nicolay, there'd be something else he'd find to do. John Hay wouldn't stand gloomy at the window, embracing his "hypo," his old familiar hypochondria.

"What?" said Abraham Lincoln once more, forcing himself to turn around.

"This," said Hay, glancing up briefly. In one hand was a pair of scissors, in the other a small sheet of paper.

"Hmmn," Lincoln grunted. He didn't move. He couldn't, not with one foot still lingering in another time. Must he move on? Did he have a choice? He was here, locked into his own time, here to live out the balance of his life. An hour ago he had been elsewhere, living another life, ninety years from now. It had not been a dream. In his pocket was proof, though a proof that would be nothing but a puzzle to anyone but himself. A copper coin, with ONE CENT inscribed on the reverse. The other side bore the usual references to LIBERTY and trusting in God, and an impossible date, 1955, and the blasphemous portrait of himself.

Outside were trees, leafless. And gray skies. And a country at war. Lee won't manage another miracle, will he? Lee and Joe Johnston linking up, drawing out the inevitable. More lives. Deaths. It was as if there were two clocks, one here and one there, ahead. Both ticking on, and himself listening to both. He took out his watch—a few minutes after eleven, correct according to the clock on the mantle. Coincidence? The whole time he'd been there he hadn't thought once to look at his watch and see what time it was keeping. Could he just stand here by the window and ponder the mystery of time, an observer?

No. It would be like loving a child and fearing for its life. So you lock the child in a room and keep it from the world, the world from it. And the child turns into an object, outside of time and without life. Like wishing a sunny day could go on forever, and the wish coming true; gone is the stillness of night and the quiet of the stars. And dreams.

He turned from the window. Later today he intended to present a proposal to his Cabinet that would end the war, end the bloodshed. They would shake their heads. Welles would note in his diary, "The President has matured a scheme to promote peace and end the war. It did not meet with favor. There is such a thing as overdoing forgiveness." So why go ahead? Why give Old Man Welles ammunition for his cannon?

"There," said Hay, who had risen from the desk. "What do you see?"

Lincoln sighed. "Do I need my glasses?"

"No," said Hay. "But you do need to think. Tell me what you see."

"Is it some sort of puzzle?" Lincoln asked. Hay had given him a small loop of paper he had been working on with scissors and a pot of glue.

"Sort of," said Hay. "But that's too general an answer."

"Are you asking me to read your mind?" said Lincoln. "I can do it, you know, but it takes concentration. And energy. Nothing received without expenditure. The law of conservation. The times balance upon the head of a pin. The whole earth teeters, verges on toppling, and John Hay asks me to inspect his slender loop of paper."

Hay was smiling and so was the Boss. "Well, what have we?" said Lincoln. "I see." He squared his shoulders, and with parade-ground voice commenced: "Honored Secretary to the President of the United States of Harmonica, Generous Ladies and Distinguished Gentlemen, Worthy Serpents. Before us we have a single piece of common paper, in length six to eight inches, in width somewhat less than two inches. A dab of mucilage joins the ends of what was once a rectangular strip of common white paper, so that now it forms a loop. But," Lincoln's left index finger emphatically stabbed the air, "not a common loop such as encircles the cylinder of a cigar." He was in the courtroom now, and judge and jury were as intent upon the attorney as the ox on its goad. "I repeat, not a common loop," and with thumb and forefinger he traced the loop twice around. "And herein lies the twist. Not a metaphor, but a literal twist. And that, Gentlemen of the Jury, Honored Secretary, is the story of the Loop of Loops."

"Very good, sir, but that is not the whole story," Hay responded. "There is a German mathematician by the name of August Ferdinand Möbius. He is presently the director of the Leipzig Observatory and a correspondent of Joseph Henry. He is the inventor of the strip of paper there in your hand." Hay smiled.

"And that completes the story? A trifle of biography?"

"No," said Hay. "I have here a pair of scissors. What, I ask you, would happen were you to slice lengthwise through the middle of this loop with this incidental pair of scissors?"

"There would then," said Lincoln, "be a cut extending non-transversely through the loop with the effect that—" he stopped. The picture so suddenly in his mind's eye was of Mary, knotted in the bedsheets, an impossible tangle of cotton and person. And Mary's dreams, a mirror of a nation in rebellion with itself, her family fighting on both sides of an equation. "I do not know the effect," he said. "Ordinarily I would say there would then be two loops, but I know you and August Möbius would not bother to invent a puzzle with such a trivial solution. To expedite the moment, I will say the obvious: two loops, each half the width of its parent. Two twisted loops, that is. The scissors, if you please."

Hay raised his hand, one finger extended. "I forgot something, a question, two questions."

"All right," said Lincoln.

"How many sides to the present loop, and how many edges?"

"Two?" Lincoln scowled. It reminded him of the games he and Willie used to play, the obedient father willing to endure any ignominy the child could offer. "Well, it looks like two edges, this and that."

Hay shook his head. "Trace your finger along an edge and see where it goes."

Lincoln was already doing this. "Aha!" he said, one finger now on the opposite side from the other and still in transit. He could see its destination ahead. "So—it has a single edge. And I have the suspicion that the number of sides will not come out two. Yes, I see." He had run the loop once more through thumb and forefinger. "One edge, one side. And I am wondering what application this strange loop might have. Not as a belt for a lathe, unless the lathe were to churn the legs for a table that might serve its food both atop and—in a manner of speaking—abottom itself. To serve a seamless meal that begins nowhere and never ends. Oh, if only the food could be found to match the wonderful properties of this table, the never-ending apple with a core both out and in and a matching skin on the out- and inside. Where were we?"

Hay, smiling from ear to ear, handed over the scissors.

"Thank you," said Lincoln. "Well, let me see. It's hard to start, isn't it. But I think I can manage." He launched the scissor point into the paper strip and sliced around, catching up to the beginning. "Just as I thought. Or as you led me to think. You know you shouldn't have asked me your two questions before I cut. You gave it all away. Single-sided John Hay. Now what? The loop is twice the size. No, no, no. Twice the length."

"Is that all?"

"Yes, that is all. Is that not all?"

"How many edges, how many sides?" asked Hay.

Again Lincoln took the loop through its loops. "Hmmn. May I notch an edge? Never mind, I'll just do it. There now." Again the loop looped through his fingers. "It appears this loop no longer has the property specific to Professor Möbius's initial loop."

"Perhaps not," said Hay. "Perhaps you'd care to slice it from gullet to gullet once more?"

Lincoln shook his head. "I'm a busy man, John. This evening the Cabinet meets to reject my proposal to distribute four hundred millions of dollars to the sixteen states pro rata their slave populations in return for a cessation of all resistance by the first of April next."

"To reject it? You know that?"

"Yes, and that's what makes me a busy man. It takes good time to look the hypo square in the face, to take its measure, and declare it the most excellent of hypos, a most melancholy hypo, a hypo of the highest order and deepest degree. All this takes time."

Hay scratched his cheek. "You're thinking they won't settle for compromise? Not now, with Sherman on the loose and Grant eating up General Lee?"

Lincoln shook his head sadly. "No. They will sooner spend lives than dollars. They wish to see the South flat on its back and its throat bare. And I, fool that I am, wish there were but one edge down there, so that before long we could come back to the beginning with the lesson learned and lives still to live." Lincoln's eye caught the hands of the grandfather clock. "I think Mary should be up by now. Unless I am mistaken, Madame Elizabeth is due at high noon to confer with Her Majesty upon the subject of a hemline or two. Thank you for the lesson on the virtues of thinking twice before taking sides."

◆ X ◆

This House of Houses

5 February 1865

MARY TODD LINCOLN HAD BEEN AWAKE for a good hour. It was almost noon and still she hadn't had a full night's sleep. She had sent word round to Lizzie to put things off till two. She rolled over onto her other side, knowing it would make no difference. When she was a little girl in Lexington, before Mama died, she used to crawl into the big bed, and Mama, without even waking, would take her little girl in her arms, and together the two of them would sleep till God knows when. By the time the little girl woke, Mama would be long gone, and the child would be curled up, lost deep in the down comforter. Then Mama had died and that was the end of that. Daddy brought his new wife and her family into the house and love flew out the door. And Mary Todd had learned to follow rules.

Well, at least she had some say in the rules nowadays. There was no one to stop her from getting up in the night and wandering through the rooms. It was like a haunted house since Willie died. What wouldn't she give—no, she wouldn't think about it this morning, or afternoon, or whenever it was. She pictured long-faced Dr. Charlemagne Chambers gathering them into his circle to summon the spirit of Willie. And Father Abraham doing his best to keep from saying something about this darn foolery. She could read his mind like an open book. She should be the one raking in the dollars, Mrs. Lincoln, the Kentucky Mind-Reader. Don't ask the question unless you are willing to face the answer. She could spruce up her act, draw spirits from the land of the dead, and promise to read their minds, maybe even better than Chambers with his fancy New England accent. She too could undertake a course of study with Mesmer in the old country—if Mesmer were alive. Mr. Lincoln said not a word, but you could see the deep sadness in his face. Why did she put him through it? Because without him it had no chance of working. It would take the lure of his father to draw Willie back.

She wasn't hungry. Her last stop on the midnight ramble had been the kitchen for a bowl of wheat biscuits with warm milk and butter and white sugar. Good thing they kept the stoves going till after midnight. That was one benefit of living in this house of houses. She loved the sneaky feeling of getting away with something. Eating by candlelight, taking her time, with the shadows deep in the four corners and no one to scold her, then tiptoeing back upstairs to let the warm milk do its magic and bring sweet oblivion.

"Mary?" The door opened gently, and in peeked Father. "Don't you want to be ready for Madame Elizabeth? I heard you tell her to be here about now. It's nearly twelve." He entered the room and lightly closed the door behind him.

She blinked her eyes, though she was already used to the light. It was one thing to sleep in late like a daughter of privilege, but it was another just to lie here and stare at the ceiling. "Lizzie won't be here till later. I postponed things a bit. Sometimes I wish I were a cat."

"So you could sleep any- and everywhere."

She nodded. He too was a mind-reader. Finished her sentences for her, when he put his mind to it. "You haven't told me much about Hampton Roads."

"Not much to tell. Met with Aleck Stephens, and Judge Campbell and Senator Hunter. Seward was with us, you know. They came on board the *River Queen*, but they had their instructions from Jefferson Davis and were looking for conditions. That man seems to think the last four years have left no deep impression."

"I never did care for Jefferson," she said. And it was true, she didn't. Too stiff a turkey, strutting about like he was cut from different cloth than the rest of us.

"They didn't know the Amendment had been passed. That put the damper on their hopes, not that Aleck had any great hopes to begin with. I do like that man. You should have seen him. It was raw out there, and don't ask me where he got his coat, but it would've fit a grizzly. When he stepped out of it, it was the littlest ear from the biggest shuck you ever did see."

She could picture it. Aleck Stephens, the Vice President of the CSA, was even shorter than she was.

"His nephew is a prisoner at Johnson's Island. I had asked if there was anything I could do for him. Aleck was a good friend when we were in the House together."

"I remember," Mary said.

"He asked if I could have his nephew exchanged, so I did that first thing and requested to have him report here. The lad must be special to his uncle. You might like to talk with him. He'd most likely value a voice from home in this cold city."

"I would like to do that," she said. "So it came to nothing?"

"Nothing," he echoed. "Well, we had to show that we were open to any reasonable offers. My conditions were plain as plain can be. Go home, I told them, get your states to give up the rebellion, and organize as soon as possible into law-abiding governments. Forgo slavery. Then we will talk about conditions. They don't know a bargain when one jumps in their lap. Aleck of course did, but he can't go against Davis, not when Davis set up the meeting. Damn that man. Damn the whole stiff-necked bunch of them. And Lee too. More Virginian than American. That's the virtue for you and me of being born in one state and coming to live in another. Home isn't quite home, but then our allegiance isn't as narrow, is it?"

She nodded her head in agreement and wished she were home. His arms were at his sides. Fine arms still for chopping wood and splitting rails, but for a long time now they had had trouble finding their way around a woman.

"Well," he said, "just thought I'd check," and off he went. He hadn't been even a full stride inside the room. She half sat up, leaning on her elbow. The fire was going strong—as usual she had slept through its waking. She must rise from this bed, mustn't disappoint him.

She rose and donned her slippers, then stood by the window, her crossed arms holding her elbows in close. The chill hadn't worn off yet. Another gray day most likely. She parted the draperies a bit. Below, in the yard, stood her husband's two goats, their heads raised, sniffing the clear air and staring into the distance. If their master were here by her side they would know it as surely as the fox its den or the miser his hoard. Their bearded faces would stare up at the window in vacant affection as though they too understood he was more than just a father; he was the Father of Fathers. Her they ignored. "Damn fool goats," she muttered.

Pets. After Willie died she gave away everything that would remind her of the dear boy, that would make her think of him in his white shroud and cold grave. Out went his toys and pets, even his pony. She shivered. What matter if a room is warm or not, when the cold is in you, down deep in your bones? During the rare nights when her husband did share her bed, she'd cling to him, like a dog sucking the marrow from a bone. She knew it kept him from sleeping and in the end drove him away, back to his own bedroom, or to the couch in his office, to the narrow bed in the Soldiers' Home, or the company of Grant in the field.

He had not always been repelled by her presence alongside him. She thought back to when they were first married, boarding at the Globe Tavern on the corner of Adams and Third, meals and washing included. Back to when she was the one kept wakeful half the night in his long arms. Back when he still thought of her as Molly. It was no surprise that Robert was born nine months and three days from the date of their marriage. It wasn't an elegant life by any means. Yet already she had had her sights set on this very house, this mansion. When had they picked up the habit of calling each other Father and Mother? Obviously after Robert was born, but how soon? It had been just a different name at first, no more than that. But words take on weight. She turned at the sound of the door opening again.

"Morning—or afternoon," said Lizzie Keckley. "I don't mean to disturb you, Mrs. Lincoln, but I thought it best I come a bit early. I know how you hate to rush."

It was true. She and Time were on uneasy terms these days, neither pushing the other too hard. Lizzie knew to be patient, and Mary had come to rely on her to pick out the pearl earrings and necklace, the bracelets, the red roses for her hair. "It's no bother, Lizabeth," Mary said. "Besides, I need someone to drag me away from my thoughts. There are days when I think I could turn to stone just standing at a window if no one disturbed me."

"One of those days, is it, Mrs. Lincoln? Don't I know how hard it is for you when the President is away? But he's returned—I passed him on my way in. He said he and Mr. Hay were off to the War Department and they'd be back shortly, for the reception."

"Yes," Mary said, "he was here just minutes ago. It helps to know he's close by. I don't know why I am so dependent, like those goats of his. His pet wife."

"Oh, those goats," said Lizzie, crossing the room and drawing the draperies. "They live for the sight of that man. Worse than dogs. Give me a cat any day. They know their own mind. But words are words and deeds are deeds, like they say. And I'd say it's time we got going."

Such a resolute woman—having bought her way out of thirty years of slavery says something about a person. "Then you'd best turn up that lamp, Lizabeth. You'll need what light you can get to perform your magic. I do wonder why you put up with me, though I'm glad for it. I'd be lost otherwise." Lizzie nodded all the while, hearing and not hearing, readying the tools of her trade. You'd have to fall down dead to occasion her failure. As Father might say, the woman could put a smile on the face of an ox. "God knows," Mary said, "I don't make life any the easier for Mr. Lincoln, and don't you deny it."

Mary's complaint had no effect one way or the other. Lizzie brought a tray filled with fruit over to the dressing table and stood by with comb and brush waiting for Mrs. Lincoln to be seated. When the brush gently began its work, it was as if the tangles of Mary's whole person were coming undone. "Lizzie," she said after a dozen strokes, "would you mind telling a story—like the one of Mr. Bingham and the altering of his hard heart?"

The brush hesitated. She could see Lizzie in the mirror, thoughtful. "Mrs. Lincoln," she said finally, "most stories that I have to tell give me pain to go over. I tell those stories so folk will know who I am, will know my story and know that I have not always been a familiar of folk like yourself. Now that I am on the shady side of forty, I may look like one thing, but most of my days have been fettered. Most days my feet could not point where they chose. My life has been eventful, my recollections distinct. But I don't find real satisfaction going over the wilderness of those stories more than I need to."

"Lizzie, I didn't mean one of those stories, fraught with pain. Like the story of the white man who persecuted you—how long was it you were under his thumb?"

"Four years, Mrs. Lincoln, four years. And the child that I brought forth was the only child I ever did bear."

"I'm sorry," said Mary, "for what you lived through." Her voice faltered. She wanted to say more but didn't want to sound so helpless, so pitiful. She wouldn't say that if she were put to the trials Lizzie Keckley had stood up to, she didn't think she could manage, didn't think she could keep her chin up, her eyes dry, her thoughts clear, let alone make her way in the world. Grief could drive her mad. Father said so, and he had warned her that the asylum on the hill was waiting. But how do you compare tragedies? Lizzie's life, hers. She'd sooner have never been born than live through Lizzie's pain. But what about her own life? Can you avoid the battles that life brings, the sorrows? You cannot say to Mama, "Not me. Choose yourself another child."

"Yes, Ma'am," said Lizzie. She had resumed the slow and steady brushing, stroke after stroke. "I know that your sorrow for me is genuine and not just words."

"Thank you," said Mary. "Though to be honest, I don't know that I can see another's sorrow, being so clouded with my own." She sighed audibly. "I sound pitiful even to myself. I had a hard time sleeping last night."

Excuses. From the mirror she could see that Lizzie was in her own world. As we get older, she thought, further along, our lives turn inward and we take in less and less of the world and more of ourselves, our recollections, our reflections. She lowered her eyes, and shards of a dream came into view. She could picture a river, brackish and sluggish, meandering, losing itself in the marsh. Trees, old, bent, and withered, hung with Spanish moss, loomed overhead, their trunks hidden in shadow. And behind her was Father, silent, seeing what she saw, yet saying nothing.

Mary waved her hand in front of her eyes to dispel the vision. "I guess," she said, "I just wanted to hear the sound of your voice. You know my mother's name was Eliza."

"And your stepmother too, if I'm not mistaken."

"You are a resilient person, Lizzie. Just when sentiment is about to have its day, you give the door a nudge and quicker than a flicker it's gone."

Lizzie shrugged. "Resilient, yes. Without resilience I'd have sunk long ago." She paused, hairbrush in mid-stroke. Her lips were pursed, her chin raised. A gathering of forces.

"Lizzie," Mary said, "I won't stop you. Tell the story you want to tell." Mary said no more, didn't say that what she really wanted, had been wanting for two years and more, was a story that would work magic, a soothing story. She wouldn't ask for Willie to be alive again. How could she ask for that? But she could ask for a story that ironed out the wrinkles, that worked them from the damp shadows into clear and seamless calm. She could hope for that.

Lizzie took a deep breath. "Three years ago my son left Wilberforce with the three-month troops and went to Missouri. But I'm not telling his story, how he was killed in Missouri, on the battlefield when General Lyon fell—the gallant General Lyon, as everyone said. I like to think it isn't just generals that are gallant. The women I sewed for, they used words like *brave* and *noble* and so did Mr. and Mrs. Walker Lewis that I took rooms with. Even my friends. To console me that my son had died for a good cause. How could I doubt the cause? I had told myself the same thing. It's when they told me that death comes to every one of us—I say *they*, because it was more than one that said it."

Mary looked up and saw Lizzie's jaw set, her eyes narrowly focused on an invisible adversary, sorting her words just so. Then Lizzie resumed. "It was like they were reminding me of what had slipped my mind, that it's natural to die, that sooner or later all of us will die, and our flesh and bones return to the earth. Did they expect me to take heart from their words?"

Mary shook her head in commiseration. Most likely she had said such words too.

"I know," said Lizzie. "Life is a mystery and death is an even greater one. Folks would go on and tell me of an early death of a loved one, a child, a wife, a sister. They meant well, to lighten my load. 'Lizzie,' they would say, 'He knows when the least sparrow falls, and takes note. And every note joins the swelling chorus, and if you listen carefully you will hear your son's voice singing with the chorus, singing the song of living and dying.' They even used the word 'joy.'"

"'Joy,'" said Mary. "'Joy'?"

"Yes, 'joy.' It didn't make a difference really, but I wondered about their words and their honesty. I wondered."

"At least no one talked to me of joy."

"No," said Lizzie, "I can't imagine they did. Not even Reverend Gurley. Anyway, after I got word of my boy's death, my heart was dry, like a stone. I went on with my sewing, kept up my routines. But the dryness, like the wing of a butterfly left on a summer's windowsill, wouldn't leave me. And then one morning, I heard this awful commotion outside my window. I got up to look. Jays. There were five of them, cawing and taking turns, one after the other, diving down from the big old pine tree, swooping close to the ground, then flying back up to the tree. They did this again and again. I looked at the ground and all about I saw feathers, blue feathers, and gray. And what was left of a wing. That and the beak and some of the skull. What the cat had left behind. I wondered, what do the wise old birds about town say to those five jays, diving one after the other? Do they say, 'Take heart, my dear fellows, for sooner or later death comes to us all. The fall of a single jay is part of the divine plan'? I don't think so, even if the birds could talk. All morning long I kept rising to look out the window. I would linger, with my forehead pressed against the cool glass. Then because I couldn't stay that way all day long, I would go back to work. But I wasn't really working, wasn't paying attention to my needle. I had the image of my son before my eyes. The image of a baby, then a boy, a lad, a young man. And lastly, a body, lying lifeless in Missouri. Plan? What plan? Toward dinnertime the jays ceased their cawing. When I went outside all the feathers but one were gone. I didn't know which cat to be angry with."

"I guess not," Mary said softly.

"Dinnertime came and went. I fixed myself a bite to eat, then I went back to my sewing. I miss my boy. I had hopes to see him be something in the world, but that won't come to pass. Instead I tell you his story. My story. You know, Mrs. Lincoln, I think your hair's been done ten times over."

◆ XI ◆

Another Landscape

11 April 1955

J OAN MATCHAM'S EYES struggled open. The bed was all hers. She gritted her teeth and told herself she wasn't going to cry. But why not? What difference did it make? No one was there to shake his head at poor, hopeless Joan.

Her chest was heaving, and like a breathless child, she let her tears flow. "Oh, oh, oh," she whimpered, both hands knotted in fists above her belly. When she got her breath back, she couldn't decide whether to laugh or turn her fury on the Fates for dealing her such a fortune. She wouldn't say *misfortune*. "Oh, Abe," she said aloud, as though he had just boarded a train eastward bound, and her hand was gently waving its farewell from the platform.

Her hand was waving, she realized. By now all his trains would be antiques, with bulgy smokestacks and drive wheels two stories tall. Her hand was in one century and himself in another. She looked for the clock. Holy Jesus! A quarter after one. She should be sitting at her desk.

She pushed the covers aside and swung her legs over the edge of the bed. She was naked as a jaybird. She grinned. It was no dream. No, it wasn't. Though where would she go for proof? Her purse, for one thing—her money hadn't spent itself last night. And hadn't he said that when he checked into the Orrington, he'd signed his own name and given his Springfield address? Not that she was about to draw the Orrington's attention to their guest register. Beth was a witness, and Rusty. Teach Rusty to talk, that was the ticket.

She looked out the window—another sunny day. She should call the department, but she didn't budge. No. The History Department could do without her for one day, and she could do without them. Besides, she needed to talk with Beth. To see him through her eyes. Not that she had any doubts. "I mean, look at this room," she said softly. "I don't live like this, with last night's clothes caught in a tornado." Oh, it had been real all right. Abraham Lincoln had been here, and he was not at all presidential.

Anyway, she'd better call the office. And she'd better remember to kill this lilt in her voice. She dialed.

"Fran, it's me. I'm not just late—I'm not going to make it today at all. I'm dizzy or something. I don't know. I fell back asleep and can't seem to get myself going. If you need me in the morning, let me know. Otherwise I'm going to give myself the day off. Sorry."

She set the receiver back in its cradle. Everything should be that easy. Of course, it helps if you haven't missed a day of work for five years—who wouldn't believe you?

What about his clothes? she thought with a start. *Had he tumbled back to his century naked?* But they were nowhere in sight. They must have made the trip with him, his notebook and spectacles and all. Not a trace. Why hadn't she asked for something, a token, a sign of his presence here with her.

Her eye caught a young woman across the street, dressed all in green with a red stroller. Joan snared the corner of her lip between her teeth, her eyes fixed on woman and stroller till they passed from sight. What were the chances of being pregnant? she wondered. Eyebrows would be raised, that's for sure. Joan shrugged her shoulders. A long shot. Well, no matter what, she'd better get going, before Beth got away. Though she had a feeling Beth wasn't going to be out and about today, not after last night.

Brushing her teeth, Joan looked back toward her tousled bed. Why couldn't they have had one more day? But deep inside she had known they wouldn't. Knew it deep in her bones, knew it to the core. They both knew. And when had she last felt so free? She looked at herself in the mirror. When Emily was a baby, a child? Certainly not since the crash, that was for sure. Emily, the only baby she'd ever had, her Emily, the fruit of a one-night visit, betwixt and between. Well, time would tell. Half a dozen weeks. Then a visit to Lorraine Riggs, her friendly gynecologist. And then concocting another story. Or no story at all. She'd better give Beth that call. But not before breakfast. She'd best eat. Give gravity a boost, something to fix her feet to Mother Earth.

JOAN SAT AT THE BREAKFAST TABLE, where she ate all her meals. She never used the dining room anymore. The Schuberts, the family who'd sold them the house, had redone the kitchen just before the war, ripped out the wooden cupboards and the porcelain sink and the built-in icebox in the pantry. They had replaced them with the Servel refrigerator and the stainless steel double sink that looked as dull as pewter unless you polished it with Babo. The dark blue formica counters made her think of Greek islands floating on clear waters. Instead of wood, there were metal cabinets above and below, painted white, with chrome handles curved like crescent moons. It was very modern, very sanitary, very sterile.

Why did she notice all this now? Yesterday, when they had eaten their omelettes, such thoughts were far from her mind. What had he—it was so hard to say his name, Abe—thought? Who knows? He might have thought this kitchen was no more and no less than ordinary in this time and place.

She spread a bit of raspberry jam on her English muffin and took a bite. It was almost two o'clock, and her day had hardly begun. Beth sounded odd on the phone, not shaky from the accident, but as if she were choosing her words carefully. Strangely, Beth wasn't at all reluctant for her to come over, even said she'd been waiting all morning for the call. It was Joan who hadn't wanted to rush right over. Who wanted to savor her breakfast, her coffee. To relish the calm before the storm.

JOAN PARKED IN FRONT OF BETH'S. She had driven carefully, eyes on the road, looking left and right at intersections, while thinking about the business at hand. Beth answered the door wearing sunglasses.

"Come in," Beth said, removing her glasses. "I wasn't certain it would be you."

"Oh my," said Joan. "You got a doozie." Both eye sockets were violet and green. "It's kind of beautiful, the way they match."

Beth shrugged and closed the door. "It's Joan," she said to the parrot. "Come on in the kitchen. I'm dying for a cup of tea."

Joan followed along, set her purse on the kitchen table. Beth was running cold water into the kettle. "Your parrot's kind of quiet today."

"What do you mean?" said Beth, and Joan's heart skipped a beat.

"I just meant that last night it carried on a regular conversation"— she fumbled for the name—"with Alfred. Alfred Abrams."

Beth didn't turn, hadn't noticed Joan's fumble, was setting the kettle on the burner, reaching in the cupboard for the box of tea. "I guess. Last night's pretty fuzzy for me. She's a funny old bird, can talk up a storm if she has a mind to. She's family. Don't ask me how old she is."

Joan studied Beth from behind. She was taller than Joan remembered, and the effect of the straight skirt and the plain blouse made her seem rigid, as if she were posing for her portrait.

Beth arranged a plate with squares of cheddar cheese, saltines, and a sliced red apple. When the water came to a boil, she filled the teapot, set it on the table, and sat down. "Oooh," she said. "I feel like I've been run over by a steamroller."

"It's no surprise," said Joan. "It's a miracle you're no worse than you are. It makes me shudder even to think about it."

Beth nodded. "Have some tea. Do you mind pouring?"

Joan filled both cups, added a bit of sugar to hers. Beth sat there breathing deeply, her eyes closed, her legs stretched under the table.

"Are you sure you're all right?" Joan asked. "Your kids ought to be getting home from school. Maybe I shouldn't have come over so late."

"No, it's all right. Ben and Naomi stay at school on Mondays for orchestra. The problem isn't just the accident. It's Ira and me, we've split up—it's been in the works for a long time. Last night was the frosting on the cake. I was hoping for one last chance to talk, but what can you say in a movie? And you saw us afterwards, going through the motions. Drink your tea while it's hot. Besides, Ira has an apartment on Lake Shore Drive near his office. I don't know why

I care one way or the other." She brushed the hair away from her forehead.

"No, I don't mean that," Beth said. "I'm trying to be civil—you know me. Well, maybe you don't. I make the best of things. We're human beings, and he is the children's father. He's not the worst man on the face of the earth. But something about your friend really got on the wrong side of Ira. Anyway, that was the last straw. You can see for yourself Ira doesn't give a damn if he's civil or not." Beth shrugged.

Joan sat there, nibbling on apple and cheese. Yesterday was no dream—that much was clear. But what to say next? "Last straw, what do you mean? Was it something Alfred said?"

Joan could see Beth thinking back over last night, weighing the moments, sorting the words. "No," she said. "Who knows. Everything's poisonous right now where Ira's concerned. He said if he ever laid eyes on that S.O.B. again, he wouldn't be responsible."

"What's that supposed to mean?"

"God knows. But he wouldn't let go of it. Like a dog with a bone. I won't repeat everything Ira said. He thinks of himself as the cock of the walk. The games men play! 'No one gets the upper hand on Ira Silverman.' Just where did your Alfred Abrams drop in from? Another planet?"

"He might as well have," said Joan.

"Figures," said Beth. "Did he spend the night? That's the best way to lose a man."

Joan smiled wanly and shook her head. She wanted out of here. Didn't want to watch Beth Silverman hollow out the universe. She had gotten the answer she needed. "Beth," she said, intending to say something about how things would get better. But instead she heard herself asking about the car.

Joan finished her cup of tea—it didn't taste like tea, didn't taste like anything. It was time to go, she said. They promised to get together again soon.

Home Sweet Home

5 February 1865

Lincoln wandered along the hallway. How hard it was these days to find words to exchange with Mary. The danger was that once he found them, Mary would launch into territory best left unexplored. Money was a dangerous topic, of course. Money for clothing, money for the boys, or just money in general. Oh that he had never run across the order for the black camel's hair shawl—$1000! Alexander Stewart, Her Majesty's Thief —Mary, Mary, forgive me, Mother Mary. And then, the more his Mary owed, the more she ordered, in hopes of keeping the greedy New York lions at bay. He had noted three new hatboxes in the far corner of her room, stacked up like the layers of a wedding cake. Why, the boxes themselves cost more than a month's rations on the Potomac. When you got down to it, the boxes cost more real money than the hats inside.

Suddenly he envisioned Joan Matcham's bedroom, as in a stereopticon's panorama: the chenille bedspread and the crazy quilt for catnaps folded at the end of the bed, the chest of drawers with its odd assortment of this and that—perfumes, he reckoned, combs, brushes—whatnot. A desk and chair, and on the desk a jar with pens and a few books, the red and black one a ledger for sure. It was as if he was seeing all this for the first time. The two small Turkish carpets on the floor, the pine boards running crossways. The door to the closet was nearly closed, but open enough so that his eye could take in a handful of gowns, simple things that an Elizabeth Keckley could turn out in an afternoon, a snip here, a stitch and a half there, set in the sleeves, turn up the hem, and it's a dress. No seed pearls by the thousand, no lace and ribbon, no ruffles. Dresses, not costumes.

And whose beady-eyed portrait was staring down at him? "You just mind your own business," Lincoln said out loud. "There's a war going on, and maybe the writ of habeas corpus did get suspended. So what!" The grim visage relaxed a little and went back to its quiet business of decorating a wall. He should have asked its name while he had its attention. He never had gotten around to a proper tour of this home sweet home. He nodded a goodbye, shrugged, resumed his stroll, and for no good reason whatsoever, went down the stairs and turned left toward the entrance hall. Up ahead he could hear singing, or tuneful muttering, hard to tell which. Ah, it was Edward, perched on a ladder with a trowel and a bucket of plaster.

"Howdy, Edward."

"Afternoon, Mr. Lincoln. How was your trip?"

"Necessary, but not much to show for it—like pulling weeds—not a harvest to get you through the winter. But the boat ride's always welcome. And the fresh air, and the music too."

"Yes, Sir. I was downriver one time—President Taylor took me along, then up the bay to Annapolis. Come nightfall it was a regular show. Enough to wear out your shoes. The dancing, I mean."

"I guessed as much," said Lincoln, though it was hard to picture white-haired Edward clogging along to the accordion and fiddle. "And how come you're up on a ladder on a Sunday?"

Edward smiled. "I know what you're thinking, Mr. Lincoln. What with you being gone, there's not much coming and going and my services aren't called for, so there's a chance for Edward to put time in with his friends at the Block and Tackle, and most times I would've, but last night I gave the Good Book a short turn, said my prayers, and went to bed. Then I skipped church this morning. Say what you will, but some Sundays my sins can wait their turn."

"I understand," said Lincoln, "I understand. My sins don't go by the calendar either."

"Well," said Edward from his perch. "I best get on with my plastering," and slip-slap he was back at work. He was as tactful a man as Lincoln had ever met. You'd think we were all equals, Fillmore and Pierce, Taylor and Buchanan. And yours truly. He had not spotted a book by Edward on the Northwestern library shelves, though he could easily enough imagine a title—*My Life with Eight Presidents, Or, Deep Dark Secrets of the White House.* Carpenter was there, *Six Months at the White House with Abraham Lincoln*, and Hill's *Recollections*. Even three small volumes by Billy Herndon with an odd title, unless you know the man—*The True Story of a Great Life*, by Billy and a man named Weik. Which could only mean that Billy had finally given up the ghost and got somebody else to finish it for him.

Lincoln headed across the hall and up the other stairs. He should be using these free moments to write his own book while there was still time. *Still time?* Now what in tarnation did he mean by that? He paused. He had been thinking about every odd Jack writing his inside story about the man on the face of the penny, and his own version of the story untold. And then came the jump to time running out. Like the myth of the three fatal sisters and the one with the scissors ready to cut a life short. His life. Premonitions, dreams. Good thing Mary wasn't privy to his thoughts. He resumed his climb, step by step. Ford's Theater. Well, he could avoid it, and instead get struck down by a disrespectful horse on Tenth Street, be carried inside the theater, and dutifully expire. A revision of the script, but acceptable nevertheless to the clerk in charge of Reorderings of Divine Providence.

"John," he called out, "if you can hear me, you must forgo this turning of the universe inside out and outside in. There's work to be done, straightforward work."

Lincoln emerged from the stairwell, and there was John Hay, right on schedule, his hand on the latch, the look of a scared rabbit etched across his forehead. "Sir?"

"Calm yourself, John. I want you to accompany me to Mr. Stanton's headquarters, where I will invite consideration of my proposal for compensation and an end to the war. Mr. Stanton could lend his weight to the project. I can't do it alone. You know from your tour of Florida and I know down to the marrow that the war will end and swords will be turned back to ploughshares, but that knowledge is not sufficient for the Secretaries of the Cabinet. Old scores need settling. Jeff Davis must sit down to his humble pie. Sit, eat, and choke. That's their hearts' desire, you know. General Grant already is asking what he should do with the old coot should he fall into his hands."

"I have my own opinion there," said Hay, his lower lip curled against the upper.

"And you learned this from the Quaker ladies who came by Thursday last?"

"Quaker ladies?"

"Yes," said Lincoln. "The ones who said Mr. Jefferson Davis's prayers would have a better audience on high than yours truly."

Hay's eyes rolled. "And why might that be?"

"Well," said Lincoln with a smile, "take that attitude and I see no good reason to give you the benefit of the considered wisdom of those upstanding Pennsylvania Quaker ladies."

"My apologies," said Hay, clicking his heels and squaring his shoulders. "Let me rephrase my question. I wonder what those Quaker women had to say?"

"Still a trifle ingratiating, but I'll let it pass. Said the second lady, her gray hair piled high atop her head: 'Because we all know Jefferson Davis is a praying man.' And, said the first, 'What dost thou mean by that? Isn't Mr. Lincoln a praying man?' And returns the second, 'Yes, but the Lord above will think he's joking.' "

"And," said Hay, "you're telling this story to me—not a joke but a true story—to spare Mr. Stanton the agony?"

"Yes, and my agony as well: it pains me to cause Mr. Stanton such suffering. Get your coat and hat, John. Time's a wastin'. I'll meet you down in the hall."

"Yes, Sir. Give me a few minutes to check my desk, get my things, and I'll be down."

"No rush," said Lincoln. He tried to imagine his own son coming into such easy manhood. Robert already had such a serious brow, and Willie—no, he wouldn't go that route.

Lincoln turned and headed back down the stairs. John had been such a comfort in those dark days. Serving his country more than he could ever know. His roots lay on this side of the Atlantic, in Pike County, Illinois; but more than anything, John longed to travel, to wander the streets of Paris. Pike County would not contain him for long. We don't have to go home to be at home, thought Lincoln. We take home with us wherever we go.

This notion of home, maybe it accounted for his feeling so much at ease in Joan's century. You'd expect him to be more off balance. But the truth was he was hardly daunted. He supposed it was like learning a different language: the words sound different, but the ideas are the same. We each learn to speak a different way, but we can always find common ground. It's what they call translation. What he had done was translate time. What a notion! Such a pity there was no one here to tell about it. Not even John, the one person he would even consider.

No question though, John would love the tale. So just how would he tell John this story? From beginning to end? Would he say that one moment he was setting down his pen, and the next he had skipped ahead ninety years? No, that would be telling the story too fast. He'd have to describe how it felt like the moment when your attention starts to wander and a daydream begins. You're neither here nor there but on the way somewhere, and then with a jerk you return back where you belong. "What was that all about?" you wonder. Some say such moments are kin to the tingling you get when someone walks on your grave.

Of course the element that made his story different, and not *like* daydreaming, was coming home with such a crystal awareness of the time away, the time in between, not to mention the coin from that other realm. He could not have dreamed the lights in the store windows and the automobiles, the very words *automobile, toaster, hamburger, airplane, movie, television.* "One moment I was at my desk," he would say, "and the next it was like I was cast overboard. Then swimming back to shore, and not knowing how I had gotten so far asea. Then how my feet found the land once more, and everything was rightside again."

He could picture John Hay listening, nodding, taking it all in. He would have his doubts, of course, though the penny might quell them. John knew when a story was serious, was real, and the story-teller in earnest. Of course the ultimate question might then occur to him: Why was it Abraham Lincoln who was chosen for the journey? Would he ever know the answer? He could see himself telling the story up to a point. What he never could tell, not truthfully, was the other journey, the journey back. That he had been lying upon a bed, as bare as a newborn, and by his side a woman. And himself recently within the woman, and—oh my God! How could he not have thought of it till now?

Something was at his pants leg. "Tiger! What d'you want? Some attention?" Lincoln bent over and picked up the kitty, stroked its chin, nestled his beard against its fur. "You've got your engine going, don't you? Well, I don't blame you one iota. I too wish I were in someone's arms. So what's your considered opinion? Tell me what you think of the thoughtless Chief Executive." Hard to read Tiger's reply. Hard to read his own reply. And what a thought, he thought, to have engendered a child in another century. But what if, what if? Not that his thinking would matter one iota. And Joan, dear Joan, what story will you have to tell? If. Kin to the story of the Frog Prince? This was no joke. A child. And which way did he wish it? Yes or no? "It's not up to us, Tiger. Not up to us. A little late for that."

"JOHN, I HAVE AN UNUSUAL REQUEST." The President and Hay had just popped their heads into the telegraph office at the War Department to see if there was news from either Grant or Sherman, who was now making his way north through South Carolina. Dave Bates, the telegrapher, just shook his head *No*, his finger never leaving the key. One wonders what language his children will grow up speaking.

Perhaps that was the link between his time and Joan's, this new-fangled device. At a Smithsonian lecture Joseph Henry had explained how it worked, with electromagnets and relays and batteries and miles and miles of wire. Even the oceans wouldn't withstand it, if Cyrus Field has his way. And if you can extend a message across space, why not across time?

"A request, Sir?"

"Yes," said Lincoln. "Rather a personal matter." Hay smiled expectantly. The lad at times was childlike, an innocent. Yet Lincoln knew full well that Hay had another coat, or was it the same coat inside out? At any moment his tongue could blister your skin worse than Aunt Sally's iron. Lincoln had seen Hay do it, more than once. Best not give him too much time to think. "All right," said Lincoln, taking the leap. "I present a hypothetical situation. Are you ready? We have some minutes before the reception."

"Of course. Does it involve a message?"

"Yes," Lincoln said thoughtfully. "But this is different. Not like your mission to Frémont or our slippery number with Greeley. This has nothing to do with the war. As I said, a personal matter. I need to send a letter."

"A letter? Doesn't sound very hypothetical."

"I suppose not, but there's a trick to this letter: I would wish to delay its sending." Images of an envelope passing from one hand to another flashed before his eyes.

Hay eyed him curiously. "Anything like the letter you had the Cabinet sign blindly before the election, which I cut open afterward?"

Lincoln thought a moment—he had written out his plan to support McClellan had the general been elected president; then he had the Cabinet sign it on the back without reading its contents; next he had folded it every which way and pasted it closed.

"In a way it is like that," he said. "With that letter I was clearing my conscience, doing my best to put politics out of the question. What was important was to save the country—the instrument didn't much matter. John, I don't know quite what I'm doing with this letter. Conscience is a part of it." Hay was scrutinizing him. "It is a letter for future delivery, for delivery after my death."

"But," said Hay, and then he didn't say.

Lincoln filled the vacant moment. "Its delivery will be after your death as well, John. I mean for this letter to go a long way forward."

He could see the wonder in the young man's face. "So you mean," said Hay, "to entrust to me a letter for delivery, say, into the next century?"

"Yes," replied Lincoln, "well into it."

"And you need for me to hold this letter till such a day that I find another youth to entrust with it. Does the chain go further?"

"Perhaps," said Lincoln. "I know within a day or two when I want it to arrive. Barring any accidents, it could work." He was speaking to himself as much as to Hay. "Will you help?"

Hay smiled wryly. "Exactly how far ahead?"

"To nineteen hundred and fifty-five. June, mid-June. The eighth would do. Not before. I don't know how fast the mails work then." By June, he figured, Joan Matcham would know, one way or the other. It was his turn to smile, picturing the expression on her face. "Evanston, Illinois," he added.

"And you have composed this letter?"

"No," said Lincoln. "I thought I'd better have the messenger before the message. To tell the truth, the notion has just occurred to me. It was Dave Bates and his magic key that put it into my head. I don't need an immediate answer."

John stood there, mulling it over.

"Here comes our man," Lincoln said, waving a distant hello. Charles Sumner, Senator from Massachusetts. Sumner made him edgy even though they held the same beliefs. He was such a strident man, and so volubly an abolitionist. There was always reason in what he said, and every speech so proudly memorized, but how often did he get your vote? It was hard to take your eyes off the man, what with that stride, the swinging cane, the bright whistling. Sumner waved back, his cane performing a pirouette.

Lincoln turned to Hay. "Did I tell you Mary said the good Senator couldn't believe I said 'turned tail and ran' in a state paper? Guess Massachusetts don't got no wild critters to put you on your mark, and ready, set, go."

Hay chuckled. "You've got me picturing Charles Sumner hightailing it through the woods, with Lord knows what in pursuit. But to tell the truth, if I could afford it, I'd wear lavender trousers too."

"You would? I may have to rethink my device of the letter. Can you trust a man in lavender pants with the secret of your life?" Lincoln gritted his teeth, regretting his careless words. Hay had shot him a look. "I know what I just said, John, but the matter here is like nothing you would ever imagine. Now you'd better lead me inside before Mary has a fit."

They entered the Executive Mansion side by side. With a nod Hay headed for his office and Lincoln toward the reception room. He envied young John, meandering along with no one to answer to. John could drift up to his room, lie on his bed, sit in a chair with his favorite book, head over to Willard's for coffee with Senator this or that, drop in on Chase or Seward, twiddle his thumbs in a closet, ride to Arlington with a picnic lunch. He could do damn near anything. Unlike himself.

Hell's bells! Just this once, and he flew up the office stairs, entered the library, and shut the door firmly behind him. His heart was pounding. His eyes took in his surroundings; his heartbeat slowed. Books, books, and books. To think there had been a time when a single book was a treasure, and here was a sultan's treasury. Even the piano danced to their tune. Row after row, stacks and heaps. He looked toward the brown leather chair and imagined himself sitting intently, a shawl loosely draped about his shoulders. In the days before the good Lord had given him General Grant, he used to send Hay over to the Library of Congress with a long list of titles, and he would read about Napoleon at Austerlitz, Nelson at Trafalgar, Caesar in Gaul, looking for patterns. But no war had ever been like this one, so many men in arms, such potent arms themselves, and the generals learning their craft in schools, trained by the book, taught to look like soldiers. Why should so many of them turn feckless, turn tail?

He remembered the night when Meigs shook him awake at the Soldiers' Home and urged the immediate flight of the Army. "Get the men on transports. Kill the horses—they can't be saved, no time." The man spoke like a telegraph. McClellan was locked in at Harrison's Landing, Stonewall Jackson was loose and, if you took Meigs' word for it, would be there in minutes. It took a while to get the story out of the poor soul, his face white as a ghost despite the frantic midnight ride.

And then there was Halleck, who wanted to be the General-in-

Chief, and "responsible for results"—his very words. But after the second battle of Bull Run he was unnerved and deplucked, and ever after he evaded any responsibility and was no better than a bespectacled clerk whose main concern is the sharpness of his pencil.

Yet both men had graduated from West Point, and high up. It took himself, a man not known for bravery, to sustain their sinking courage. To judge from Grant, the best generaling is learned in your uncle's general store, dealing not in maxims, but in goods by the yard and pound. And when the time comes, you remember that the man across the line is no different from you, and you plunge ahead. Thank the Lord for General Grant.

Grant's Commander-in-Chief wasn't quite alone. From the fourfold boundary of a small silver frame on the wall, the eyes of Thomas Jefferson were looking down at him. Lincoln met him eye to eye. Jefferson, the author of the Bill of Rights, his the words that are writ in our hearts. All men created free and equal. Not, White men are equal, and forget the Black man, forget the Indian. An idea so easy, so ready, you could grasp it in your hand. And women too would have their day.

Joan. Why couldn't his hand grasp hers as easily as his mind could reach forward? She was just across the threshold, so close. In his letter he would say that she was in his thoughts, that he did remember, that it had not been an idle time, a time without regard. He wanted to say that time was twisted athwart, that yesterday was tomorrow and tomorrow was yesterday. He wanted to tell her that he kept thinking about all they had said to each other in the night.

It was so little like the language of the day, this language of the night. He and Mary certainly talked in the night, but not with those words. *Who,* he wondered, *could have taught us that language? Not our parents. Nor our friends, nor our brothers and sisters.* Or could it be that he and Mary were the exception? That lovers did talk their way in and around the act of love? He had clear recollections of lying beside Joan, conscious of himself and where he was, what he said, what he thought. Could he trust the memory? Would she think it ghoulish to receive a letter from the other side, the land of the dead? Was her sense of time as twisted as his? They had talked about time repeating itself, their meeting by the bench again and again. But was that talk before or after?

She would know the handwriting, would know the letter was from another century. She would know the signature, the "A" and the "L" woven together. Joan Matcham would know it was real, that it all had happened. If she denied him, she'd be left with a void, never to know they had driven in the car together, gone to the museum, dined, had seen *East of Eden*, spent time with Beth and bedeviled Ira, had rescued Beth, and then gone home. But she wouldn't deny their story, any more than she would deny her own shadow.

He thought again about what he would say in his letter, that he remembered, that he cared. That it was no dream. That he regretted nothing.

✦ XIII ✦

Shadows into Stories

5 February 1865

DEEP INSIDE, WHERE HER HEART should be, a silent voice said, *I am empty*. Lizzie hadn't let her plead illness but insisted she go on with the reception. "Yes, so true." Her token responses were more than enough to keep Mr. Sumner going. She took in his words and replied when necessary, but she wasn't there, wasn't present. She had listened to Lizzie's story of the grieving jays, had understood that the whole world grieves, that her grief was not unusual, was ordinary. That life goes on.

"We are not what we were in the beginning," said Charles Sumner. "We have shrunk in character, and only now is the pendulum sweeping back. When the air has cleared, Americans will know that the Founding Fathers and the Constitution spoke for liberty. Liberty—why, the word is written on the face of the least coin in our pockets."

He droned on, phrases out of speeches, his words like straw. She had come so far, had come to the Executive Mansion, had brought her husband to this apex of democracy, to this horrid war, this horrid city. "Yes," she said, and high overhead the light glinted from the polished crystals of the chandeliers. Mary Todd was nobody. Without Father, she was nobody.

"Left to its own devices it will wither away"—Sumner was speaking directly of slavery. "That was the intent of the First Fathers. What they had not foreseen was the last-ditch resistance as that withering accelerated. The more slavery was denounced, the more the slaveholder searched for new roots for his malignant progeny. At times it seems that this dying institution has us all by the throat. How else can you explain that in eighteen hundred and fifty-two, little more than a dozen years ago, I was one of only four senators who voted to repeal the Fugitive Slave Act?"

It was hard to pay close attention. Sumner would do well on a desert island so long as he didn't know it was deserted. She was the opposite, drowning in a sea of living beings. When Father was away she lived in a darkened house, peering outside. And where was Mr. Lincoln?

The Senator was waiting for her to respond to his speech. He was a good friend and deserved better.

"I can't explain it," said Mary Todd Lincoln, gathering the strands and holding them tight. "Yet I might say that I understand how slavery clings to our lives like the spider's web to cloth. My grandmother, and my step-grandmother as well, the Widow Parker, wrote in their wills that their slaves should be freed at their death—including Jane and Judy, who lived with our family. You see the contradiction, don't you?"

Sumner shifted his stance, glanced toward the window. She had leapt beyond his understanding; for him slavery was largely an abstraction.

"In our minds," Mary pressed on, "we know that it is an offense against humanity. And so with our last breath we give voice to that credence. But until then, until that uttermost moment, we lead a daily life, and we do not willingly give up the comforts of the hearth. Would you be a servant to yourself? Would you perform your own daily tasks? Would you cook your food, clean your house, launder your clothes? Or do you prefer to buy those services?"

"A mother, or a wife, would perform those tasks," said the Senator.

Mary looked up at him. Did he understand that he had just compared a wife to a slave? "Yes," she said, "a wife might cook and clean, but in the Lexington of my childhood, if you could afford her, Mammy did the cooking and cleaning, not Mother. Our principles are not always convenient to our practicalities."

"I would never own a slave," said the man of principle.

"Nor, I think, would I. I can grasp the platitude: He who would be no slave, must consent to have no slave."

"Platitude?"

"Yes, and if you wonder at my less than certainty, it is that my present circumstances make that choice too easy. I have nothing to lose by its abolition. But remember, Charles, I am a child of the South. Slavery for me is no abstraction. It was a vital fact in my life."

Her eye caught the roomful of persons in splendid dress. She lowered her voice and pressed on. "Without slavery, life would not have been as comfortable, so in honesty I must give pause. I grew up knowing that Mammy, who raised me, whom I loved like a mother, might at any moment be sold down the river. She knew it; we all knew it. The trader is everywhere, the slave pens close at hand. When the price of hemp goes down, nothing is sure. The institution is unthinkable, but its beneficiaries who live with it day in and day out find excuses, justifications. They do not see themselves as villains."

"Perhaps," he said. "But times have changed. If ever I had any sympathy for the South, it is gone. We can never go back to those days of self-deception. Too much blood has been shed. Slavery is dead, though the vestiges cling like the spider's web, as you aptly put it. It is time for the country to move on. If the slave is no more a slave, what then is he? One of us? Does he vote? May he work for a wage, receive a public education, serve on a jury, acquire a passport, practice the law? When I ask these questions, I feel as if time has taken fright and run back, and Chief Justice Taney is again our hard-driving shepherd. It is as if we ran a trying race, and now we must run it all over again. The slave may no longer be slave, but he is still no more than a beast of the field, and we use him no better. If we do not press forward, it is May of 1856 once more, and my blood is spilled on the Senate floor for naught."

"The assault," she said softly. In all their conversations it had never come up, though anyone hearing the name Sumner would immediately think of nothing else. She had been unfair, she realized. He had himself been victim to a fit of Carolina choler. She knew the story well—who didn't? He was still a young senator when Congressman Brooks walked onto the Senate floor, approached the seated Sumner, and struck him first with the whole cane, and when it snapped, kept on and on with the broken handle, and no one did a thing. Both men in the instant became heroes. The South Carolinian received canes by the dozen from admirers; and Sumner's empty chair for three years spoke more eloquently than any words the man might have said. The first blow of the rebellion, though few understood it at the time. So he too had lived with pain and sorrow.

"Afternoon, Charles, Mary." The back of Father's hand brushed Mary's fingertips. "Lost track of time," said Lincoln.

"Welcome home, Abraham," said Senator Sumner. "I won't ask how things went with the Peace Commissioners, though I might hazard a guess."

"I expect you could, and with a little luck it might turn out to be correct," said the President, "like the sow who wondered at the commotion outside her pen."

Sumner squared his shoulders. "I'll not ask how the simile of the sow goes, but I do have a firm notion about the conference."

The President smiled. "You're sure now? The sow's name was Portia, and her seven shoats were named after the seven hills of Rome."

"No doubt," said Sumner, "and she was wedded to a Brutus."

"Not that I know of," said Abraham with a straight face. "And to tell the truth I've never heard of hogs marrying. Customs were simple in our neck of the woods. But Portia might have known a Brutus. The name does ring a bell. I would like though to hear your version of the conference."

"Well," said Sumner, "the commissioners continue to view the war as mutually inaugurated. Hence they speak of a cessation of hostilities, a mutual cessation. I expect they played up the misery of the daily slaughter. As though they had been drawn into war against their will. As though the South had not done its best to extend the boundaries of slavery to the territories. As though it were not for a fundamental principle that we undertook this war. What would they term it? A misunderstanding? An old feud blown out of proportion?"

"Yes," said the President. "We heard those arguments at Hampton Roads. The tally of death, and still coming on."

"And then," said Sumner, "you outlined your simple conditions: that they disband their armies and reorganize their legislatures within the domain of the national government. In closing, you informed them of last week's passage of the Thirteenth Amendment to the Constitution."

"Very close, Charles. Strange to say, they did not know that my proclamation of emancipation had been extended by Congress."

"I can imagine their surprise," said the Senator, "that you are not a lone wolf up there, but that the pack runs with you. Their only hope for a truce would lie in your being out of tune with the rest of us."

"And thanks to you," said Mary, "Mr. Lincoln and Congress are in harmony."

"I would hope so," said Lincoln. "Be assured I'm a man of my own time, but I can look ahead. The Founding Fathers wanted the institution of slavery to wither away. Someday it will be unimaginable that it held together for so long. Mary, by any chance did you catch the name of that young man, the German fellow by the buffet with Joseph Henry? I know his face from somewhere."

"No," she said. "He must have come in while Charles and I were talking."

"I don't know him either," said Sumner. "Well, I'd best get back to work."

"Thank you, Charles," said Mary, and Sumner was gone.

"He's a good man," said her husband, "and a true friend. Now to satisfy my curiosity." Leading her by the hand, he set out toward Joseph Henry.

She thought of the room as a sea dotted with islands. They would land on the shores of one conversation, exchange information with its natives, then set sail for the next. From Feejee to the Sandwich Islands. It was as if they were their own Exploratory Expedition, gathering specimens for the Smithsonian. Two fresh congressmen from New York had joined the collection—with the inauguration little more than a month off, there already was a shuffle of "out with the old and in with the new." Come morning, she wouldn't remember their names. Finally they approached Joseph Henryland and set anchor.

Henry and his friend dusted the crumbs from their fingertips and shook hands with the President and his wife. The young German, Ferdinand Zeppelin, was a count, though he seemed uneasy with the title, shrugging at the designation. Henry explained that the count was a cavalry officer who had spent much of the last year as an observer with the Army of the Potomac.

"That's it," said Lincoln. "You were with Wright at Fort Stevens— that's where I've seen you."

"Yes," said Count Zeppelin, "on the parapet. We were afraid you would get your head knocked off."

Mary caught her husband's quick signal—*drop it*, it said to the young count, though the hand that held hers didn't so much as quiver. What could she do with him? She couldn't put him under lock and key, couldn't keep him from the men in the field, couldn't tell him that his place was here, that he was elected president, not general. Not that she hadn't said all that, but it was like talking to a stone wall for all the good it did.

The count's eyes shifted her way momentarily—she could see his mind searching for a safe path. "But I am less interested now," he said, "in the art of war. Professor Henry and I have been talking about a different theater, a theater in the skies."

"Ah," said the President, "so you're a balloonist. Then you must know Thaddeus Lowe—our aeronauts fly under his wing."

"Yes," said Zeppelin, "Lowe and I have talked together a great deal and also flown together. I think no one in the world knows more about the art of ballooning than he."

"Fits my estimate of the man," said Abraham. "You know he sent me a telegraphed message from his balloon, early on in the war. It was an odd message, but what are you expected to say when you're tapping out dots and dashes?"

"I remember it," said Mary: *The city with its girdle of encampments presents a superb scene.* Such strange phrasing that it comes back to me at odd moments."

"It's a good thing," her husband said, "it wasn't me or Edward Everett up there, or the signals would still be flowing."

"I doubt it," said Joseph Henry. "The battery might have other ideas."

"May I ask," said Lincoln, directing his attention to Count Zeppelin, "if you consider ballooning a hobby, or is it something more?" Zeppelin cleared his throat. "It's much more. From my first flight, in St. Paul, Minnesota, it has consumed me. Currently I am obsessed with the idea of purposeful flight. A balloon is fine for meteorology and for observation, but I should like to do more than drift. I should like to have command and control over the direction and destination."

"So you have an invention in mind," said Abraham, "a balloon not at the mercy of the winds. Can you picture such a vehicle becoming an ordinary mode of travel?"

"Exactly," said Zeppelin. "A vehicle that is directable. As it is now, the shape of a balloon doesn't matter much. Actually, one would wish it to have as much wind resistance as possible, like a sail, since it is the wind that drives it. But another kind of craft would be what the pneumaticists call *aerodynamic*, shaped precisely to minimize the effect of wind. It would require a rigid frame to contain the balloon, and an engine to propel it. I can see it in my mind's eye."

"Promise me that you will preserve your vision," her husband said. "Though I wonder if you have ever considered a different sort of powered flight, following the shape of the birds. That I can envision. Thanks to Professor Henry, we feel free to dream almost beyond imagining. Who knows what may come to be? Pikes with motorized vehicles racing from city to city, electricity flowing from a central station to power the cities, and all one has to do is fit a plug to our local connection and we have power to run lamps, stoves— who knows what else? Machines to launder our clothing, to make bread into toast, to cast our shadows into stories."

They were all staring at the President. Mary was accustomed to his flights of fancy, but here was a full-blown picture of another world.

"Shadows into stories?" said Joseph Henry. "I'd say you're doing that already. When you retire from the presidency, I could find a place for you at the Smithsonian."

"Doing what?" Mary asked. "He used to be handy with a broom, back in his Denton Offutt days—or so I'm told. But it sounds as though before long they'll have mechanical brooms, and no use for the likes of Mr. Lincoln."

"Don't be too sure about that, Mary. Even an electric broom needs a helmsman. But I suspect Professor Henry had a more genteel position in mind. My title could be something like Assistant Surveyor of the Clouds, Second Class."

"Of the clouds?" said Count Zeppelin. He was having trouble sorting out what was fancy and what was real.

"I think," said Henry, "that Mr. Lincoln has gotten wind"—he grimaced at the word —"of my recent experiments upon the velocity of the winds at high altitudes by timing the speed of the shadow of a cloud across a measured plot of land."

"And that worked?" asked Zeppelin, his eyes wide with astonishment.

"Of course," said Henry. "And why not? We already use sun and shadow to tell the time. At any rate it helped in our search for the best fog-signal apparatus to arrest the attention of the mariner."

"And," said Lincoln, "you have determined that the bellowing of a mighty ox works best?"

Henry smiled broadly. "No, that was not our determination, though I wouldn't be at all surprised to find it was effective. If the ox could be trained to cooperate."

"And if the mariner understood what this mighty ox was doing on a foggy shore," replied Lincoln. "You can see, Count Zeppelin, that Professor Henry commands our esteem, or we wouldn't play so lightly with him. In these troubled times we take great solace from his lectures at the Smithsonian."

"Mr. Lincoln exaggerates," said Henry, "but I do think the mind benefits from any respite it can attain from daily strife. Otherwise I don't know how we could endure the sights from our windows."

All the men were nodding in agreement. Mary, the only mother among them, nodded too. What respite had they for the troubled heart? Joseph Henry was a good man, meaning well. His only son, another William, had died the same year as her Willie. *She would get through this*, she thought to herself. *She would get through*.

✦ XIV ✦

Down to the Raisins

5 February 1865

A BRAHAM LINCOLN LAY IN BED. He often slept in his own bedroom, and tonight was no exception. He stretched his legs, felt the blood surge and calm itself. Strange, how it was always a wonder to lie down at day's end, a surprise, like the taste of something brand new. Why, he wondered, had he not done this sooner? As though he couldn't remember during the course of his day that this rich pleasure awaited him. He inhaled deeply. Exhaled. It reminded him of sexual desire: how you could perform the act time after time, and still be surprised when the moment came, and there you were, mingled in ecstasy. *Well,* he thought to himself, *if you did remember it, if your memory were so complete, so perfect, that it recapitulated the moment, you would never need to do it again.*

His eyes were open, tracing familiar outlines, exploring shadows. No way to fall asleep. He closed his eyes once more. After a late supper he had walked with Hay over to the telegraph office to read dispatches. In a world of flux it was good to have routines, to follow a pattern. He would open the drawer at the cipher-desk and begin reading dispatches from the top until he came to the one he had read on his last visit. He would then announce for the benefit of the operators that he was "down to the raisins." They all knew the story of the young girl who begins her birthday feast by eating freely of raisins. Then during the night the child is taken violently ill, and the doctor arrives as she is casting up her accounts. The genial doctor, inspecting the black objects, remarks to the concerned parents that any danger has passed, as the child is "down to the raisins."

Lincoln had spent a good hour reading dispatches, first at Major Eckert's desk, then on Dave Bates' couch. Sherman was in South Carolina, in Robertville. Now that his men had crossed into the state that had launched the secession, they were angry. Foraging wasn't enough, so they were putting homes to the torch. They hadn't taken Georgia so personally. He could understand the distinction, as the memory of Fort Sumter was still fresh for them. It would take a deliberate mind to say *No* to such an impulse. A *No* that would be considerably easier here in Washington than on a muddy road in Carolina.

Nothing would stop Sherman, that was clear. And Grant had a clear edge over Lee. Thomas and Sheridan were sure hands. Before much longer the day of surrender would certainly come. It couldn't play itself out, like stubborn children at cards, holding on to the fours and fives, in vain hopes of a miracle. God forbid. It mustn't go on till the last soldier is killed, or captured, or dies of exhaustion. Or goes home a deserter. It would have to be Lee, not Davis, who finally gives up. Hell would freeze over before Jeff Davis would surrender his mad dream of two countries, two Americas. If it were left to Davis, he'd put out a call for soldiers ever younger, ever older, on down to the last man. Yes, it would have to be Lee, who must possess a kernel of sanity. Who must know that his game of feinting left then right, pulling back, and closing ranks must draw to a close in a matter of weeks. Who understood that Grant's Army of the Potomac was like a relentless ocean swell wearing at the shore.

There was a time when Lee thought his was the tide, himself the force eroding the fragile northern shores. And so his plan took shape, like clay on a potter's wheel. He fought defensively, reasoning that it was not a war to win, but a war not to lose, hoping that the European powers would see the growing stalemate and urge the undoing of this new-fangled experiment in democracy. And finally that the wearied North would concede. Gettysburg was Lee's big mistake: hungry-eyed and over-reaching, Lee cast himself as a giant-killer. And now the election had come and gone, and the country had said, "Go forward. Carry on."

Oh but Mary hated Grant, called him "the Butcher." As though Grant enjoyed the bloody hands, the bloody fields. But the crank must turn, and the walls of the vise must close. It wouldn't be enough for Richmond to fall—this had never been a war for territory, but a war against an army. There was the nut that had to crack. Only Grant could do it. Lincoln could talk peace and indemnity, and today he had, but the Cabinet had refused. They wanted to let the illness run its course, to see every last raisin cast up.

Now here he was, abed. Anyone would say he had spent last night here in his bedroom, and the night before on the *River Queen*, but he knew he had not. He could imagine a little book, a slender volume hidden on the crowded shelves at the Northwestern University library: *Lincoln's Sudden Visit to Evanston, Illinois, With a Tabulation of his Movements about Town*. It would chronicle how Abraham Lincoln had arrived on foot in downtown Evanston on a Saturday evening, signed the register at the Orrington Hotel, spent Easter Sunday in private pursuits, then passed from sight toward midnight.

By one reckoning he had spent last night in her bed, Joan's, and the night before he had slept at the Orrington Hotel. By another he had slept here on this bed in the Executive Mansion. He didn't know how long he had slept by Joan's side. "Joan Matcham," he whispered. How strange to let his lips give shape to that name now, here. He had confessed to her that he thought of Mary, though that had been afterward. And before? Then his thoughts had been elusive and vague, deliberately so, to quiet the notion of betrayal, unfaithfulness. But it was done and could not be undone. What if Mary were to know? He had heard stories of unfaithful women and had seen into the man's mind, the anger and the grief. What the man felt, would the woman feel too?

Years ago, when he first ran for office, he had made it an element of his platform that women should achieve the ballot and be no different from men before the law. Precisely what was he thinking? Did he have in mind the possibility of a genuine relationship of like minds, of equals, of men and women not walking different ways, but living joined rather than separate lives? Once upon a time he and Mary had been much closer, though they had fought like wildcats often enough. Once they had walked the same path. That was no longer the case. Could he find his way back to her? He didn't know. Maybe, when this fierce war was done, he could descend from this unexpected peak, return to the plains, come home from this other century and find his way back to Mary.

He rose from his bed, on tiptoe made his way to Mary's bedroom, and slipped in beside her. Her face was slack in sleep, but he could read a story of pain in her features. Why had he come here? To share her pain, or to salve his guilt?

Outside there was a bit of wind, and the house creaked ever so slightly. The downy covers were up to his chin. He was tired, and he would sleep well once sleep made up its mind to come indoors. He pictured Joan outside, indecisive at first, then entering the house, walking lightly across the room. Her robe falls to her feet, and she slips into bed alongside him. She's cool from the winter night, her soft breast brushing against his chest. He shuddered. It was Mary, the mother of his sons, by his side, sleeping gently. She needed her sleep. And he needed his.

✦ XV ✦

On Lafayette Square

21 March 1865

LAFAYETTE SQUARE, AFTER LUNCH, and the rain still pouring down. Across the way were the White House and the Departments of War, Navy, State. With her stationery box on her lap, Sarah Prentiss let her mind drift.

At her desk by the window sat her old schoolmate, Elizabeth Blair Lee. She was writing to her husband, Captain Samuel Phillips Lee, whom she wrote often and who, according to the newspapers, was presently at New Orleans. Elizabeth's promise when they first married was to write a letter every day that her dear Phil was at sea, a prodigious quantity of words as the days and years mounted up.

"Blast!" cried Elizabeth, crumpling her paper into a ball and hurling it across the room. A mild epithet for the lady. There were times when it seemed she had picked up her language in the forecastle of her husband's ships.

"Blots again?" Sarah asked in a cringing voice. Elizabeth had already crumpled up one page of her letter, then smoothed it out as she started anew.

"Yes," she hissed. "Everywhere—well, not everywhere, but enough. One too many—that's certain."

Over the years Sarah had thought about Elizabeth's marriage, whether it was a plus or a minus to have separation thrust upon the conjugal union. Elizabeth's letters to Sarah did not speak directly to that question, yet one noticed that serenity was central to Elizabeth's

138

life, the continuity of an even keel. Though from the sailor's point of view, an even keel is not such a good thing: better to have the wind on the beam than to lie becalmed.

Outside the wind was picking up; she wouldn't be surprised if the rain changed to snow. Not in a beehive of years could she imagine making Elizabeth's promise, let alone fulfilling it, to write her husband those letters day after day. It seemed remarkable to her how opposite lives could be.

"Done and damned be the blots!" Elizabeth exclaimed triumphantly. "Tomorrow's letter can pick up the pieces."

"Mistress of the Pen," toasted Sarah. "Long may she thrive."

"It's not that noble a victory," said Elizabeth. "A goodly portion takes as its subject the pen and its faults." She handed over the letter.

Sarah took it, careful not to smear the half dozen blots, and began to read:

Washington 21 March 1865

Dear Phil
This makes the third letter I have commenced to you in the last hour—but ere I get half thro—they have got covered with blots from this miserable pen—but I have no other just now so must run the risk—
I recieved your's of Thursday 15th and was very happy by its coming— The cheering of your letter helped me greatly for Mother has been urging me to see the Doctor to examine this lump on my right bosom— In Jany. the whale bone in the body of my dress hurt me some but after I cut it out I forgot it entirely until I discovered this small knot & for a few days it has been on the increase— I dont write to alarm you

Sarah looked up, her eyes meeting Elizabeth's, and Elizabeth nodded. "Read on," said the nod, and Sarah's eyes dutifully returned to the letter. Elizabeth hadn't mentioned the lump—it could be anything, it could be nothing, but now what struck Sarah was the thought that she couldn't imagine ever writing anything so intimate and direct to her husband. She read on—

but you remember
the bitter mortification when I found you had been sick in
Phila— I made up my mind then that in a true marriage with
true affection neither husband nor wife would keep secrets no
matter how great the pain— Tho this may annoy you far away
know that it is a comfort to my feelings to share this little lump
of annoyance which has never given me the least pain except in
the day that the whale bone hurt— Even then it was so little
that I bore it all day without coming home—
Mr Johnson is still with us & continues to improve daily in
health & cheerfulness— I wish there were some way to scotch
the rumors of his drunkenness but know of none— As Vice-P to
Mr Lincoln his is no mean task—
Sarah Prentiss sits across the room from me reading, or pretend-
ing to— Blair has been enjoying Sarahs time but today is at Sil-
ver Spring— I think the weather will turn even wetter— You
know how I smell it in the air—you always say I am better than
any barometer— Sarah is edgy to move on from Sen Fessendens
who she says has an over watchful eye as tho she were a child—
Beside she does not greatly enjoy his wit— Sarah took me last
evening to the lecture at the Smithsonian— It was the first time
I had been there since the fire in Jany. & the damage is not as
bad as I imagined— Mr Henrys private rooms took the worst
of it & his collections and journals suffered badly tho he seems
cheerfull— The P was at the lecture & I saw he was very careful
not to smile when Mr Henry closed his introduction with the
usual addition that the Smithsonian Inst. is in no way respon-
sible for this course of lectures, nor is the Washington Lecture
Assn. in any way responsible for the Smithsonian Inst.— You
remember the gale of laughter when it was Mr Greeley for the
Radicals— Poor Mr Henry— Tho yesterday he was all smiles
as the lecture was by a German astronomer & mathematician
named August Mobius— Sarah P had made the acquaintence
of Prof. Mobius when she crossed the ocean & we spoke with
him after— Most of his lecture was about the new mathemati-
cal science of topology which I remember as the science of the
top of things though the lecturer used the word surface— It got

interesting when he talked about the shape of the universe— It
never occured to me that the universe even had a shape let alone
whether it was this or that— You would like how he compared
the universe and the ocean— I dont think of the ocean as
having a shape either, other than what it takes from the land
beneath— Sarah said to me after that this was the point of the
Professors simile— I wont go on & you can read the report in
the paper—
We talked with Mrs Lincoln & Capt Penrose after the lecture—
The P & a small party have been invited by Gen Grant to City
Point & you must know what that means—

Your affectionate Lizzie

I had nearly finished indeed & the pages nearly perfect when
these blots lit on my papers— Add one more

"It never ceases to astonish me," Sarah said, "how your letters have
at their foundation such an understanding. Miles of ocean might
separate you and Phil, but as soon as you write 'Dear Phil,' in a sense
he is already present, already sounding out your words."

"Well," said Elizabeth, "it hasn't always been so. Were Phil here—
the flesh and blood Phil—we could mistake the other as easy as
apple pie."

"Easy as apple pie?"

Elizabeth smiled. "It was almost the first thing I taught him, how
to make an apple pie."

"Have you ever found a lump before?"

"Yes," said Elizabeth. "When Blair was two and still nursing, I noticed a knot. It was merely a congestion of the milk and I knew that,
but it made me think. Mother's right: a woman after forty ought to
be careful of her ailments. I will see the doctor. Mother is like me in
many ways. It takes so little for us to fear the worst, and so we see
disaster in the smallest of signs. If Blair has a fever I hold my breath,
no matter how common a fever is. We wonder, *Is it now?* But para-
doxically, knowing how we exaggerate, we go to the other extreme. I
wish we could keep to an even path. I would be hopeless at sea; I'm
afloat enough as it is." Elizabeth stopped, a rueful smile on her lips.

Sarah said nothing. Her own life was like shapeless clay compared to Elizabeth's. If someone were to ask for her philosophy of life, what would she answer? Nothing. Her life had not been so pathless before the night of the river's flood and Andrew's and Meg's deaths. Meg just six years old; were she still living she would now be a woman well into her twenties. Sarah did what she could to avoid thinking back to that time, to Meg, but at any moment, in a flash, it could all be there in full. And with it, the pain.

She felt the warm clasp of Elizabeth's arms around her, Elizabeth's handkerchief gathering their tears. "Friends," said Sarah after a moment. "I believe in the touch of a friend."

✦ XVI ✦

Ghosts

21 March 1865

ABRAHAM LINCOLN CONSULTED HIS IMAGE in the mirror. The tie was straight enough. The person within the clothes was another matter: warts, unruly eyebrows, the pair of milkjug ears, a beard that never did live up to expectation, skin as slack as dried potato, sunken eyes. What an inventory! He consulted his watch. "Mary, it's six on the button."

"Almost ready," she sang out from her dressing room.

He nodded to his reflection. "And don't you forget it," he mouthed, darting his pistol finger at the face within. Things you can do when no one is watching. "The carriage waits," he said matter of factly. He had spent a good portion of the day with Commander Barnes working out details for the trip. Grant's telegram yesterday morning had been a felicitous surprise. Grant had invited his Commander-in-Chief to his headquarters at City Point for a day or two, suggesting that the rest would do him good. Lincoln's answer was immediate: he had already thought of going after the next rain, and he could go sooner if need be; Mrs. Lincoln and a few others would probably accompany him. It would be more than Grant's day or two. Barnes had suggested chartering the *River Queen* to accommodate the President's not inconsiderable party, with his own vessel, the USS *Bat*, providing protection. They would depart early Thursday afternoon and should arrive late Friday, rain or shine. He had telegraphed his son, Captain Robert Todd Lincoln, to tell of his plans, reminding him not to make it public. The trip would do both his parents good.

Mary appeared, smiling and in fine array, and he extended his arm. He caught Elizabeth Keckley's smile of approval from the dressing room. Where would they be these days without Madame Elizabeth? She had even done some nursing for him in the past week, appearing with chicken broth when he was laid up and the Cabinet had to meet at his bedside.

A final flutter from the hand of Elizabeth Keckley and they headed down the stairs, Mary saying how glad she was to see him so recovered, how feeble he had been at the opera last week, Miss Harris not wanting to speak of it but casting worried looks the whole evening long. Alfonso Donn, a new doorkeeper, stood tall and respectful and spoke carefully. "Good evening, Mr. President. Mind the rain. The carriage should be here momentarily."

Mary's eyes were on the sky—they wouldn't be outdoors for any length of time, but one of them usually expressed concern for the other. Not that it ever resulted in either returning for a fitter garment. The carriage pulled up. Burke, the coachman, a wiry colored man, bowed slightly to Mrs. Lincoln and turned to Lincoln. "Good evening, Mr. President. To the Willard?"

"Yes, please," said Lincoln, handing Mary into the carriage. In a couple of minutes they were across Fifteenth Street and in front of the Willard Hotel. Dinner and then Grover's Theater, for a French opera, the name of which escaped his mind. If he didn't have his nose fastened to his face, like Mother Sarah used to say, he'd forget that too. Though forgetting wasn't his problem lately. He kept remembering that other time, other house, other bedroom. And other coach, his eyes fixed on the glowing lights of the dashboard and wondering how long before the spell would shatter. He willed his eyes to open. *Not now*, he said within, and deliberately he pictured his slant-top walnut desk back in Springfield, where above and to the left the door opened onto sixteen cubbyholes, four by four rows of them, labeled *Bonds*, *Contracts*, this form and that, all the way down to the lower right-hand corner and *Kickshaws*, where Joan resided. He filed her away in the desk of his mind, for the time being.

His gaze lifted. They were inside and seated at their table talking of cotton, his mechanical self carrying the conversation forward, like the hand that shakes a hundred or a thousand other hands while knowing nothing about who's attached to any of them. "Cotton," he said. "And tobacco. If I have to hear General Singleton's name one more time—"

"Was Orville Hicks by again?"

"Yes, but he didn't get far, not with General Grant convinced that tobacco is being exchanged up here on the Potomac for bacon and that Singleton is at the bottom of it. General Grant calls it a deep-laid plan for making millions, and he says that when it comes to millions, all other interests fade, including duty to one's country. Grant says he has less objection to whisky being traded."

"And Orville?"

"Orville thinks I'm afraid of Mr. Stanton and that's the reason I hesitate. He has a legion of men behind him. Judge Hughes, Senator Morgan, others."

"And what is Orville's contribution to this picnic?"

"Me, I suspect. I'm sure he puts up some money, too. It would be indecent otherwise." Lincoln fell silent. War was bad enough without such crass complications. "I suppose he's like most folk, wants his money to breed more money. You know, one guinea begets another."

Mary had a sour expression. She had a good idea how long this grim game had been going on. "Access," she said, "access to the President, who just happens to be an old friend."

"Yes," he said. "He has access to me. But I always add that it is subject to the approval of General Grant, that nothing is to interfere with the primary object."

"Coward!" she said vehemently.

"I know. It's like having your cake and eating it too, except it's no piece of cake. Cake of soap maybe, that doesn't wash very clean. Mr. Stanton hates it too. He's opposed to the whole scheme of trade in foreign products. Life was so much simpler when Orville and I were small-town lawyers and not very sure where the next dinner was coming from. Oh, Mary, he wears us down. He's afraid the war won't last long enough to make his killing, and so he importunes us. Mr. Stanton just returned from the front today, and there's Orville at the War Department, first in line like a child for a prize. I think Orville talked nothing but cotton and tobacco. I'll tell you though, our Mr. Stanton can show a dry wit. He takes Orville by the arm, and not until they come to the portico does he turn to him and say in an ordinary tone of voice: 'By the way, that tobacco that the troops from Fortress Monroe burned, the two hundred thousand pounds purchased by General Singleton in Richmond and sent to Fredericksburg'—can you picture Orville now? With his heart in his throat. 'Well,' says Mr. Stanton, 'that wasn't General Singleton's tobacco after all. Strange what stories get in circulation.' And there they part. Orville speechless for once in his life."

Mary raised an eyebrow, and he paused.

"I'm sorry. I manage to forget myself, don't I? Tell me about your day."

"I did get out. Stopped by Stuntz's. There was an aeronautical display in the window, with model wagons and everything. There was even a balloon painted like the sky, like Mr. Lowe's. Good thing Tad wasn't along, though I may take him to see it. But it wasn't for sale. I did get him a set of toy soldiers, an Indiana regiment, very like the troop last Friday."

Toy soldiers, thought Lincoln, and he tried to imagine war as a game.

HE GLANCED ABOUT, A CHILL ACROSS HIS SHOULDERS. Mary had just set down her water glass. On all sides folk were at various stages of dining, and white-clad waiters bustled about with trays. He turned sideways, feeling a gaze upon him, and a pair of eyes dark as midnight met his. Lincoln studied the face, handsome, with unruly hair like his own, and a flourishing mustache. It was the actor Wilkes Booth, knife and fork in hand, intent upon his dinner plate.

Lincoln returned to his own dinner—all that remained on his plate were a couple of dun-colored legs, a third of a crab's chest, and the buttery sauce tinged now with green.

"Food like this brings out the worst in us. Mindless machines that devour whatever is set before them."

"Only if it's a crab," said Mary with a smile. Her plate was lily white—swept clean with a piece of bread.

He looked at his watch. "We could divide a piece of the apple pie, and then we should go." In an instant the waiter was there and back again with a single wedge of warm pie, vanilla iced cream on the side.

Mary set her fork down. "It's been so long since I've done any cooking—I miss picking berries, peeling apples, watching a crust turn golden, then smelling the steaming hot pie on the counter."

"It's been too long," he said.

"Sometimes," said Mary. "I wonder if the Mrs. Lincoln here in the capital is the same as the one who used to live back in Springfield. The Springfield Mrs. Lincoln was a brighter woman who saw where she was headed."

He nodded. He wanted to tell her it wasn't so, but it was true. A weight as heavy as a leaden cloak descended upon his shoulders. Her voice sounded so high-pitched.

Mary continued: "Her home was the center of the world, and she had everything she wanted right at her fingertips. Her three boys, her husband—most nights of the year she had her husband. She had a comfortable house, food on the table, warmth, family, friends."

"Yes," he said. "We had all that, but—"

"I know," she said. "Time doesn't stand still; events don't step aside for our convenience."

"There's a river, and downstream is this great rock."

"You mean slavery, don't you?"

He nodded again. Waters were rushing, breaking against the rock. They had come such a long way, the whole country had. Rivers have but one direction. Down. How does water ever get upstream? For the life of him he couldn't see how it ever got back to the source.

"Four more years," Mary was saying, "but not all of them need be years of war—tell me that's so."

He straightened his shoulders and shifted in an attempt to cast away the leaden cloak. "No," he willed himself to say. "No, this war is coming to an end." He tried to picture Tad as a young man, back in Springfield with his family and friends. But even with the war winding down and certain to be over before year's end, the picture frittered away. If there were a crystal ball on the table instead of the remains of apple pie and iced cream, it would show him nothing. But that was just his own story. The country's future—he hoped he could help with its telling, leading it to a clear ending, or what passed for an ending.

Mary had nodded to a table by the door. She had caught the eye of Preston Blair's daughter, Elizabeth Lee, a dependable friend for Mary, which was a rare thing. Old Washington did not quickly befriend the Lincolns, not when parting with the Davises had been so hard. Like so many families, his and Mary's included, the Blairs and even the Lees were fighting on both sides of this war. Perhaps the Davises were too. What family didn't have its black and its white?

He had thrown the Blairs to the wolves—Radical wolves—in exchange for reelection, asking Montgomery to resign as Postmaster General, and an equally cursed necessity, reassigning Captain Samuel Phillips Lee, Elizabeth's husband, from his command of the North Atlantic Blockading Squadron to the Mississippi. Demoting him from Acting Rear-Admiral to Captain. Bitter days, thought Lincoln. He remembered asking Preston Blair how it could be good policy to sacrifice true friends for a false one, or worse, for an avowed enemy? Preston had sighed. "What good are personal interests," he had said, "when the salvation of the Republic is at stake?" Such faithful friends, worth their weight in gold, and that included Elizabeth Blair Lee, who at this very moment had poor Vice President Johnson living in her home.

"Did you care for that last bite?" asked Mary, looking at his plate.

"No," he half-lied, "here, you take it." His thoughts returned to the Vice President. He would be no easy house-guest, yet how he managed was of national importance. Washington was certainly not his element. It had taken the next thing to a direct order to bring him out of Tennessee in time for the inauguration. Imagine saying he might put off his appearance till "after the first Monday in April," his very words. A full month after the inauguration. The Cabinet had shrugged their collective shoulders and directed the Commander-in-Chief to send a telegram: "Unsafe for you to not be here on the fourth of March," and if that wasn't clear enough, "Be sure to reach here by that time."

Duly, Johnson had arrived, and oh, what an impression he had given. Lincoln took their word for it; he had missed the first stages of the Vice President's talk, had sat with eyes closed, thinking how different these times were from when he gave his first inaugural address. So much was unsettled back then, no one knowing who he was and how he would handle the disaster, Secretary Seward expecting to take up the reins of government in his wise and experienced hands. Waiting for Johnson's speech to wind down, Lincoln had thought ahead to his own words. He would call for forgiveness without malice, for binding up the nation's wounds, urging that we must forget about sides and think of one nation, a Union. It was Davis who spoke of two countries. And so Andrew Johnson's words had slipped by unheard. Of course the papers had finally reported on the speech, taking their text from Johnson's own draft. It wasn't a bad speech, as printed. Just drunkenly delivered.

It was time to get a move on. Lincoln glanced at the receipt, left the money for the bill on the table, and rose to his feet. A young couple were now sitting at Wilkes Booth's table.

"All was perfect," the President said to the beaming waiter. "I about die for crab like this. It's only fair, of course, given that the crab died for me."

With a smile Mary led the way out, passing by the table where Elizabeth Lee sat. "Good evening, Elizabeth," she said.

Elizabeth Lee looked up, swallowed, and returned the greeting.

"Evening, Elizabeth," said the President. "Isn't that pie something! And how is Mr. J doing?"

Elizabeth Lee considered the question before replying. "Quite well, Mr. President." She was speaking low, and though eyes were certainly on them, their words would not be overheard. "He has improved very much in his appetite, though I don't think he ever was a hearty eater. His breakfast he particularly delights in, and now that there are but few of us at table he talks well, though the moment strangers appear he loses all cheerfulness. You know, when he first came he was the most mortified, sick, and hurt man I ever saw. Mr. King gives us hope of Mr. J, says he can resist temptation if he will, for he knows by experience. Excuse me, Mr. Lincoln. This is my friend from childhood, Mrs. Prentiss, just back from England and visiting the city."

Lincoln extended his hand. "Pleased to meet you," he said. "My wife, Mary, Mrs. Prentiss."

"My pleasure, Mr. President and Mrs. Lincoln," said Sarah Prentiss, her eyes meeting his.

He managed to keep his balance. It was Joan, the very image. The eyes, the hair, everything but the attire.

"London, ah, London, you say?" He was stammering. Elizabeth Lee had said England. She had caught the small difference—a glint in her eye said so, and she was letting him boil in his own juices.

"Yes," said Mrs. Prentiss, "I was with my brother at the Legation, but now he's married and I am cast off."

A short silence ensued, no one knowing quite what to say after this oddly personal remark.

"Well," said Elizabeth Lee, "you mustn't let us keep you. I hope you are going to Grover's. I hear from Father that the Frenchman's opera is very fine. And if I may, I will tell Mr. J you asked after him."

"Yes, please do, and yes, it's Grover's for us." So ended the brief conversation.

"WHAT," SAID ELIZABETH LEE, "was all that about? You look like you've seen a ghost."

"I don't know," said her dinner partner. "I assure you, as the words came out of my mouth I was in horror."

"In horror? I only meant that to my ears it was as though you had skipped a beat, taken a step or two more than expected. And that Mr. Lincoln seemed contributory to the moment. I had the distinct impression that you two had met before."

"No," said Sarah Prentiss, "never. But I felt in the presence of an old friend. Am I usually so flippant? And with the President of all people?"

"Not at all. Though I think you need not dwell on it. It was just a passing remark. And our dinner has been so joyful, so rare a night on the town for two women long in the tooth, that I can see how the tongue might be unlimbered."

Sarah sipped her coffee. She would let it go, would not dwell upon it. But deep within she noted a stirring, like something long asleep now awakening.

Elizabeth laughed aloud, a soft chuckle. "I am doubly glad now that we will be at the opera to see the White Lady with all her attendant mystery. Our night out from Mr. Johnson."

"SUCH IMPERTINENCE," Mary said when they were clear of Willard's and back in the carriage for the short jog to Grover's.

Lincoln said nothing. Silence, he knew, was the soundest palliative when the green demon had clenched its talons onto Mary's heart. He could feel her seething, waiting for the slightest word of denial. He glanced out the window. Burke was pulled up close to the theater, now advancing to the carriage block where Crook, detailed by Mr. Stanton, waited to escort them inside.

"Mind your step," said Lincoln as he handed Mary out.

Folk stood aside from the entrance. "Evening, evening," he murmured, glad to be on neutral ground. He accepted a program and let Mary lead the way up to their box. As the door to the box swung shut, he caught a last glimpse of Crook. Come hell or high water, Mr. Stanton would have his way. At least he didn't go to Hill's extreme of bundling himself up in his cloak outside the bedroom door, with an arsenal of pistols and bowie knives, waiting for the safety of the dawn. They were kindly efforts, he knew, but it was by Providence that he lived and by Providence that he would stay alive.

Seated, Lincoln slipped on his spectacles. François-Adrien Boieldieu's *La Dame blanche*, and in parentheses for those unable to guess at the French, "The White Lady." Première at the Opéra-Comique, Paris, December 10, 1825.

"The story is Sir Walter Scott's," said Mary, "or the two stories are his. *The Monastery* is one and *Guy Mannering* is the other, both Waverley novels of course."

"Of course," repeated Lincoln. "I'm not entirely ignorant—just by half. This is the one you saw in New York?"

"One of them." She was trying to be civil. "Would you like a rundown on the story?"

Taking his humble demeanor for assent, Mary launched into the plot. "A young English officer appears at dusk in front of a Scottish castle just as the lady of the castle gives birth. If Boieldieu were stricter with Sir Walter, the young man would cast the newborn's horoscope and tell the father how the stars warn of three hazardous times in the boy's life."

"Only three?" said Lincoln.

"Three," said Mary firmly. "This is comedy, not tragedy. Shall I go on?"

"Please. My lips are sealed."

"I'll be quick—here are the musicians. Just the main points of the first act."

He rocked back—grateful that Grover's supplied him with a good-sized chair—while Mary told of the ghost known as the White Lady, the old Count's missing heir, his beautiful ward (a soprano) who doubles as the ghost, the false steward, a hidden treasure, and Dickson, the tenant in whose place the young Englishman offers to answer the summons of the ghost. And finally the climax: the pretty young ghost recognizes the hero because she had once nursed him back to health.

"All this in the first act?"

"No, not all. The scene inside the castle, with the ghost and George, that's the next act."

"George?"

"Officer George, our hero," Mary paused. "Thank you for the fine dinner."

"My pleasure, Mother," he said, patting her arm. The curtain was rising, and the stage was filled with song and dance. They both loved the theater, although Mary's taste ran more to opera and his to dramatic productions. With Shakespeare Mary got fidgety, whereas with opera he was content to accept the spectacle without burdening the performance with concern for significance. Adrift, he found himself wondering, *Who was that friend of Elizabeth Lee's?* If she were once again before him, would he see that she bore only a mild resemblance to Joan? But in that instant at Willard's, she had seemed the true coin of Joan. A coincidence, as in opera. But he was no romantic hero, and Elizabeth Lee's childhood friend was no ghost. Unless from the future.

The curtain rose, and onstage strode a stalwart young man who could be none other than the hero, his voice already rising in song. Lincoln leaned forward, studying the façade of the tenant's house, the faces and figures of the chorus. It's nice, he noted, how all the pieces fit together. The villain can snatch away an heir, falsify a will, scheme for treasure. But the stars have their story written down, and no matter how adroit he is, the villain cannot change a single line.

Nor can the hero. He had said as much in his inaugural address regarding this terrible war: *If God will that it continue, till every drop of blood drawn with the lash shall be paid by another drawn by the sword, it is the judgment of the Lord, righteous and true.*

He considered his own story. Born in Kentucky in the year 1809, born again in Chicago, Illinois, in 1955, dies (date to be determined) at Ford's Theater. Good thing this was Grover's, not that you couldn't be taken ill at Grover's, or fall down its narrow steps and that fall precipitate another at Ford's, but the last nail in the coffin. It was a good thing that come Thursday he would leave this city with its thousand and one complications and join Grant, where the only theater was the theater of war.

◆ XVII ◆

Proverbial Joan

5 June 1955

J OAN MATCHAM SAT AT HER ROUND salmon-colored kitchen
table sipping good Darjeeling tea. She glanced at the kitchen
calendar one more time. April was done, May had come and
gone, and the dawning of June had confirmed her suspicions. She
had had a notion of what was looming on the horizon ever since
the morning after. The precedent of her first pregnancy foretelling
the next. She had also thought about lightning striking twice. And
the single swallow that does not make a summer's day. Yet lightning
had struck twice; and one swallow was sufficient. In a word, she
was pregnant. Her periods missed and the brief bout of morning
sickness already receding from memory. Assuming the pregnancy
was not a hysterical one.

Tomorrow she would see about an appointment with Lorraine
Riggs, her gynecologist since before Emily was conceived. It would
be awkward, to say the least. She could picture the encounter, the
doctor's token question, the patient's reply, her smile frozen on her
face. *I'm fine, maybe more than fine. I think I'm pregnant. Yes, I'm
forty-two. Who's the father?* Followed by a sickening grin. *Oh, it was
an older gentleman, though not so old as all that. His name was Abraham Lincoln.* Lorraine would look askance. *I'm not being evasive. It's
Abraham Lincoln, the president after Buchanan, the one before Andrew
Johnson.* Or she could define him by his words: *It was the man who*

believed that a house divided cannot stand and who lived with malice toward none and charity for all.

Would it be better to quote the old ballad: there came a knock at the door, and the pretty lass home alone; and when the stranger was gone there were still two within? No, she didn't catch his name.

But there would be no false stories, not with Lorraine. She was Joan, who swallowed the canary and couldn't keep it from singing. Joan, the goose that laid the golden egg, or would lay it early in the new year. Proverbial Joan, that's who she was. Joan, unable to conceal her joy.

Yet she had not been able to keep this an absolute secret. She had begun to keep a journal again, a diary. She had bought a perfect-bound book at The Bookshop with pages lined, a vellum cover, and the endpapers stiff and marbled like a choice book from his own time. She turned to the first entry.

Wednesday, April 20, 1955—I am not sure where to start. Further on in these pages I may tell a full story, one that obeys the clock and calendar. I will try not to be literary but to tell a straight story in straight words. This story needs no embellishment—it has that baroque element without need of more from me. It is ten days since he came into my life, ten since he left. Less than a day to meet, to love, to be gone. Whether I go on and tell this story in full depends on whether I am pregnant or not. That wasn't easy to write, not that I fear it or do not wish it. It's almost silly the ways in which I wish it were so. Wanting proof. As though it would be a little boy born with those hands and that beard, and that laugh. Of course it could be a girl. He has never had a daughter. And I have never had a son. So it's an even shot for both of us. If I am not pregnant, the story can come and go with me. Without the ocular proof it would lose too much in the telling, worthy of no more than a benign smile. But if I am. If I am, the father of this child is Abraham Lincoln.

I repeat, the father of my child is Abraham Lincoln. I shiver at having written his name so baldly, so easily. Two seven-letter words to stand for the single person. It all began when I saw him sitting on a bench overlooking the lake, and it didn't cross my mind that he resembled the man on the five-dollar bill.

Joan smiled, remembering the moment. At first, she had seen nothing more than a man, a man too old to be a student, who casually reached down and petted Rusty. She had told him how Rusty got her name, which brought Emily into the story, and since it was Easter Sunday, the next thing she knew she was crying. Joan found it hard to keep the sequence straight. Good thing she could write all this down. She resumed her story.

From there on the conversation wasn't ordinary anymore—by ordinary I mean the way it is between strangers who steer clear of intimacy. With my salt tears the ice was broken, and we were no longer strangers. We started to walk, and walking, it made sense to introduce myself, which I did. He then blurted out who he was, that his name was Abraham Lincoln, and I didn't know what to think. Somehow, I hadn't made the connection. I hadn't seen the resemblance. Yet strangely I accepted what he said, didn't send him on his way. Gradually, as the day wore on, seeing him in my rocking chair, the bushy eyebrows, the craggy face, the lanky legs, I came to know that he was the real thing. And at the deli when he wrote out the note to Stanton and I saw his handwriting, I was certain.

She closed the diary. It was exactly twelve o'clock, Sunday, the fifth of June. She lifted the lid from the small brown teapot—empty. In one hour she would be sitting at Cooley's Cupboard across from Tom Matcham. Joan grimaced. She and Tom had met quarterly ever since Robert's death. As executor of Robert's estate, Tom had taken on the responsibility for his sister-in-law's economic well-being. They would be scheduled to meet again (she counted out the months on the fingers of her right hand, July, August, September) in early September, and again in December. And she would be due (her fingers once more counting the months), as she already knew, by mid-January. By December he would definitely know what was up. What could she possibly tell him?

Absurd. It was absurd. Who would have expected Joan Matcham to appear in such a romantic plot? Tomorrow she would call Lorraine Riggs' office. What story would she tell? Well, let tomorrow tell its own story.

✦ XVIII ✦

At Sally's House

1 April 1865

THE SUN HAD NOT YET RISEN, and the rain kept on and on. It had poured all the day before and all that night, a sodden finish to the month of March, and now April was splattering oleaginous mud halfway up Emma Slaughter's parlor window. Sarah Prentiss stared blindly into the rain-splattered gloom. Whatever had possessed her to come to Richmond? Was this truly where she wanted to be, in rain and wind likely to blow you off your feet? Was she in flight? Or simply adrift?

Across the room was a square piano, what her mother termed a *megatherium*—you wouldn't want to quarrel with anything so huge. Sarah hadn't touched it. And now the grandfather clock was chiming: six in the morning. Time for night to fall and day finally to rise. Sarah peered outside once more.

Looming darkly in the thinning shadows was the Confederate balloon, the *Jefferson*. It had survived the stormy night. Who would expect that such a flimsy looking thing, fashioned of silk and cord, less than the very air itself, could endure this havoc of wind and rain? Ever since she had arrived in Richmond it had been tethered there, on the lawn of the Davis mansion, ballasted with a dozen bags of sand fixed to its netting. Its mission, presumably, extended no further than observation, but she had to wonder, given the number of times Jefferson Davis had come out to inspect it, testing its ropes, questioning the aeronauts, patting the wicker basket as though it were a faithful dog. He would depart, apparently satisfied; but before long he would be back to perform the ritual all over again. To be truthful, she could sympathize with the old goat-beard. It was bad enough to trust yourself to the inch-thick planks of a sailing vessel, let alone this basket of wicker. Such sympathy did not, however, endear him to her.

Farther across the lawn she could make out his portico, and below it the hint of a framed doorway, a ghostly edifice slowly taking on substance with the rising sun, as though released from a spell and coming into being.

She should have known that Richmond would be no better than Washington, merely an exchange of capitals—USA for CSA—each with its White House, its gaunt president. And they were drawing closer, these two men, for the buzz around Richmond was that President Lincoln had abandoned his stately mansion for General Grant's headquarters at City Point on the James.

The morning after meeting President Lincoln at Willard's Hotel, Sarah had run into Emma Slaughter at Center Market, and one thing leading to another, Sarah had agreed to accompany Emma and her son Jourdan through the Union lines and home to Richmond. Emma and Jourdan had traveled north for medical treatment, and once the eye specialist had rendered his Philadelphia judgment, they intended to return home. An odd war, one hand turned against the other.

From Center Market she and Emma had gone to Elizabeth Lee's, a brief reunion of Madame Sigoigne's pupils. Just one hour later Sarah was sending her card up to President Lincoln requesting a pass to Richmond.

Here everyone was still asleep, or if awake they were savoring the warmth of lying abed under down comforters. Sarah rearranged the quilt on her lap. She was at sixes and sevens. She had fixed herself a pot of tea and now what? She thought once more of attempting the labyrinth of Eugène Sue's *Wandering Jew*. The longer she ignored it, the more it weighed.

Sarah wedged off the tin lid from her stationery box. On top was the closely written first page of her letter to her brother Richard, a

sketch of her trip back to America. All that was fine. What wasn't so
fine was the ripening of her anger over his courting Charlotte Wel-
man and deserting her, his widowed sister. Her pen had scratched a
broad X across the page. Eventually, she had gathered her wits and
begun again, a letter addressed to both husband and wife, a proper
mouse of a letter, with a skitter of joy here, a dash of sunshine there.
The semblance of an older sister so happy for her baby brother and
the carrying on of the family name.

Sarah's eye caught the sheet of paper beneath her X-ed out letter.

*Allow the bearer, Mrs. Prentiss, with ordinary baggage to pass
from Washington to Richmond & return.*
March 22, 1865   *A. Lincoln*

She remembered being ushered into the office, President Lincoln
standing with outstretched hand, waving aside her apologies for
interrupting. "Of course, Mrs. Prentiss," he had said. "I remember
you as plain as air." He shrugged and smiled, and here in this dark
room her own smile echoed his. First words can be so awkward. She
had explained about how hard-pressed Emma was to manage the
house and also nurse Jourdan, and that she had offered a helping
hand. "And the father?" Lincoln had asked.

"Colonel Slaughter was killed at Nashville in December."

"War," he said flatly. "Your friend must have friends in Richmond. It's not the best time to be there. Wars are won when armies
are defeated or surrender. But Richmond is not just any city; it is
their capital, a symbol, and so much of the war has centered on it. I
would dissuade you, if I could."

His eyes were so kind. She had noted that, and his genuine smile,
and his hands so gracefully folded palm to palm. She had been
struck by his patience, as though he were not the president but a
friend giving advice. And before she realized it was happening, he
had drawn from her the fuller story, the story of the storm, of Meg's
body washed up on the bank of the Kennebec River, with never a
trace of Sarah's husband. The story of her grief. She told how Emma
had come to Waterville from Boston, where she had been visiting,
and how Emma had kept her going, helped her rise each morning

to face the day. Sarah hadn't wanted to tell this story, but in telling it she was reminded of the story Elizabeth had told her, of Willie Lincoln's death three years before.

"Your friend's son—" he had started to say, and then he sighed deeply.

"I'm sure Jourdan will recover," she assured him. "The problem is more his cantankerous nature, trying to persuade a child of what is good for him, a child who doesn't want to be confined to his room, let alone a darkened room."

"I understand," he had said. They were both sitting now, he at his desk, she alongside, and she had noted his ready pen, a small-barrel Gillott like her own. "You are serving as a friend, and in these dark days the unconditional love and service of a friend means all. I will write the pass, but may I impose one condition? You will use your best judgment of course, but should Richmond fall before you return, you must not give way to the ensuing panic. Do your best, please, you and the Slaughters, to hold your ground. Tell me the whereabouts of the Slaughters' home, and I will direct our soldiers to watch out for you." Then he had written the pass, waving it in the air to let it dry, offered it to her without letting it go. As they both held the pass, he wished her a very safe journey. Then he had said, "Don't trouble yourself that you put me in mind of my Willie. I catch myself every day talking with him as if he were with me." He released his hold, and the pass was hers.

Sarah heard footsteps, and the parlor door slowly opened. Three inquisitive faces appeared: Caesar the calico cat, Ginger the chocolate spaniel, and old Sally, almost as wide as she was tall, wearing a calico babushka and a starched white apron. "Mrs. Prentiss!" she cried out, her chest heaving. "You like to give me my death. Since Colonel Slaughter was killed, this house has been like a tomb, but I wasn't expecting no ghosts. I would've sworn it was the Colonel's mother herself sitting by the window. The years don't matter to the dead."

"Sorry if I gave you a scare, Sally. It's just me."

"I see that now. My granny talked with ghosts regular enough— more ghosts than you got fingers—and I thought my turn had come. I'll get some porridge boiling in a bit—goes good with coffee. It gets me how you folk can drink that watery tea. And Thomas will be by soon with a pitcher of cream—Thomas from cross the way." Sally's head gestured in the direction of Jefferson Davis's Executive Mansion, and her voice turned to a conspiratorial whisper. "What some call the White House, though there ain't but one White House, far as I's concerned. And I don't say that because this one is what I call gray. Mrs. Davis, though, no one could find fault with that woman. Oh, and that nice Captain Harding, I invited him to breakfast, I hope you don't mind. I'll take these with me."

On that note Sally made her exit, tea tray in hand, with Ginger and Caesar at her heels. The woman could do ten things at once— Sarah had seen at first glance that with Sally on hand, the house, so to speak, ran itself. What Emma Slaughter stood in need of was moral, not physical, support. Every woman's household should be blessed with a Sally.

And Cyrus Harding, a classmate of Richard's and another of Sally's conquests, was coming for breakfast. Sarah had run into him the day before, hands in his pockets, awaiting exchange and given the privilege of the city thanks to Alexander Stephens, but little more. He and Stephens, somewhere in the web of things, were inhabitants of the same family tree. She had always thought of Cyrus as a cool man, a person with the perfection of a well-oiled machine, cogs and gears clicking along in his head. But now in want and hungry, he was not so cool, so mechanical. He had spent three weeks in Libby Prison, the old tobacco warehouse by the river that had been confiscated after the battle of Bull Run to house Northern prisoners. It was notorious in the North, a by-word for the worst that the aristocracy of the South could dream up, though once she was in Washington Sarah had wondered if Libby could possibly be worse than Old Capitol Prison. Hearing Cyrus Harding tell his story, she imagined her brother in Harding's place—*There but for the grace of God*, she thought. Richard wouldn't have survived; Richard was too soft.

Harding had been reluctant to speak about his experience, but eventually he told her how he had arrived in Richmond and been stripped of his coat and blanket and left without food for two days. Then the prisoners had been marched to the prison, made to climb three flights of stairs, and issued one shabby blanket for every three men. The two daily meals, at ten in the morning and five in the afternoon, consisted of a few ounces of stinking meat and some musty wheat bread made from unsifted meal, mixed with water and a little grease from the rotten bacon. Occasionally they were given a scoop of boiled beans or soup in place of the bacon, but neither of these was any more palatable.

"You would think they meant to starve us," Harding said. "None but the toughest of men can keep alive with such usage." He shrugged, both of them aware of those he had left behind. But he had smiled as he told of the joy of a good scrub, of putting on clean clothes free of vermin, and of his wariness not to eat too much. "I thanked God," he said, "when we arrived in Richmond, but I thanked all else when I passed out of that building, sick but still able to navigate on my own."

He was such a different man now from the one her brother had brought home for the holidays. Warmer, with less starch in his bones. Back then he had been so sure of his authority, his destiny. How blind they all had been. Couldn't they have seen this storm on the horizon? But then again, neither of them had ever seen a manacle or known a slave.

Sarah gathered up her letter box and book. There was a hollow feeling in the pit of her stomach, as though she were hungry, but she knew this emptiness would not be satisfied by a meal. She was waiting, that she knew, but she hadn't an inkling of what she was waiting for.

✦ XIX ✦

A Majesty of Minds

1 April 1865

O ne more message," said Abraham Lincoln, "just in case. Mr. Stanton doesn't miss much, but I'm uneasy nevertheless. What if our coachman isn't there to greet Mrs. Lincoln? Small things—" His voice faded. He didn't need to spell it out, didn't want to, that Mary was like a taut wire and ready to snap. Her outburst on the reviewing field with Mrs. General Ord was enough to last a Methuselah's lifetime—that the wife of a mere general should dare to ride by the President's side, and in such array! With that feathered Robin Hood's cap, as though she were the Empress Eugénie herself!

"I understand," said Sam, two words that went a mile. Sam Beckwith's tent was right next to Colonel Bowers' larger canvas establishment, which supposedly was Lincoln's official headquarters. But Lincoln preferred this one, calling it "the telegraph office" and wellnigh living here since his arrival at City Point more than a week before. Their folding desks were at opposite ends of the tent but within arm's reach of each other. General Grant—nobody's fool and not one to miss a trick—had directed Sam to report to the President, who was a direct link between the Army and the War Department.

Initially, Grant had suggested a visit of a day or two, a short rest to do the President some good, but Lincoln wanted more than a few days, and more than rest. It was possible that if the thing were pressed, in a matter of days the eastern front would collapse. Sherman and Grant were like the two jaws of a nutcracker, and Lee in the center had nowhere to go. And so two days had stretched to nine, and now with Secretary Seward heading back to Washington and Mr. Stanton already there, the Commander-in-Chief (which was none other than the son of Thomas Lincoln) could easily be spared for another week at the front. And then! Lincoln could picture it: the two generals, Grant and Lee, and Lee's officers and their horses, and the men, standing, waiting for the last turn of the screw that says *We're through*. The end of this desolating rebellion. He could all but taste it, like a peach so ripe its juices run down your chin. Amelia, Farmville. Maybe Buckingham Court House or Appomattox. The surrender. His being there wouldn't make a bit of difference. The war didn't need him to end—but oh how that moment would warm a heart half frozen.

Sam was back to ciphering, either composing the next telegram or deciphering the last. Lincoln reached for a telegraph blank and uncapped his pen:

HEAD QUARTERS ARMIES OF THE UNITED STATES,

City-Point April 1 5/45 1865

Alfonso Donn
Doorkeeper, Executive Mansion
Washington, D.C.
    Have Burke, coachman, have the enclosed carriage
sent to the Arsenal Wharf at 8 o'clock Sunday Morning &
remain until Mrs. Lincoln's arrival.

A. Lincoln

"Sam," he said, reaching across the tent with the telegram. "Not urgent. They're not being chased by pirates like the *Polly Ann*."

Beckwith turned, his head cocked, his smile wry: "The *Polly Ann?*"

"You don't know the story of the escape of the *Polly Ann?* On the Erie Canal, and the pirates catching up, and one of the crew ordered the pilot to 'heave to.' When the vessel 'huv to,' the sailor leaped ashore with a bag of oats and scattered them along the tow-path, a liberal scattering. That done, he hopped back aboard and on they went. And when the pirate's craft came along, skull and cross-bones crackling in the wind, daggers drawn, blunderbusses loaded with shot, no amount of persuasion would induce the mules of the *Jolly Roger* to proceed till every last oat was consumed. A happy ending, for the *Polly Ann* and for the mules, if not for the pirates."

"If I didn't know it before," said Beckwith, "I know it now. A true story, you say?"

"Would the President of the United States of America tell anything but the truth? No need to reply." Lincoln sighed and stood. Truthful is what he was not these days. In his pocket was the penny, his penny, the penny of himself. And should something happen to him? Of course he could dispose of it, a solution that defeated the necessity, which was to cling to the artifact, his certificate of sanity. He would be wise, though, to keep the coin away from Ford's Theater. Though doing so smacked of superstition.

Lincoln bit his lip. A voice within was waiting its turn, the voice of conscience. He closed his eyes. *How easy*, said the voice, *how easy never to think aught of the callow husband, of his infidelity.* Eyes still closed, he thought: *But I know, I can't solve that now. Not now. One thing at a time. I can't dot every* i, *cross every* t. "Sam," he said, "think I'll take half a stretch before the rain picks up again."

He stepped outside. Say what you will, but he had taken care of Mary for the moment. He had waved farewell as she and Mr. Seward stepped aboard the *Monohasset* early in the afternoon. And in Washington she would be met at the wharf. Tad they had allowed to stay behind, a welcome distraction for the men and a permanent clog for Captain Penrose, thereby undoing Mr. Stanton's intention that Lincoln have an escort and guardian. Lincoln did, except the Lincoln with the escort was Tad.

The camp was situated on the bluff overlooking the James, and Lincoln followed the boarded path running alongside the corduroyed road that led down to the wharf. Any minute now the rains might recommence—with a wind like this there was no telling. In the sky, among the fleeting clouds, shone what few raggle-taggle stars the heavens could assemble. Below, the waters ran without any great rush—the James, a river of water, not blood. General Sherman, when he and Grant were aboard the *River Queen*, had spoken of battles where the blood ran in streams down the hillsides and pooled at the low points. And more blood would flow before the last shot was fired, but then it would be over. Thank the Lord.

Lights were on at the sheds by the wharf—loading and unloading didn't wait for the sun to shine. In the channel an array of ships were moored: steamers, sloops, a brig or two, transports, the *Bat*, the *River Queen*. It took so much to sustain this war—Stanton told of purchasing more than three million pairs of trousers, seven million pairs of stockings, two hundred thousand camp kettles, over thirteen thousand drums, fourteen thousand fifes. Drums and fifes, imagine! *How many tents?* he wondered. He looked back toward the encampment, its row upon row of tents dotted with the occasional campfire (wood—especially dry wood—was scarce). Closer to the bluff were a goodly number of log huts, Grant's headquarters. Of course General Grant himself was a few miles south, before Petersburg. Lincoln picked out the tent he shared with Sam. Now that the South was on the downhill, he did delight in being the main conduit of news from Virginia to Washington, at the same time passing on to Mr. Stanton his own impressions:

> *Arrived here all safe; Robert just now tells me there was a little rumpus up the line. . . .*
> *Grant has been out since yesterday morning. . . . Last night, when it was dark as a rainy night without a moon could be, a furious cannonade, soon joined by heavy musket-fire, opened near Petersburg and lasted about two hours. The sound was very distinct here, as also were the flashes of the guns upon the clouds. It seemed to me a great battle, but the older hands have scarcely noticed it. . . .*
> *There has been much hard fighting this morning. The enemy drove our left from near Dabney's house back well toward the Boydton plank road. We are now about to take the offensive.*

Voices approaching. He recognized the accent of Joseph Henry's visitor from Germany. Things may have thinned out some with Mr. Seward and Mrs. Lincoln now on their way up the Potomac, but no sooner had the *Monohasset* got up a head of steam downriver than upriver came the *State of Maine* with a delegation from the Smithsonian, or more precisely, from NASUS, the National Academy of Sciences for the United States—himself an honorary founder. It was a delegation of five: Joseph Henry, Asaph Hall, Asa Gray, Count Zeppelin, and the newcomer fresh off the boat, August Möbius, Hay's puzzle-maker, not to mention an astronomer or mathematician, or maybe both. A majesty of minds. What, he wondered, if he were to show them his penny from the next century? A temptation mightily to be resisted.

Suddenly he remembered his dream from the dark hours of last night, of looking at himself in a mirror—which he did little of nowadays since growing his beard—and realizing his hair had grown sparse and what little there was had gone from gray to white, and then behind him—her head and shoulders framed in the mirror—Joan Matcham, but her hair long and done up like Sarah Prentiss's. And then he didn't know which one it was, or whether he was here or there. There was more to the dream, but all he could remember was a dog with stripes like a tiger, maybe not the same dream. Or was it a tiger with a body like a dog? In any case, it was another dream not to report to Mary.

"Gentlemen," he said.

"Mr. President."

"So," said Lincoln, "which way do you think this weather will jump?"

"Well," said Joseph Henry, "none of us is a meteorologist, but with this wind from the northeast and the fierce look of the sky, only a fool would bet on anything but rain. If it were coming from the other direction, I'd simply telegraph St. Louis, ask how it's faring, and predict their weather by morning. But until we have meteorological observatories at sea and a way to communicate those observations—"

"A wireless telegraph, you mean?" Lincoln interrupted. He was cheating and he knew it.

"No," said Henry deliberately. "I was thinking of a cable such as we have laid across Chesapeake Bay, with relay stations in mid-ocean. But imagine, a wireless telegraph! Wouldn't that be something, like a surface without friction. Have you any other fantastic ideas for us?"

"Now that you mention it, I might have one or two." How could he say *No* to such an invitation? "Small things," he said, "handy things, like an electrical saw, small enough to fit in your hand; or a self-propelled velocipede, light-weight and geared, for man, woman, and child—a replacement for horses, much as I like them. There's a thing I'd call a "flash-light," hand-held again, with batteries no bigger than your thumb. But you men are the ones who have the liberty to play with ideas. To quote Shakespeare, I'm just a 'vile politician.' "

"I told you our Mr. Lincoln was an unusual man," said Henry. "You know he has patented a device to make our rivers more navigable by lessening a vessel's draught of water through a system of adjustable buoyant air chambers. An ingenious proposal. He's a man of vision."

"The model at least worked," Lincoln said, "though I do not expect to grow wealthy with the application. But speaking of vision, I do have a question, one question, and then I'll let the men of science do the talking. Do you ever wonder why the heavens are not brighter at night? It may seem like a trivial question, especially tonight with stars scarcer than wings on a wolf. But as a boy I used to wonder about the stars—there seemed so many of them in the sky, just about everywhere you looked. And now telescopes see more and more of them, filling in spaces the ancients thought empty. With all these new stars, I wonder why the skies at night are as dark as ever?" Lincoln sighed. "At times I'll go to any length to take my mind away from the main business."

"No," said Möbius, "your question about starlight is not trivial. Just because men fight wars does not mean that we must put our minds to sleep. If you have other thoughts on the subject I should like to hear them."

"Remember," said Lincoln, "I am like a child in such matters, but I've wondered if it could be anything like a train whistle receding with its signal, not just growing faint, but also lowering its pitch.

What if starlight were doing the same thing? Receding. And so the stars rushing away from us would have a faltering light. Surely there's a pattern up there; they can't be going helter-skelter or we'd really see fireworks."

"Asaph," said Henry, "what do you think?"

Asaph Hall cleared his throat. "President Lincoln, indeed what you ask is not insignificant. One traditional explanation has been the cosmic dust, but as you say, each new generation of telescopes finds new stars, so dust does not seem to be the answer. And besides, cosmic dust is a factor only in certain regions of the sky."

"Quite right," said August Möbius, his German accent distinctly British. "I like this notion of the stars receding, hurtling apart. And you have hit it on the nose: the heavens cannot be a locus for a melange of vectors. They are not like this nation with its railway trains flitting every which way. Nor can I picture a universe that is just so big and no bigger, a universe fixed in its extent, as the Church of Rome at one time would have had us believe. The great Isaac Newton thought the entire heavens were as far across as light would travel in two years. Bessel, judging the parallax of the star 61 Cygni, tells us that it is thirty-five million million miles away. Six light-years, as he terms it. I do not think we have begun to plumb the depths of the skies."

"Agreed," said Asaph Hall.

Möbius nodded thoughtfully. "May I ask, Mr. President, do you wonder about other such matters? I could listen the whole night long to such questions as yours."

"Perhaps," Lincoln replied. "I am also interested in time."

"All sentient living beings are interested in time," said Möbius, "but you have not yet posed its question."

"In time I will phrase my question," Lincoln said, smiling at his inadvertent joke. "My question is this: How rigid are the walls of time?"

Silence filled the air. "The walls of time?" Joseph Henry repeated.

"How odd to think of time having walls," said Count Zeppelin. "I wonder what would be walled in and what would be excluded."

"I take it that you speak metaphorically," said Asa Gray. "The metaphor I am accustomed to is of time and the river, time flowing like a river, a river without beginning and end. I don't understand your question about the walls of time, but I am a botanist, not a physicist or a philosopher."

Lincoln hesitated. Having asked his question, he wasn't sure how far to go. "Yes, I have also heard the maxim that time is like a river. But a river meanders. Isn't it Hotspur in *Henry the Fourth* who teases Glendower about dredging a river—is it the Severn or the Trent?—changing its channel and thereby making the river shorter? As though time could skip a beat. You would wake, not into tomorrow, but into a later time, discontinuous with the present. I was thinking just now of a switchman whose lever throws the train from the main track onto a shunt, but of course that would still ensure a continuous flow. For there to be a break, as I picture it, you would have to climb out of your flowing river and slip into another."

"I too have been thinking about your question." It was Möbius taking his turn. "Euclid and his geometry describe a world of two dimensions, as if the planet were flat and not a sphere. And now we think of the universe as a giant sphere compounded of a host of lesser spheres. A leap of faith. And time, does it march like a soldier, Euclid's soldier? Might it not dance? I too wonder at time's path. But I am an old man on my last legs."

"Time is such a funny business," said Asaph Hall. "Every one of us knows how time can fly at one moment or grind to a halt in the next. But such a notion of time, however vital, is non-scientific. There are also those who hold that time is merely a human invention, Descartes for one. But in my opinion I don't think he has the answer when he says time is no absolute. No more than if he were to declare that space is something we have dreamed up."

"Please," said Hall. "Let a yard be a yard. To tell the truth, I am beginning to find this conversation unsettling. I prefer to stand on solid ground."

"Which I think there'll soon be less of," said Joseph Henry, pointing to the skies. No stars were now visible, and the wind had risen to a higher pitch. "While we talk, nature moves on."

"Look! Look!" cried Count Zeppelin, pointing upriver. "Can it be a balloon? It must have broken its tether."

"Over there," said Gray, pointing into the darkness.

Lincoln squinted, picked it out, sweeping along the shore not a hundred feet up and heading their way, its envelope a lighter gray against the dark sky.

"Ahoy, down there," came a voice, faint but clear.

"Ahoy," they called back, and at the same moment Lincoln and Count Zeppelin spotted the mooring line whipping behind the car as its course took it across the bluff, barely twenty-five feet now above the sodden ground, and both men hot in pursuit.

"Who are you?" one of the others called up, and Lincoln heard the reply: "Captain Cyrus Harding of the Ninth Massachusetts and his friends escaping from Richmond. Join us." Lincoln had the lead, Zeppelin at his heels, the coiling line almost in reach. Lincoln snagged it, held on, and was borne aloft, his legs running on air. "Hold tight," called a bearded face peering over the edge of the car. "Hold tight. Reel him in, boys."

And then the line tore free, spun away, and President Lincoln's feet were once more upon Mother Earth. "Farewell," he called up. "Fare thee well."

✦ XX ✦

The Presidentess

2 April 1865

S HE HEARD A FEEBLE KNOCK, followed by a tentative "Mrs. Lincoln?"

"Come in," she called out. She opened her eyes. Her headache had ebbed. She'd rather tell them not to come in. *Give a woman a few minutes' respite. Leave her in peace.* The library, an octagon like the Blue Room below, with its many volumes, was an island of calm and refuge. Hadn't she been serving the mad god of war until a soul could cry out *Enough!* They took Willie, and now they were scheming for Robert—Captain Robert. As though the elevated rank guaranteed impregnability. And Tad had stayed with his father at City Point. Two fools sitting flush in the palm of Mars.

And she was a third fool. But she would have her pound of flesh, and good red blood too. She had come back to Washington only after she extracted a promise that she would return when Richmond fell. To spite that traitor, Mr. Jefferson Davis, to cross his threshold—no longer *his*, but now *hers*. She didn't need to review the troops. Let Mrs. General Griffin, or Mrs. General Ord, Mrs. General this, Mrs. General that, glory in the game of war, sitting their horses like cut-outs on a magic lantern, each in perfect proportion, and President Lincoln drinking it in, his thirst like a well without a bottom. The troops loved it too, loved the pretty ones. More fools. There was a superstition that in death the eye retains the image of what it last beheld. Look closely at their eyes then, the dead ones, what do they hold? Smoke and flames? A bullet frozen in time? Or visions recalled at the last instant? A sweetheart, a mother? Mrs. General Ord's painted face? If it were up to the Presidentess, as the papers called her, General Ord would have been cashiered for the insolence of his wife.

Absurd woman, herself. The absurdity of keeping Chase from the Supreme Court for his daughter's opinion of the President! *We are not accountable for our wives.* They had never said it so directly, not in her hearing. But it came down to that, said or unsaid. That was the story that would stick in history. Forget Mrs. Lincoln at the hospitals, consoling the wounded. Forget her compassion. And think of her long-suffering husband, berated before the staff, before the massed troops, before a stunned Mrs. General Ord. What difference did it make? Richmond would still fall, and she would sit on Jeff Davis's throne, would laugh at his sour apple tree, whether he hung from it or not.

"Telegram from Mr. Lincoln," said the trepidacious face at the door. "Sent early this morning."

"Thank you, Parker. Just set it on the table."

"Yes, Ma'am."

Parker retreated. He might as well have been wearing kid gloves. But to be fair he was a good enough Parker, not uncaring.

The sheet of paper lay there unread, and Mary went back to her thoughts.

Last week on the *River Queen*, on their way to City Point, with the fouled drinking water tormenting them all, her husband had dreamt that the White House was burning. His telling of the dream had left her stunned. Her home aflame! Where her children lived and died. Though it was not really her home. Why was it so hard to picture herself back in Springfield, the two of them walking hand-in-hand across the threshold of their own home? Had some bitter curse from Robert E. Lee declared that they must endure his fate, the loss of homestead? That picture was so clear—herself a wanderer, whose foot never would climb a flight of stairs to her own bedroom. The doubt was so absolute, a spasm from deep within, rising, rising, till she could barely breathe. She willed herself to relax.

After his fiery dream, she had sent a telegram to Ellen at the White House—she could read the operator's mind as his eyes had scanned the text: *Send a telegram, direct to City Point, and say if all is right at the house. Everything is left in your charge. Be careful.* At least there was no direct reference to flames to raise the telegrapher's eyebrows still further. Nor was there any reference to her husband and his horrible dreams. Would he ever learn not to tell them? Though she understood why he did. You can't clasp these black visions close to your heart, all yours and no one else's. When was his last dream of innocence?

Suddenly it was back in all its glory, her own dream whilst on the *River Queen*, coming home. He wasn't the only one with frightful, alarming, wondrous dreams. She glanced out the window—it was such a gray day, all color drained from the sky, from the hills in the distance. Even the trees down by the river had given up their fresh coat of green. In the dream she had also been looking out a window, but such a window as she had never seen before. In the foreground were what she could only call villas, like pictures of Spain or Italy—Greece perhaps—washed by bright sunlight. Like a quick and steep staircase their tiled roofs descended to the sea. Behind them were even steeper hills, with row upon row of olive trees, though she couldn't see that from her window—she knew it. Low trees, with gnarled limbs, and dark brown olives bitter to the taste. She had picked one and tasted its bitterness.

Beyond the lowest villa, beyond the pebbled beach, the sun shimmering on the water, a small bay, emerald green, and beyond the bay an isthmus, the water choppy and the tips of the waves sparkling. And beyond that, another country with mountains in the distance, fishing villages on the shore, women in black dresses, children in brightly colored clothing. How she knew this landscape so well was a puzzle. Usually she had trouble seeing clearly at a distance. And the isthmus still echoed with the cries of battle, an engagement at sea, such as Antony and Cleopatra might have fought against Octavius Caesar, banks of oars rowing furiously as Antony gave chase to the fleeing Egyptian queen. What window could yield this vista? Only a window in dream.

She hadn't been alone in the room. In that small room with its dull, unpolished marbled floors and whitewashed walls was a friend. *Mrs. Lincoln*, she had said, *I am Margarita Spalding*, and then they had spoken of ordinary matters. Of the view from the window which presented the sun and water, and the bitter olives. And how they had walked along the shore beneath the shade of so many rows of olive trees, a path that led to one bay after another, Margarita and herself. Where the path was narrow and steep they had held hands, fore and aft, Margarita leading, Margarita a tall woman, not young, but younger than herself. A mother, like herself.

Where is your daughter? she had asked Margarita. The answer, plain and simple: *At home.* A sufficient answer, within the dream.

It had not been difficult walking along the path, though she wore ordinary clothing, these very shoes. It would have been even easier wearing such shoes and such a dress as she had worn as a child to pick blackberries, in Kentucky. They had spoken of their childhoods. And she had noted in Margarita Spalding a curious reluctance to keep the conversation in the here and now. They had said nothing of her being the wife of the president, of President Abraham Lincoln, the mother of Robert and Tad, of Eddie and of William Wallace Lincoln, her Willie. Nothing of the great war wracking the country. Nothing of Jefferson Davis or his generals or their wives.

They had stopped at an inn or tavern, more likely, where the path descended close to the water's edge. They had sat outdoors at a small table, and Margarita had ordered lemonade for them, and dark bread and butter, and fried potatoes. Despite the shade on the path they were both thirsty. There were voices inside the tavern, the high-pitched call of a child for its mother. Though *mother* wasn't the word the child used, it could mean nothing else. Margarita knew enough of the language to converse with the waiter. It wasn't English, wasn't like French. The reckoning settled, they had walked beyond the bay with the tavern. Then, coming to a high hill with a bay below that was wider than any they had seen and the descent sharper than any thus far, they had turned around. They retraced their steps to the inn, where they had another pitcher of lemonade—such thirst. Then through the groves of olives, and back to the path bordered with dock and thistle, back to this villa, back to the present and visions of Cleopatra flying home to Egypt and her Antony in mad pursuit.

Lizzie Keckley was at the door, smiling. "Afternoon, Mrs. Lincoln. Welcome home."

"Lizzie, how are you!"

"I'm good, Mrs. Lincoln. How was your trip?"

"All right. It was all right." Lizzie was looking at her steadily. "No," said honest Mary Lincoln, "it wasn't all right. I lost my temper and made a fool of myself, before everybody. Poor Mr. Lincoln. How I berated him. I don't really wish to talk about it. Not right now."

"Why should you?" said Elizabeth Keckley. "Who would hang dirty linen on a line?"

Mary Todd Lincoln laughed. "Not I. I never would, never should. Does the name Margarita Spalding mean anything to you?"

Lizzie scowled. You could see her turning over a host of names and faces. "I knew a Mr. Spalding once. In Petersburg, a chandler. He had a daughter or two, but I don't know that I ever knew their names. I have known a Margarita or two, and a few more Margarets, but none named Spalding. Why do you ask?"

"It was a name in a dream and I've been wondering about it. Such a vivid dream. And usually in my dreams if anyone talks I don't remember it. But she said 'My name is Margarita Spalding,' going out of her way to tell me what she knew I didn't know."

Lizzie nodded. She placed great stock in her dreams. "Once I dreamed I had a book in my lap. It was called *Bermuda Leaves*. And when I woke I didn't know whether it meant leaves on a tree or something or someone leaving who was called Bermuda. I never did get a chance to peek inside. It still troubles me, like an itch I can't get to."

It was Mary's turn to nod.

"Well," said Lizzie, "I heard you were back and just thought I would pay a quick visit. And Parker said there was a telegram for you from Mr. Lincoln."

"Yes," said Mary Lincoln, "he left it on the table and I've been on my way to pick it up. You can see how far I've got. Mr. Lincoln, he will say nothing about my temper—he never does, but I cannot rid myself of the sadness in his eyes as I lit into him tooth and nail."

Lizzie sighed. "These are troubled times, win or lose. Let's see what the word is from City Point," and she handed Mary the telegram.

Mary rose to her feet and together they read it over.

HEAD QUARTERS ARMIES OF THE UNITED STATES,

City-Point, April 2. 7/45 1865

Mrs. A. Lincoln,
Washington, D.C.

Last night Gen. Grant telegraphed that Sheridan with his Cavalry and the 5th. Corps had captured three brigades of Infantry, a train of wagons, and several batteries, prisoners amounting to several thousands. This morning Gen. Grant, having ordered an attack along the whole line telegraphed as follows

"Both Wright and Parke got through the enemies lines. The battle now rages furiously. Sheridan with his Cavalry, the 5th. Corps, & Miles Division of the 2nd. Corps, which was sent to him since 1. this a.m. is now sweeping down from the West. All now looks highly favorable. Ord is engaged, but I have not yet heard the result in his front"

Robert yesterday wrote a little cheerful note to Capt. Penrose, which is all I have heard of him since you left. Copy to Secretary of War

A. Lincoln

"Heavens!" said Lizzie. "This is some news! I do take it for a prophecy of the end. If General Grant says 'highly hopeful,' it must be that and more. This may be the fall of Richmond we've all been waiting for."

"Yes," said Mary Lincoln. "Mr. Lincoln has promised me that I can be with him on that day. Will you come with me and take me through Petersburg?"

Lizzie beamed. "Home, of sorts. The eyes may be bitter that see

Elizabeth Keckley returning, but I wouldn't give up the chance for a million. How soon do you think it might be?"

"With Sheridan sweeping down? Two days or three, less than a week. Not that I want to count my chickens too soon. But it's time to plan and not be caught short. Remember how they thought I was the conduit to the rebels, back when the news was bad day after day? A spy, the mysterious channel. Weak, vain, and underbred. And remember how General Halleck demanded my exportation? At the least, a free talker, they said. And that not even from the Copperhead press. 'Say nothing,' said Mr. Lincoln. 'Don't grace them with a reply.'"

"I remember," said Lizzie. "Dark days. Well, I will leave you to your good news. You will need to get a good night's sleep, one sea journey after another. I will say nothing till the word is officially out."

Mary waved goodbye. She must organize her party. Senator Sumner should be with them. And Senator and Mrs. Harlan with their daughter Mary, her son Robert's girl. And the Marquis de Chambrun. All of us banqueting in the halls of Jefferson Davis. It was impossible not to gloat.

Her dream had been one bit more, the ring. Mary summoned an image of the path, with the villa in sight, and Margarita Spalding saying that if you hold a ring up to the sunlight you will see your true love. But with the sky so clear, the light so true, Margarita had held her own ring up to the sun, and Mary had held her pinky ring up to the light. *The other*, she had explained, *her wedding ring, it no longer comes off and on easily.* She smiled now at the small lie. It hadn't been off in years. Looking at the light, and like a fool, not watching the path, she had stumbled and dropped the ring, and could not find it after. Her mother's ring. Still staring out the window, reflecting upon the kindness of Margarita Spalding, Mary Lincoln raised her right hand to the rays of late, slanting light, palm upward. As she knew, now, and had not known the moment before, on her little finger, there was no ring.

The Harvest

6 June 1955

I T WAS ONLY 5:20—Joan Matcham was ten minutes early. Not until she parked her car did she notice the name above the door: *The Lincoln Clinic*. Of course, given that it was situated by Lincoln Park and the Lincoln Park Zoo. Not that she wasn't seeing his name everywhere these days. She filled out the nurse's form, medical history, family history, personal history. She glanced around—an office is an office, but Lorraine Riggs' was different in subtle ways. For one thing, the chairs in the waiting room were comfortable. And the pictures on the wall were unexpected: Gauguin's South Seas woman holding a basket of fruit, and Van Gogh's field of wheat. A vase with freshly cut tea roses sat on a table.

Joan had called first thing in the morning. "We have nothing till a week from Thursday, but we do have a cancellation for late this afternoon, half past five—Mondays are our late day. I know it's short notice. Can you make it? And remember we've moved from Rogers Park."

"I think I can," Joan had said. Then she had to resist the impulse to carry on with the rest of *The Little Engine That Could*, the little blue-faced, determined-at-all-cost-to-make-it locomotive huffing and puffing its way over the mountain and down into the station. Emily's favorite story once upon a time. Oh, Emily.

To be on the safe side, Joan had left work a bit early, but rush hour was going the other direction on the Outer Drive, and besides, Lorraine's office was near North Side. She had brought along Tolstoy—you never know when the world's going to stop revolving or an elevator will stick between floors, and then what? Not many books were small enough to fit inside a purse. Everyman editions, Oxford World Classics. Hence Tolstoy. *The Cossacks and Other Tales.* While waiting to see a gynecologist? Better *Tales of Love and War.* Ah, the nurse was beckoning.

Joan was weighed and measured, handed the classic white gown and a paper cup. She shed her clothes, slipped into the gown. She sat on the edge of the gurney and waited a minute or two. Enter Dr. Riggs, a few years older than herself, her brown hair flecked with gray. Their mothers had been friends from way back. Chatter, chatter, and then Joan's unpremeditated words, all rehearsed speeches forgotten: "I'll get right to the point. I think I'm pregnant." She held up her hand to forestall the question on Lorraine's lips. "You know I'm not married, and I know you're going to ask who the father is, and—well—let me say it right off—I can't say. Can't say who he is. I just can't say. It's just that—"

"Slow down. Slow down," said Lorraine Riggs. "The world isn't coming to an end. And without an examination we don't know, or I don't know, enough of the story. Let's not get the cart before the horse. And besides you're free to tell me what you will or you won't. Just because we know each other doesn't mean you're obliged to bare your soul. How much do you know of my private life?"

"Not that much. Damn little. Sorry," said Joan. "That caught even me by surprise. I guess I didn't realize how things had built up in my head, like a pressure cooker, then all at once the cap is off and whoosh."

"I understand. Shall we proceed with the exam? And we can continue from there?"

"Fine, of course." Joan lay back, closed her eyes, relaxed, and then it was over.

"Okay, good," said Lorraine. "When you're dressed come on down the hall to my office."

Joan put her clothes back on, glanced in the mirror. Same old Joan, maybe a little flushed. The door to the doctor's office was open. Lorraine Riggs looked up and gestured to a seat across from her desk. Joan sat, her hands folded in her lap. It was the doctor's turn to speak. The moment of truth.

"Sometimes I wonder," said Lorraine, "why Mondays are longer than other days of the week. Of course I know the answer."

Okay, Joan thought. She could prolong the agony as well as the next person. "I didn't know you had moved. Any special reason?"

"More space, lease ran out. A parking lot. Ants in my pants."

"It's nice," said Joan. "Good name for a clinic. It has a certain ring."

"Lincoln Park?"

"I like the sound of it."

Lorraine squinted doubtfully.

"Well, I like Lincoln." To put it mildly, Joan thought.

"You like Lincoln?"

"Yes, it just so happens I do like Lincoln." She was playing with fire. "I wouldn't mind living on Lincoln Street."

"Fair enough," said the good doctor. "I once chose a house because it was on Mulberry Lane and I like silk."

"My mother loved silk," said Joan. She had a sudden vision of her mother in her black moiré kimono with the slender gold collar, her mother younger than Joan had ever known her, except as an infant and beyond the bounds of ordinary memory.

"Mine too," Lorraine said with half a smile. Then, hardly missing a beat, "I'd judge we'll have the results in a couple of days. Assuming it's positive, I put the due date in mid-January."

"I was hoping you might know something from the examination."

Joan could see Lorraine weighing her words. "Usually," she said, "I wouldn't venture an opinion this early on the basis of an examination. But judging from the size of your uterus, plus the missed period, chances are the test will come out positive. I'd like to see you monthly. You're more than a trifle old to be having a child, but since Emily's delivery was normal, I see no reason to worry. How old was Aunt Anne when you were born?"

"Mother was nearly forty-five."

"That's about what I would've guessed—like mother, like daughter. May I ask one question?"

"Yes, of course," said Joan, "though I won't promise an answer."

"As you say, you're unmarried—I'm not asking about the paternity of the child. That's not my question." Lorraine hesitated, and Joan saw the question hanging in the air between them.

"No," she said firmly. "I mean to keep this child, to do everything in my power to carry it to term. It isn't because I find the idea of abortion anathema. I want this child." She could feel her chest heaving, anger rising.

"I'm sorry, I'm very sorry," said Lorraine. "I didn't mean to upset you. I was going to say, somehow—well, just to make sure you know what you're doing."

"It's all right," Joan said. "To tell the truth I don't know exactly what I'm doing. I haven't begun to think things through. But I'll take my chances. My eyes are open, and I'll see what I'll see. A good part of me asks whether I've taken leave of my senses. Am I treating all this as a lark? The answer is, I'm not. Granted, it's a surprising turn of events—to put it mildly. You're right to be asking me if I know what I'm doing. You're right to go beyond the surface. Babies aren't toys." She was babbling, like a windup doll set loose and no stopping it. She clamped her lips together.

"I'd say you sound good and healthy. Keep that up. Most women in your shoes would be at their wit's end."

"Whatever the reason, I'm not."

"Can I ask one more thing?" Lorraine said with an odd smile.

"Okay," said Joan. "This one I can guess. It's about the father."

"Right," said Lorraine. "The father. I don't need a name, but I'd like to know a few things regarding his background, his state of health."

Joan nodded. "I understand that. I can't name the father, for reasons I can't reveal." Silence. "I don't mean to sound like I'm testifying before HUAC and rat-faced Joe McCarthy. It's nothing untoward. There's no dark story behind the conception, and he is, as far as I know, a healthy man."

Joan heard what she was saying, knew that the tense was wrong, though Lorraine couldn't guess it. Abraham Lincoln was not a healthy man, death being a condition of utmost ill health. A grim joke there. Joan went on. "Blood type, I have no idea and no way of finding out. That's one more thing I'll have to chance. And I have the means to support this child. I work to escape boredom. I have yet to devise a story to avert the opprobrium of bastardy. Such an odd phrase."

"Yes," said Lorraine. "I might have some suggestions there, or counsel if need be. There's no rush by the way—you're my last appointment." She had caught Joan's quick glance at her wristwatch. "Unless you're in a hurry."

"No," said Joan. "No hurry. No hurry at all. And I want to say again how thrilled I am to have this child. And to be talking about it. I can't tell you just how thrilled. Even though you don't have the test results, I'm sure it's true." Her voice sounded more shrill than thrill—the lady doth protest most extremely. But it was true. She hadn't been looking ahead with any great clarity of vision.

"In fact, tonight I'm going to celebrate," she said. "How, I don't know, but it will be alone. The father, for reasons, uhm, can't be part of it, other than the part he *is* of it, the child in my womb I mean. I will say that it was the first time I—" (again she had launched herself into a sentence and couldn't see a way to escape gracefully)—"we were together." Joan sighed in relief—not so bad.

Lorraine was letting her boil in her own juices. What the hell, Joan said to herself. "It struck me I'm something like Mary, the Virgin Mary. She did have—" (Oh no—Joan was lost again; why was the word *sex* ruled out? Can't do it in public; can't say it aloud.)

"Sexual congress?" Lorraine filled in.

"Yes, congress with—oh my—"

"With God."

"With God?" said Joan in horror. How had they landed here?

"I suppose. He's called the Father," said Lorraine. "Only one way I know to get to be a father. May I ask how deeply religious you are?"

Joan shook her head. "Not at all religious," she said. "Not in the usual sense."

"Well," said Lorraine, "I've never heard an explicit description of Mary's conception—I'm sure it's there in the Bible somewhere, mysterious, ectoplasmic, but I'll bet there's no discussion of God doing it with Mary. She conceives without sexual intercourse such as you or I would picture it. And, I'm sure, without pleasure. How the planting takes place is not for a doctor to work out. I just reap the harvest. *Trust me*, he said, maybe. An old line if I may say so. One last question? May I?"

"Yes, ask on, though again I don't promise an answer."

"You said you were planning to celebrate. What would you say to having dinner with me? I promise it isn't just to weasel a story out of you. I can't say let's have a drink, because I tell my patients to avoid alcohol, and tobacco."

"I'd love it. And alcohol I can spare. Remember, I'm an Evanstonian, born and bred. Any ideas where to eat?"

"It's your celebration; it should be your choice. But Zarantanello's isn't too far from here. Sinful Italian cuisine. I ration it—no more than once a month, and I'm due."

"Sounds wonderful," said Joan.

"Fine. Let me tell Natalie she can close up, and we can be on our way. I'll meet you at the door."

Joan picked up her purse and walked back down the hall. What would Abraham Lincoln have made of this interchange? She was going to have to work out a routine, come up with a story.

MONDAY AT ZARANTANELLO'S was slow—a few well-mannered couples following the rules for demure public behavior, plus one exuberant family with four daughters, all in their mid-to-late teens, all six as effervescent as a glass of freshly poured ginger ale. Lorraine leaned across the table. "I've never been here on a Monday before. Weekends it's jammed, and there are specials later in the week. That's Mama and Papa Zarantanello with their daughters. Imagine hair like that!"

Joan nodded. She had been admiring precisely that, each of them with a single lustrous braid, black as night. And voices and gestures that said *This is home.* "I figured they were family. Oh, I recognize the oldest one, from school—she's hard to miss. I've seen her in the History office. Hey, they've got a chicken lasagna."

"It's delicious," said Lorraine. "I eat everything here but the squid, and that's my failing, not theirs."

Joan grimaced. She wouldn't even have brought it up.

Lorraine looked up from her menu. "Cannelloni is tempting, that and a salad, and in honor of the occasion I'll have my usual glass of Chianti. Ready to order?"

A few minutes later their salads were served, and a few bites into hers Lorraine looked up. "I've been thinking what I'd do in your situation, a woman, an independent woman, and no spring chicken, finding myself pregnant. I've had a fair number of young women in that fix, but I'd be a different case."

"Yes," said Joan, "you would, and I am."

"Anyway," Lorraine went on, "I can see myself trying to carry on with my life. I'd look for support among friends. I suppose I'd work less, lean on my colleagues. I'm blessed not having monetary problems. I just realized," she added, "I've been assuming you're not contemplating marriage." A pause, a pregnant pause.

"No, absolutely not. Besides, it's not an option. That's no reflection on the father. He's no cad, far from it. It's just how things are."

"Do you have an idea how folks at the university will react?"

"Sure," said Joan. "Shock, disbelief. If I were a faculty member, I think they'd expect me to resign. Northwestern's a Methodist school after all. But I'm only a part-time secretary. I have a good record. The staff would support me. And if I were discreet, took a leave of absence—I'll do that anyway, for a couple of years at least. It's one of those things that will just have to sort itself out. It's kind of like working my way through this meal," and she deliberately took a bite of salad. "Bite by bite. Every step leads to the next. That's how things were, step by step, with the father I mean." She could elaborate, but didn't. "I don't see myself going off to Aunt Nelly's ranch in Wyoming for twelve months, the year when I become great with child—what a phrase! As though I'm as big as a barn. And when I reappear in polite society I'm the same old slender Joan. But that's a story where the child is left behind, and I won't live that story." Rarely had she heard herself sound so emphatic.

"Lorraine," Joan said then, "can I ask, have you ever thought about marriage?"

"Never, not even tempted. I like my freedom too much. I have friends, and they go a long way. Mother and Dad gave up on me years ago. Luckily there's a brother to tend to the family tree. And pardon my saying it, but this world will manage quite well without another baby."

"I wasn't thinking much about babies either time. Emily was conceived at the Palmer House on the one day Robert had leave. Poor Robert. He would have objected to these noisy Italians. Actually, I'd like to have another daughter. I can't picture myself with a boy, raising a son, manliness and all that."

Lorraine laughed. "If worst comes to worst, you have a few years before that will be a concern. From what I can tell, babies are babies. It's the parents who make them conform to expectations about gender. Nature's too busy the first years to worry about manliness or femininity."

"I guess. Emily was mostly Emily, her own person. So now I've got a picture in my head of a little boy sitting by my side, and we're reading the same stories Emily and I read. I'd been looking forward to Robert Louis Stevenson with Emily, reading the books I had loved as a child, *Kidnapped* and *Treasure Island*. She was still too young for Stevenson. A boy would be all right." The child Joan was picturing was a tall, lanky boy with tousled hair, a cross between Abraham Lincoln and Huck Finn, a good-hearted child, and loving. She had begun to read Emil Ludwig's life of Lincoln and recalled Lincoln's love for Sarah Johnston, his stepmother, more of a mother to him than his real mother. "I'd like him to be like his father."

Lorraine nodded thoughtfully. Joan realized she had let the door open a crack, and the silence across the table was palpable. What if the door were to swing wide open? Joan had a sudden, breathtaking vision of the turn the conversation would take: *All right, since you're so nice, and so patient and understanding, I'll tell you the whole story. In a nutshell the father of my child is Abraham Lincoln, and last Easter he time-traveled ninety years forward, to Evanston. We spent the*

*day together, and you know how things go when boy meets girl. Then
he went home to finish with the Civil War. Near as I can make out, it
was February his time, 1865.* By then alarms would be clanging, bells
ringing, lights flashing in poor Lorraine's head.

"What was that all about?"

Joan's eyes rolled. "A passing thought. I'm sorry I have to be so
mysterious about the father of my child—and you don't even know
if I'm pregnant."

"Yes, I do. Though we both could be wrong. And what do I care
who the father is, though I love a good story and I smell a rich
one."

"That's just the lasagna," Joan said, leaning back as the waitress set
their dinners before them.

"A little more Chianti, Dr. Riggs?"

"Half a glass, Mary. Thanks."

"Some restaurant," said Joan, "where you can order wine by the
half a glass."

"Like I said, I'm a regular. Have some parmesan."

They ate mostly in silence. Each tried a forkful of the other's dinner and at the end both plates were clean. Spumoni was served,
and coffee. The temptation to be forthright was powerful. Lorraine
would know the difference between sanity—however implausible—
and madness. But Joan would let well enough alone.

Why hadn't she taken his picture? Silly notion. But she wished she
had some token of his being there, something like the candid photos
they take of you in Atlantic City on the Boardwalk, the two of you
arm in arm, and all at once there's the photographer with his tripod
and hood, a brief smile, and—click. Something, anything—let it be
mundane, like a gift from the Great Oz that would satisfy a simple
Kansan as to his courage, or his mind, or his heart. Something Joan
could produce, draw from her pocketbook. *See, Lorraine. It's Abraham Lincoln.*

✦ XXII ✦

The Father of Us All

4 April 1865

RICHMOND. LITTLE ROME. Is every seven-hilled city called Rome? A Rome in ruins. A smoldering Rome.

It was all happening so fast. Just two days ago, Communion Sunday, the first Sunday of the month, Davis was summoned from St. Paul's, all eyes on him as he marched stiff-legged up the aisle. Richmond's best had loitered on Grace Street, on Franklin, sweet with the smell of spring gardens. *What news? What's up?* No one knew, everyone guessed. Could it be another false alarm?

No. Lee had sent word that Petersburg was surrounded, would fall, and Richmond could be defended no longer. Sarah Prentiss had spotted Judge Campbell at six that evening, with two books under his arm, on Ninth Street, in urgent conversation with himself— they still called him Judge because he had served on the Supreme Court until war broke out. *What books?* she had wondered. Gibbon's *Decline and Fall of the Roman Empire?* Or perhaps lighter reading? Swift, Goldsmith, Bulwer-Lytton's *The Wanderer?* What cream had risen to the top of his library?

It was a scene of confusion, like leaves in a whirlwind. Anything that could move did: wagons, horses, ponies, packet boats on the canal. The governors of this false democracy, in a vast hurry, had emptied the archives, sent trainload after trainload on to the next capital. And after that? She had thought of the parable of the hare who hopped halfway to the wall, and halfway again and again. They had best get smaller and smaller trains, and hire the services of scribes expert in miniature. Sally had described the confusion at the Davis mansion—Varina Davis's saddle and saddle horse disappearing, crockery smashed, pantries emptied and nothing for the road. Word was that the housekeeper and servants had turned against Davis.

True and not true, like everything said that day. One story had it that the train with food and supplies for Lee's men, sent to Amelia Court House, had arrived and then been ordered back to Richmond for the Davis party, all in such haste that nothing was unloaded. And then to make room for the Davises and their trunks of sumptuous luggage, the supplies had been dumped in the railway yard. With news like that, true or not, the crowd became a mob. What a day! Prying open the doors of the Commissary Depot at the end of Mayo's Bridge, then plundering the barrels of hams, bacon, coffee, sugar, flour, pecans. And whiskey. Barrels of whiskey staved in, whiskey running ankle-deep in the gutters. And the treasure train with silver and gold, ingots, bricks, and nuggets, Mexican silver dollars, double eagles from before the war, crusedoes, florins, silver crowns, drachmas from Macedonia and Bactria, even the silvered face of grim Caesar—coins from the whole world over. Midshipmen guarding it, elsewise pillage. The scream of locomotive whistles and the rumble of the trains departing.

Sarah had stood her ground.

That night (the night before last, she reminded herself) there had been little sleep. A fearful explosion woke her from a hectic dream of people in flight, clad any which way, crossing each other's paths, and herself standing frozen in their midst, not knowing which way to turn. Awake, she blinked her eyes—what was dream and what was real? Not a dream, she told herself. Was it an earthquake? She got out of bed and stood at the window staring into the night, her fingertips splayed against the cool glass. Deadly silence, and then a blossoming flash of light down by the river. She drew back instinctively, her hands two clenched fists, as the explosion thundered upward. The house shook, dishes rattled, Sally sang out, and another voice cried *Save us!* Her own? Across the hallway Emma was telling Jourdan to go back to his bed. Two more explosions followed. Eventually Sarah fell into a fitful sleep.

Morning brought word that the explosions had been the destruction of the ironclads of the James River Squadron. The last troops north of the James had crossed the bridge to Manchester and then were compelled to use their sabers to make their way through the city. Ships of the squadron were fired and set adrift; the *Patrick Henry*, still at its moorings, smoldered all the long day. The bridges were aflame. Such wanton waste. Such folly. No need to seek it out.

The Arsenal and then the Armory were set aflame, and before long the shells within began to burst, at first a scattering, then by the thousand—five mortal hours their mindless bombardment endured. Sarah had seen the chimney on the Masonic Hall topple, just a wobble at first, then head over heels it tumbled like a pyramid of acrobats coming undone. She had seen cannons and their fat horses whipped to a trot up Broad Street—hard to believe horseflesh capable of such a feat. Bands played *Dixie* and *The Girl I Left Behind Me*. From the back porch Sarah watched the Negroes celebrating, their arms around each other, cries of joy, of deliverance.

The day wore on. As the army in gray fled south, another took its place, the blue, a quiet and orderly march up the river road through Rocketts and across the railroad tracks, with locked sabers at the carry, up Broad Street, through the iron gates into Capitol Square. Sarah, with Emma and Sally behind, watched as the Stars and Bars and then Virginia's long blue banner both came down. Up then went the Stars and Stripes to the strains of the national anthem, *The Star-Spangled Banner*. Weapons were stacked and soldiers turned into firefighters.

Had they had breakfast? Sarah couldn't remember. She heard that Mrs. Lee had been compelled to leave her house on Franklin Street as the flames drew near, but throughout the long day hoses kept it wet enough that no sparks set it afire. By night the fires were under control. The Federal troops passing by shook their heads. It was none of their doing, they said. Sentinels guarded the city that night, last night. After nine o'clock no one, civilian or soldier, went abroad. Shells finally ceased exploding. And come morning breakfast trays appeared for the porch sentinels. As though sanity prevailed.

They gathered in the parlor, waiting. Jourdan sat wrapped in his blanket playing a game of checkers, Jourdan the Black against

Jourdan the Red. Sarah's needlework lay on her lap. Emma sat on the piano stool, her shoulders rocking to a silent rhythm. She didn't touch the keys. Sudden shouts broke the silence. "Now what can that be?" cried Emma, her voice sudden and shrill. She was on the thin edge of things. Sarah, with Sally's help, had reminded her time and again to be calm, to be hopeful. "For Jourdan's sake," they said. Emma's impulse had been to gather her belongings and join the mad throngs in their exodus.

Sally's bright eyes appeared at the doorway. "It's President Lincoln!" she exclaimed. "He's landed!" And she was gone.

"Lincoln? Abraham Lincoln!" Emma was on her feet, as though Sally had announced the arrival of the Devil himself.

The doorbell rang. "I'll get it," Sarah said.

She opened the door and stood facing a smooth-cheeked lieutenant in blue, looking as if he should be in a classroom at this time of day.

"Mrs. Slaughter?"

"No," she said. "A friend of Emma Slaughter. My name is Sarah Prentiss, but I can get Mrs. Slaughter for you." Sarah knew her lines.

"Actually," he said, "it's you I've been directed to. You're from Maine, if you don't mind my asking, aren't you, Ma'am?"

"Yes," she said. "And you're from Boston. Would you like to step inside?"

"It's not necessary. There are orders to inquire as to your comfort, whether we can relieve you in any fashion. And to guarantee your safety."

"Thank you kindly," she said. "We are quite all right, especially now that the city has changed hands. Is it true that President Lincoln himself is here?"

"I hear one thing, then another," the soldier said, "but the word we had from headquarters was that he would be coming upriver and to expect him later in the day."

"Well, Old Sally, who was just here a moment ago, announced his arrival, then took flight."

The lieutenant raised one eyebrow. "That I don't know about. Certainly it will be a busy time. If you need any assistance, please let us know. And I will keep my eye on you here. It helps, Ma'am, that you're so near."

"Thank you," Sarah said. "I will definitely let you know of any trouble."

He departed, and she watched him head for the Davis mansion. Such an earnest young man, so sweet. Meanwhile, in clusters of twos and threes, Negroes were appearing, all heading down the hill toward the river. Sarah hadn't realized until now how deserted the city seemed, just herself and the lieutenant and now the stream of Negroes gathering, skipping, dancing, eager to greet their President. It had to be Lincoln; nothing else could account for their joy, their freedom. Then Sarah caught the unmistakable chorus of voices from below, cheering, singing. Sarah realized she had forgotten the Slaughters, and she turned back toward the parlor. Emma, with Jourdan in her arms, returned her gaze.

"What did he want, the Yankee? I suppose they'll be asking for this house?" Emma's voice was like dry leaves, without the juice of life.

"No, just the opposite. Checking if we were secure, if we needed anything." Sarah hadn't said anything to Emma about her meeting with Lincoln, except to mention that she had secured a pass. "The President must have sent word ahead that a Northern lady was in your midst, not that I have had anything to fear."

"Yes," as though the one word was all Emma could manage. She had been stalwart so long, ever since Abel had taken up arms and was killed. Now it was coming to an end, and with life less urgent, her courage would gradually dwindle till it was an ordinary life she led, a life like Sarah's, where days came and went, one so much like another. Jourdan would get better or stay the same. Quietly, the shards of a shattered life would come together, the jagged seams standing less and less in relief. The bright sun would shine again, the cool breeze would blow on summer days. Life would find its rhythm once more. But for now, like one swimmer who valiantly saves another and then collapses on the riverbank, she was at the end of her forces.

And herself, what did life hold in store for Sarah Prentiss? Where were her energies tending? Well, one thing was certain, they weren't going to fritter away in sighs. "Emma, come with me. I'm going to walk down the street and see what's going on. It won't hurt Jourdan to get out a little. It's springtime. I think Abraham Lincoln himself is here. Folk are flocking to see him." She was piling up reasons before Emma could say no. "It means the end must be near, the end we've both been waiting for. You wouldn't want to miss it."

Jourdan had come alive, but Emma was shaking her head. "I almost would. It will be historic, I'm sure. But you know what they'll say. They're already calling me a traitor for taking Jourdan to Philadelphia and then bringing you back here."

"They are? Who is?"

"Oh, I didn't want to say anything to upset you. People at church. I didn't hear it directly. Friends pass it on."

"Some friends. What are you supposed to do? Turn your back on common sense?"

Emma gestured toward Jourdan and rolled her eyes. Like a thirsty pup he was taking all this in. Emma mouthed, "Abel's people."

"What did you just say, Mama?"

"Nothing, dear. It's just a sad thing that others don't know your Aunt Sarah like we do. What a Godsend she's been."

"I understand," said Sarah. "And most likely you and Jourdan will be able to see the President from here. But I can't keep away, no matter how tongues wag. If I'm neck-deep in mire, another inch won't make much difference."

That said, she was out the door, down Twelfth to Capitol Square, past the Governor's House, the post office, then Main, and Trinity Church. It felt like the city was at her heels; not just Richmond, but the entire weight of the doomed Confederacy, its hallowed churches, its houses of government, all adding to gravity's rush. If this were a dream, her stride would lengthen, she'd lean forward and forsake the ground altogether. Flying Sarah.

"Mrs. Prentiss, this way," called a high-pitched voice.

Sarah looked up. The street was bubbling with life. A hand waved. It was young Maryann, Sally's niece, with a white kerchief around her forehead. "It's President Lincoln. He's here!"

"I know," said Sarah. "I'm on my way."

Maryann caught up to her. It was like a day at the races. They passed the St. Charles Hotel; ahead was the Masonic Hall, with the bricks from its chimney around its ankles, and four or five blocks further on was a tight knot of what looked like a squad of soldiers surrounded by a crowd of Negroes. In the middle of the knot was the unmistakable figure of Abraham Lincoln, his stovepipe hat first on his head, then in his hand. Sarah and Maryann broke into a trot. The soldiers, Sarah saw, were sailors, half a dozen in front, half a dozen behind, carbines in hand, slowly working their way uphill. It was a warm day, Sarah realized. Especially uphill.

"That him, Mrs. Prentiss? That him?"

"Yes, Maryann, it is."

"Well, hallelujah," and she skipped on ahead.

President Lincoln and his escort were marching at a snail's pace. One Negro and then another would burst in, thrust his hand at the President, and break away before the sailors could close ranks. Madness, Sarah thought. What is the President of the United States doing here in the heart of the rebel capital and the city still smoldering? But here he was, with the least guard imaginable and folk at every window. By the sidewalk, calm as a pigeon, was a single Yankee cavalryman, blocked off by the cheering people, just sitting on his horse and staring at the procession. A man broke away from the President's side and called to the soldier through the bustle, "Go to the General and tell him to send a military escort to get the President through this crowd. Quick!"

"That's old Abe!" the soldier stammered.

"You're damned right and don't let him hear you call him that! Now get going!" Whereupon man and horse came to life, like a firecracker, hooves clattering on the stones, and he was gone.

The President's face was set. The atmosphere had changed, grown quieter. By his side was a young boy, his son probably, Tad, who went everywhere with him, so she'd heard. The crowd of Negroes had thinned. The President took his hat off once more, wiping his brow, and her eye caught his. Each smiled, a quick and close-lipped sign of recognition. Then he broke away, attending to the business at hand.

Sarah kept pace with the squad. Now she had time to observe.

195

It was like a Greek phalanx, but a diamond, not a square. Or like a miniature citadel on legs with a dozen embrasures, a dozen guards. At its heart were the President and his son, then two naval officers on one side, and on the other the man who had sent the cavalryman for reinforcements. Seventeen: the dozen sailors, plus two Lincolns, and two officers, and one more. And now a young girl was dashing from the opposite sidewalk with a bouquet of roses, and the carbines turned aside to let her through. She handed the flowers to her President, and he accepted them, a simple enough transaction, but a historic moment. Someday books would record this will-o'-the-wisp fragment of the story of the fall of Richmond and the gallantry of Lincoln. They would call him Lincoln, as we call Washington, Washington.

Sarah was crying. Lincoln mopped his brow, as she wiped away tears with the back of her hand. The sun was almost overhead—so many weeks of rain and now this dazzle of day. She looked toward Lincoln once more and watched the men, their steps alternating left and right, though they didn't seem to be getting anywhere. Like marching in quicksand, or the street slipping behind them. She could barely make out their faces. It was as though time had stopped, and its gift was this frozen triptych, in the center the brave President, his son, his guardians; to the left a handful of silent citizens standing for the city of Richmond; and to the right the house of Jefferson Davis, abandoned. And herself, beyond the picture, her thoughts spinning on. This man will not live long, she realized. He should already be dead, so foolhardy his entrance into the heart of rebellion. But she understood why he was here. It wasn't the mad will of the conqueror. It was their Father coming home, the Father of us all.

The moment passed. His life could be as ordinary as any. We are allotted our three score and ten. Early death is an accident. His stride is sure, the grip of his hand firm, his heartbeat steady. If she could enfold him in her arms she would. Are we all drawn to this Abraham this way? She could almost taste the upwelling. Of what? Of connection? Of union? Of sacrifice? Of love?

On the overhead gallery that spanned the Spotswood and the Exchange Hotels, a woman stood with an American flag draped upon her shoulders. Brave woman. A clatter of hooves and the General's troop of cavalry appeared—late in the game—and fell in on both sides of the marchers. Sarah looked up at the houses lining the street. Faces staring stolidly. Any of these windows could harbor a gun, but no shots rang out. They turned up Twelfth, past Capitol Square once more. As they crossed Marshall Street, a lone officer in blue appeared, wondering at the commotion. Sarah noted his transformation when he realized that the tall man with the long stride was none other than the President. His heels clicked together, and the salute of his right hand fairly ricocheted off his forehead.

"Is it far to the Davis house?" asked Abraham Lincoln.

The officer shook his head, pointed uphill, and thank God finally found his tongue. "Just two blocks, Sir. Follow me."

Catching up with Maryann, Sarah followed the followers.

Eventually the unbelievable procession arrived. Riders dismounted, the squad of sailors divided, and President Lincoln and the others stood under the portico of Jefferson Davis's mansion, the Confederate White House. The President gestured in Sarah's direction, then said a few words to the officers who had come outside to welcome him. Sarah clasped Maryann's hand, and together the two came up the steps.

"Mrs. Prentiss," the President said. "I am relieved to see that you are safe."

"Yes, safe," Sarah said. She was still dazed that he was here at all, here in the flesh, as though someone had waved a magic wand. He had just walked through Richmond, like a stroll through a park, Abraham Lincoln, the President of the United States—Julius Caesar, Alexander the Great, Napoleon, all wrapped into one.

"Are you staying nearby?" Lincoln asked.

"Yes," and Sarah pointed to the Slaughters' house.

"Good," he said. "If I send a messenger over, would you stop by for a moment? Not right away, but in a bit. I'd welcome a friendly face and a quiet talk."

"Of course," Sarah said. "Please. Yes. Do."

Lincoln nodded and returned to the waiting men, who led the way inside. He was just a man, not a devil, not a monument. A quiet talk? Hard to imagine quiet anywhere here in Richmond today.

✦ XXIII ✦

Drunkard's Path

4 April 1865

WITH ONE EYE ON THE DEPARTING FIGURE of Sarah Prentiss, Abraham Lincoln stood by while Admiral Porter and Captain Penrose explained how they had come up from Rocketts with such a slender escort, how the *Malvern* had been unable to negotiate the narrows at Drury's Bluff because of a grounded boat, that they had done what they could, fishing torpedoes and other wreckage from the water. Then how they had abandoned the *Malvern* for the captain's gig taken in tow by the *Bat*, the little tug the President had used about City Point. Of course it was aboard the *Bat* that the marines were situated. Then the *Bat* being sent back to help Admiral Farragut aboard the *Allison*, stuck right across the stream. And of course the tug itself grounded. And remember, with the tug went the marines. Quite a story to unfold. In hindsight it looked like a conspiracy, but it was merely a chain of accidents. Eventually the journey was in the hands, or arms, of the dozen sailors. "On consideration," Admiral Porter was saying, "it seems foolhardy. It was foolhardy. Hindsight says the President can't possibly risk entering Richmond in this fashion. But one step led to the next, and each time we went forward. It could have been worse, oars breaking, injuries to the sailors, but all went smoothly. And here we are safe and sound."

"Safe, sound, and hotter than Hades," Lincoln said, mopping his brow one more time. "Nothing that a glass of cool water wouldn't pacify. I know better than to ask for lemonade."

"Actually, Sir," said a smiling corporal, "we did find a supply of lemons. I'll see what I can rustle up."

Lincoln thanked him, watched him go inside. Seeing Sarah Prentiss was and was not a surprise. He hadn't forgotten that she was here, though he didn't expect the connection to be so immediate. Somewhere he'd heard that in wartime more boys were born than girls. It sounded like a myth. Though it might fit with the ideas of Charles Darwin—it was George Templeton Strong who had suggested it. Not that he had plans to father more boys. He raised an eyebrow—how the mind rambles away when it should know better, when there's a war to attend to, and peace to reckon with.

They had talked of bridges, Joan Matcham and he, bridges across time, their impossibility and inevitability. In and around they had worried the notion, like a pen tracing a figure eight over and over. His strange letter to her, if it should work, could forge an unexpected link. Unexpected but not impossible. But this other Joan who so resembled the true Joan—had he gone loco? *True Joan!* Like a scene out of the Frenchman's opera. Is this woman not flesh and blood? Besides, he had said he would send for her. Good thing he wasn't in charge here.

He looked about. He wasn't the only one at loose ends now that they had come to the heart of (he needn't hesitate any more to say it) the Confederacy. From the river an arc of flame shot up. Until General Weitzel came back from inspecting the city, they would dawdle. He noted the house Sarah Prentiss had disappeared into, a neat two-story cottage, no larger than his own at Eighth and Jackson. Mary, oh Mary.

Back to the present. This house, Davis's, had a neglected air. Its gray stucco must once upon a time have been admirable—its half dozen pillars would give it the flavor of a temple to Apollo, or rather Zeus—none but the best for Davis. But now it seemed shabby, in need of a wash, as though it had personally undergone the long siege. Why would anyone build these houses that looked like temples for the gods? He knew the answer, Jefferson Davis's and Robert E. Lee's answer, Virginia's answer, aristocracy's answer. It had been Porter's idea, his insistent idea, that the President should personally appear in Richmond as soon as possible after its surrender, not to add to the spectacle of their humiliation, but to take up the loose reins of government and thereby to inspire confidence that restoration of order, and not vengeance, was the chief goal as the war was grinding to a close. So close to the end, and poor Mr. Stanton warning him of the consequence of disaster in the pursuit of a treacherous and dangerous enemy. *Remember that you are the political head of a nation.*

Granted. Mr. Stanton, though, like others, forgot that this was also Abraham Lincoln's nation. The President of the United States in Richmond was not on foreign soil. The nation that Abraham Lincoln captained included Mississippi as well as Maine, the Carolinas as well as Connecticut. He had telegraphed Mr. Stanton that he would take care of himself while going to Richmond, and then the next morning, as solace for the risk to his person, he had sent along word from General Weitzel of the capture of twenty-eight locomotives and hundreds of rolling stock, and of prisoners more than a thousand. Little good it would do—he could picture the helpless rage of Mr. Stanton. "Damned fool!" he'd exclaim. But Mr. Stanton wouldn't know that the President was safe so long as he didn't set foot in a theater named Ford's.

Earlier, on the march through the smoldering city, he had asked the idle question, "Is Richmond a city of theaters?" "Not particularly," Penrose had replied, mentioning the Marshall, the New Richmond Theater, the New Theater. What Penrose liked best in Richmond was Pizzini's Palace of Sweets, and he'd licked his lips at the memory. If Richmond had a Ford's Theater, Penrose would have named it. The conversation was like the echo of a conversation. An echo from the future. Had he wandered once more into the labyrinth of time. Had he made this trek before?

There must have been a time when he knew nothing but the present, a time before his face appeared on the penny's face, a time when he knew nothing but now. But with his mind now in possession of a perspective ninety years hence, he was altering that first journey. In his pocket was the penny with his homely visage and the impossible date. What time was it in nineteen hundred and fifty-five? Any time, every time, no time. He had violated time, and no longer would the question yield up comfortable answers.

He glanced skyward. Here it was close to noon, and any moment duty surely would raise its ugly head. Best get on with it. "Well, Captain Graves," he said, "seeing that we are unexpected guests and the housekeeper has departed, what would you say to giving us the ten-cent tour?"

"Yes, Sir, it'd be my pleasure." The young captain's demeanor had picked up considerable starch since he discovered that the ragged handful of sailors was escorting no less than the presidential party. They crossed the threshold to an entryway with parlors on either side. "This, I'm told, is Davis's reception room. It's hard to tell. The place is kind of stripped. His office at the Capitol is even worse, furniture broken, curtains cut in pieces, either souvenir hunters or just drunken vandalism." A shrug. "The looting was pretty bad before we got here."

Lincoln had to agree. The worn red velvet settees reminded him of the Executive Mansion before Mary and her Philadelphia designers took over and transformed it into Aladdin's palace. Nice to be able to smile about it—time heals many wounds. Lincoln watched Tad peering into a closet. Such delight. What Willie wouldn't have given for this moment; what wouldn't his father have given to give Willie this moment! *I am like Lear*, Lincoln thought, and he pictured the old king struggling to swallow his pride, to govern his heart, knowing that you cannot unbind the fortunes and misfortunes of a life. Cannot turn back the clock. The simple-minded old fool cannot ward off the young fool, cannot say, *Do not take that fork in the road up ahead. Stay at home. There is nothing wrong with the practice of the law.* The trouble is you don't know that the choice to take issue with Douglas, the desire to find a seat in the Senate, will catapult you to the presidency of the first democracy on the face of the planet Earth. Lincoln shook his head. We are all in the same boat. If Death wants to stalk you, he will, whether in Springfield or Washington. You must do what you can do, and when the time comes, readiness is all.

"This room," Captain Graves was saying, "also served as Davis's office." It was a large room, like his own office. "And this is his desk —or was his desk."

"This, then," said Lincoln, "must have been his chair." Lincoln sat, stretched his legs, crossed them. He had never imagined such a literal moment, the victor's crowning joy. But there was no victor, no war. An insurrection, yes. And insurrection knows no victory, no more than does the law. A restitution of order, of balance. Davis would speak of "our two countries," but of countries there was but one, of governments but one, of presidents but one. The Union was perpetual. Since 1861 there had been an insurrection in this state of Virginia and others. Were it less well founded, the judiciary would have arrested it. But extraordinary it was, beyond the power of conventional law and order, and it took a muster of millions to come to this moment where an ordinary citizen born in Kentucky, who had lived the vital years of his life in Illinois, a husband and father accidentally become his nation's President, should sit in a chair behind a desk in Richmond, Virginia. His sitting here at this desk turned it magically back to its ordinary condition, a four-legged plank or two of wood that pure and simple lets human flesh perform its task. If ever it was destined for the glory of dutiful service to the so-called Confederate States of America, that dream had gone up in smoke.

"Enough dawdling," he said. "Taddie, let's explore Mr. Davis's house. Lead the way." They followed the boy in this room and out, up stairs and down, forth and back. Few were their words. At any moment the stern visage of Senator Davis might appear and demand an explanation. These Virginians knew how to live. They didn't begin as apprentices learning the master's trade. No, their route took them on from grammar school to college, a route that took privilege for granted. Well, who was he to talk? His own Robert was bound upon that road of glory. But at least it wasn't founded on the sweat and blood of a race other than his own.

LINCOLN AND SARAH PRENTISS were in one parlor. In the other General Weitzel and his staff were doing what they could to get Richmond back on its feet. It hadn't been long before Weitzel had returned, then Judge Campbell had stopped by, and once again they had gone over the terms for peace: cessation of hostilities, dismissal of armies, and an acceptance of emancipation. So simple but so hard to grasp for men of Southern persuasion. Later he would present it to Campbell in writing. Perhaps Virginia could settle without regard to Davis.

So much was churning in his mind. All the same, it took an effort not to gawk. As though Joan herself stood before him in antique clothing, and today were Easter Sunday all over again. But Easter was nearly two weeks distant. "Thank you for coming by," he said.

"Of course," she said. "The President of the United States here in Richmond, in their capital. A historic moment."

"Well, yes, I guess so. I forget what I am. You get so you forget that you're in the forefront, though if I'm any example, much of the time we are thinking about peas and beans more than being presidents with their awful burdens. I am thankful that the end is in sight. That's what folk will be thinking of: that General Grant had Petersburg under siege since last summer, and how it looked as if it would never fall—the opposite of that tower in Pisa. When I was at City Point almost a year ago, it had the look of a stalemate, Grant versus Lee, and the mortality on both sides so fearful, the General assuring me he would never be further from Richmond than he was then. He's like a bulldog; once he's got his teeth into you, there's no escape. I've had generals whose greatest joy was watching Bobbie Lee change his mind and go home. The less battle the better. As though wars are won by not losing."

She nodded, her eyes so dark, under dark brows, like Joan's. She didn't know why she was here, and neither did he. "Do you think," she asked, "that the end is that near?" A question to fill the void.

"I do. Lee has been named the general of all their armies, and Lee has nowhere to go. It is my hope to be here for the surrender, though not to gloat. Rather to insure that the wounds may heal as soon as may be. General Grant is of like mind, I'm glad to say. He doesn't really need me, but Secretary Seward and Mr. Stanton will run the show in Washington well enough without me. I don't think my presence will do much harm."

"I should think not," she said, indignation in her voice.

"You may be right," he said, "if I judge of your feelings correctly. My attitude—I try not to be vindictive—may make some differ-ence, like a touch at the right moment that can help a wound to heal. And the principles we stand for are clearer to me now than they ever have been. In the beginning, when I took office, the balance was so precarious: Peace Democrats, Radical Republicans, Know Nothings, Know Everythings. I hope you don't mind my talking this through—I won't say that politics must bore you. But the day will come when there are other topics of conversation besides this tragedy."

"Yes. One wonders what will take its place in our daily lives, what other headlines, what stories, will fill the newspapers. I have no vision of what my life will be. Not that I knew before."

He nodded. "I have nearly four more years in the presidency, though like you, I can't picture my life beyond this crisis. My boys' getting older I suppose. A vacation that isn't to a battlefield. Imagine! I would like to do some formal studying beyond my narrow specialty. I'm not a knowledgeable man. If I could spend some time with Joseph Henry at the Smithsonian, or Asaph Hall at his observatory, it would delight me."

"Astronomy?"

"Yes, if you can believe it, it would. Some ten, fifteen years ago I was old before my time, and now I'm ready to be a younger man."

She laughed.

"Is that so funny?"

"No. Yes. But I was thinking of the German astronomer I met on shipboard last February."

"Professor Möbius?"

"Yes, you know of him?"

"A bit. He and Henry have been knocking heads over the composition of the universe. And just a few days ago they both were at City Point, sightseeing. Though they never drifted far from what's dearest to their hearts."

"I can easily believe it. Professor Möbius showed me a simple strip of cloth, sewn into a loop but with a twist."

"I know the very thing. My secretary, John Hay, showed me its odd properties, though I haven't had the opportunity to explore it to the full."

"What struck me as odd," Sarah Prentiss said, "was what he said

next. He asked, 'What if the universe itself were like this strip, returning time and again to itself, while we whose lives are like the
brief flicker of a candle never know that our footsteps are echoes of
lives already long forgotten?' "

"I may have heard him hint at such a doctrine. Do you think he
subscribes to such a notion, that time itself may be such a loop?"

"I have no way to judge," she said, and he, with his left hand in his
pocket, and in his pocket the penny, was on the brink of a precipice.
Step back, step back. "To be truthful," she continued, "I could not
fully grasp how the universe could be shaped other than as a void
in which the stars and planets and comets make their way, let alone
that it should be shaped like his simple twist of cloth. It crossed my
mind that the effort of following in the wake of his strange notions
was like forcing the eye to trace the design of a patchwork quilt—
the Flying Dutchman or Drunkard's Path. At times I thought him
quite mad."

"It doesn't surprise me. He and others like him delight in such
abstractions that we poor mortals cannot keep up. Yet their minds
are also fixed on the most material of objects, the stars which give us
our very lives. Or a bit of cloth."

A pause settled between them. "So," Lincoln said, wondering
what to say next, "you are comfortable here with your friend?"

"Yes, we are doing fine, especially now that Richmond is safe
again. Even Mrs. Lee has reason to be thankful to the soldiers from
the North. Did you hear the story of how they prevented her house
from taking fire?"

"Yes. Godfrey Weitzel and Lee were at West Point together, a fluid
there thicker than blood I'm afraid. And though I would have done
the same, it would not have stemmed from any warmth in my heart
for their general of generals. Soldiers love soldiers, but I am not one
of them."

It was her turn to nod. Her friend's home was in plain view beyond the garden, and he was fighting a battle against time with no
way to win. He could talk on and on and on, but before long the last
word would be said, and he would be no closer to Joan Matcham.

"I thank you," he said, "for the moment's respite. The idle moment is worth its weight in gold. I hope you will forgive the ramblings of weariness. If I may, I would like to escort you back across the road to your house."

"Thank you," she said. "Of course it's unnecessary. I cross these streets every day. You are the one who should be watchful."

"Now you sound like Mr. Stanton. But on so short a journey I can take care of myself."

All this brief time they had been standing. He had not even invited her to sit. She turned to face him directly, one step away. *This is not your Joan*, he reminded himself once more, and his arms stayed by his side. But this other Joan rose on tiptoe and gently kissed his cheek.

"I want you to have this," he said, as though her kiss were an ordinary event. How the penny had got from his pocket to his hand he wasn't sure. He pressed it into her palm. "A token. The story it tells could last a lifetime. But today brevity will have to suffice. The road, I'm afraid, has given you a second mad man. May you meet a third. Good things come in threes. We'd better go while the going is good."

✦ XXIV ✦

Confirmation

9 June 1955

A S A CHILD ON SPECIAL OCCASIONS and with appropriate supervision, Joan (then Joan Colfield) was allowed to examine her grandmother's "collections," as they were called. Hands inspected for cleanliness, she would hold in her small palm the ivory cameo and trace the soft features of her grandmother's grandmother; she would put the turquoise and silver bracelet about her wrist; she would finger the many shiny stones and wonder at their history, wonder why they were chosen. The fragile pages of the tiny leather books she would turn one by one, every page filled from top to bottom and edge to edge with a spidery handwriting so unlike her own bulky letters that bobbed up and down like a frog on a lily pad. The only words she knew for certain were the two words at the top of the first sheet: "Sarah Morrow." "Sarah" she knew because it was her middle name, one of the first words she had learned to write and then to read. "Morrow," said her mother, was a strange word, meaning the day that comes after today, a day that no matter what, would never happen, for no sooner would the morrow come but it became today. Joan knew there was a flaw in her mother's explanation but could never put her finger on it. Why would there be words that unraveled their sense faster than balls of yarn in a sewing basket? Later her mother showed her how by changing just one letter, her name turned to "Sorrow."

In 1942, on her thirtieth birthday, after her mother and father had given her the Parker 51 fountain pen, her mother had held up one finger—*just wait*, it said. And from under the table she brought forth a package that might be a box of candy or a blouse, but Joan, who was no longer a Colfield, knew it was neither. With Robert already in the service, it was just the three of them, Joan and her parents, at dinner. Joan eyed the mysterious gift. Its oblong shape, the weathered edges, were good clues, but it was knowing her mother that told her the answer. Her mother, who was born not long after the Civil War had ended, was now a woman of seventy-five. She seemed to have grown shorter in the last few years, and her step was no longer so quick. Time was telling her mother's story with less patience than before. Joan's grandmother's collections were now hers.

"I think you can be trusted," her mother said. "I was your age when your grandmother passed it on to me, left it to my care, decided I could be trusted. I remember thinking to myself that my mother was getting old. And I wondered, and she wondered too, if I would ever have my own daughter. Luckily for you, I did." Joan had heard that joke before, as though somewhere there was an unlucky Joan Colfield whose mother had never had her, a sad and gloomy child who sat in dark corners and wept at the drop of a hat.

But she was lucky Joan, she always had been. That was the story.

After that dinner on the night of her thirtieth birthday, she had walked home. Though it was after nine, it was still light, and she had looked ahead to a bath and then a cup of tea and one of the butter cookies her mother had baked for her. The box from her mother and from her mother's mother would be on the kitchen table. She would undo its satin ribbon, nibble a cookie, and gently, with both hands on the lid, she would picture her grandmother sitting across the table, a tall, dark-haired woman, slender, her own age, almost smiling. Joan had seen her only in photographs, and in only one was she a young woman.

She flinched, ducked, almost fell off her chair—something, a ball, a dark sphere, was coming at her from the side. Joan caught herself, found her balance. Her eyes had popped open. She was sitting on the couch, had been thinking about Grandmother Morrow, thinking about her thirtieth birthday, and for what could be no more than a moment had dozed off.

She had come home from work, had a cheese sandwich and a glass of milk, had taken *The Evanston Review* to the living room, then picked up last week's *New Yorker*, glanced at the reviews and the cartoons and "Talk of the Town," and had begun to think about her mother, her grandmother, the oblong box, until the sphere came at her like a rocket. It missed, passing over her right shoulder and beyond.

It was the ninth of June, sixty days since. Sixty days of being pregnant. Sixty days since he had been with her, sixty days since he was gone. For him, for Abraham Lincoln, sixty days since would put him at City Point, Virginia, where the Appomattox River flowed into the James. Two days before he had journeyed upriver to Richmond with a handful of sailors as guards. She had worked out his chronology. Deering Library had thousands of books on Lincoln and the Civil War. Richmond was a day of triumph. And ten days from Richmond—she hated to think of it but couldn't keep the foreknowledge at bay. June 17th on her calendar. April 14th on his. Good Friday. Nothing good about it.

She knew the past was a closed book. Not a good metaphor, because books can be opened. But it was like a book, if by that you meant that the words had been written and would never change, no matter how many times the book was opened. He had said he would remember her, he was sure of it. But there was no knowing. For her, it was different—she knew. Souvenir hunters may have all but ransacked the White House for memorabilia, clipping bits from the draperies, cutting holes in Mary Lincoln's precious carpets. Anything to remember him by. But Joan Matcham took the prize.

Upstairs in the bottom drawer of her dresser was the box. Her mother was almost his contemporary, born two years after his death. That her mother was born during what would have been his second term of office often amazed her, and as a child, amazed her friends. It was as though generations had been skipped. Her mother, and her mother's mother—and now herself, Joan Matcham, all in their forties when they had their daughters. Though her daughter could be a son.

It was a good while since Joan had rummaged through the old box. The urge was irresistible, and she took the stairs two at a time. She set the box on the chenille bedspread and commenced its litany. The jewelry. The smooth, round pebbles from a riverbed, gathered and saved for reasons long gone. The arrowhead, notched where it was bound to the arrow's stem. The tiny diary begun in 1866. It did tell a story, how her grandmother had met her grandfather, second marriages for both, and the birth of her mother a year later. Entries were sporadic. It told of tooth extractions, of changes in the weather, of how big baby's feet were, of finding birds' nests, of her mother, a child, spilling a bottle of ink for the second time, of birthdays and death days, of aches and pains and joys. At random Joan opened the tiny diary:

> *January 1, 1882. Sunday.*
> *New Year's Day. To church with Annie and David; a sermon by Rev. Ashford on turning over a new leaf. Inspirational. A cold drenching rain. Ride home along Lincoln Avenue, old thoughts kindled of the war years and before. Oyster soup and hot bread for dinner. Rain turning to snow and now all is white. God prosper the New Year to those I love.*

Eighteen hundred and eighty-two, the year her grandmother turned sixty-two; her mother would have been fourteen years old.

Joan closed the diary and took up a small white cardboard box with green edging. The writing on top of the box announced its contents:

She remembered what was really inside the box: not address labels, but pen points. Pen points by the dozen. Joan lifted the lid from the box and picked up a few, held one to the light:

 Spencerian Forty
Made in England

And another:

 Northern Pac Railway Co.
BANK

And another:

 R. Esterbrook & Co
Jackson Stub

Apparently they were all different—she had never noticed that, never looked closely before. How lovely, a collection. The next few:

 S. V. Sanger & Co.
Iridium

Rex Nickelene
A. W. McCloy Co.
Pittsburgh, Pa

Vidalia Line

She rummaged through for more shiny ones—without a magnifying glass it was hard to make out the writing on the dull ones. Her finger shuffled them about, and beneath them all was an old penny, dull with age. Not an Indian Head penny, but a Lincoln penny. As a little girl she had saved coins. There wasn't a Lincoln penny until 1909, and at first it had caused a flurry. Never before had an American coin borne the image of a president on its face. She loved it when a coin had a story to tell. Teddy Roosevelt had asked a Jewish immigrant with the initials V. D. B. (her coin book told his name) to design the coin in honor of the centennial of Lincoln's birth. They chose the penny because it was the coin of the common people. Of course Southerners resented the choice of Lincoln. But the immediate problem was the placement of the artist's initials on the reverse of the coin, and within a week of its issue they removed the VDB. Somewhere, maybe in the attic, was Joan's collection, and her one VDB penny. It had been years since she thought of that story. Mostly her goal had been to get all the Indian Heads, and she came close. She held this coin to the light, and froze. There, below President Lincoln's beard, was the date, 1955.

Chills then, one after the other, rippled across her back. Gently she set the penny on the bedspread. Her breathing slowed. She had opened the box of pen points often enough. But she had no memory of looking through them. She hadn't touched her grandmother's things in ages, not since Emily was a little girl. The penny had been there, all these years. She had never heard of a penny struck with a false date. How could it happen? It would take colossal stupidity on the part of the engraver. The date on this coin was real. And she knew how it got in the box, how it got back in time. Only one way. He had showed her this penny on Easter Sunday, a shiny new penny. "Imagine this!" he had said, and then returned it to his pocket. And he must have given it to her grandmother. Must have. She had been a friend of the Blairs, who lived on Lafayette Square, across from the White House. She had gone to school with their daughter in Philadelphia—Joan couldn't remember the name of the school or the name of the Blair daughter. It was family history, written down somewhere. And here it was again, the penny, back in the year of its birth. It had traveled almost two hundred years, ninety back and ninety forward.

And then it struck her. So he *did* return; he got home safely. And again she shuddered. The history books hadn't changed in the last few months. "I didn't just disappear, did I?" he had asked. And she had answered with what was almost a lie. With a truth that hid a greater truth. That the coin should come full circle!

"Oh my," she said aloud. And finding it now, not a year ago or earlier! As though the story were deliberately covering its tracks.

Downstairs the mail clanged through the slot.

Joan put the pen nibs back in their box and set the penny atop them. It was an ordinary penny, dulled by time yet newer than most, according to its date. She didn't remember noticing a 1955 penny so far this year. She put the jewelry, the seashells, the arrowhead, the little green-edged box, back in the bigger box, and put the box back in the bottom drawer of her dresser.

She went down the stairs, picked up the mail by the front door. A bill from the gas company, her bank statement, something from Field's, and last, a letter without a return address in an odd but clearly readable hand. To Joan Matcham, at this address on Hinman. Though the envelope was crisp and in good condition, it was an antique. She slipped her finger under the flap. The glue was brittle, and it opened right up. The single sheet of paper was folded in thirds. It wasn't a long letter, and her eye went right to the signature.

Chills all over again. She looked at the stamp—an air mail. And the postmark, Portland, Oregon, June 6, this year. Did she know anyone in Oregon? She took the letter to the rocker. She sat back, closed her eyes. It's a good thing her heart was strong. This could be the undoing of a girl. A girl. By now this girl was ready for anything. Let the Czar of all the Russias make a grand entrance, she was prepared. An elephant with a howdah and His Majesty, the King of Siam. Queen Victoria and Albert. But this, she was sure, this was the end of the line, the last link. And she could guess how he did it.

She focused her eyes on the letter.

EXECUTIVE MANSION

Washington, Feb 10, 1865

To Mrs Matcham, Evanston, Ill.
    Dear Joan.
        So, my little device worked. My secretary John Hay who I trust absolutely agreed to be responsible for this letter and to find others along the line. That the letter is in your hands is testimony to their integrity.

I have been back for 5 days. The trip downriver was swift but uneventful. As usual I have been busy, but that does not mean that I do not find time to think of you and say Thank you for your kindness and your hospitality. I hope that the manner of my departure neither inconvenienced nor alarmed you.

Since my return to Washington it has occurred to me that I may have left something behind, a little something. The chances are that my imagination has got the better of me. But one never knows. Once is all it takes. I am writing lightly of a subject that is quite serious and I do not wish to offend you. If by chance my visit did bear fruit, or does bear fruit, I am somewhat at a loss for words. I will not say that I was careless. I may have been thoughtless but I would not alter the moment, even if I could. There is so much more that I could say but you will have to understand more from less. From small acorns great oaks grow.

Please give Rusty my love. Yours forever

A. Lincoln

Afterword

KNOCK AT THE DOOR. Sighing, I set aside the stack of papers, capping my pen as I circle round the coffee table. Tall man glimpsed through the side window, no one I know. Twist of the brass doorknob, door opens. No coat and tie and black briefcase, not a Jehovah's Witness.

"I'm in the middle of—"

"I'm no salesman."

I can see that now that my eyes are functioning. He is tall and thin with a gray beard, no mustache, wearing a brown leather vest and long-sleeved white shirt. I look sideways at him. "I've never met you," I say.

"Granted," he says, "and I've never met you, but one of us has to take the first step."

Have I fallen asleep? Am I still in my chair, papers tumbled at my ankles? "You're not a FASRAD, are you?"

"No, I'm no android, if that's what you mean. Look closely, use that middle eye."

I start to close the door, but he shoulders past me and steps inside.

"Wait wait," I stutter.

He ignores me, marches over to the bookshelf by the fireplace, stoops over—it seems to take forever for the body to wind itself so far down, like a Brobdingnabian setting Gulliver upon the ground, or Gulliver with a Lilliputian in his palm. He withdraws a book from its upright fellows. He stands up straight once more. He opens the volume, skimming from back to front, halts, backs up a few pages, then holds it before my eyes.

I blink, stand by his side, look at the pages. Black and white photos. He points to the lower right-hand page: an illustration of a man in a top hat and three-quarter coat, in front of a tent, with army men in antique uniforms at left and right.

"You?" I ask.

"No one else. The veritable me. Posing with Mr. McClellan."

"And you've crossed my doorstep?"

"Yours."

"Have you read my book?"

"Inside and out."

"And you approve?"

He shakes his head wearily. "Is there a place we can sit and talk?" I choose the kitchen table. "Coffee, tea?"

"Water," he says. "Cold water."

I pour him a glass from the spigot. I sit across from him.

"Liberty," he says. "You took some liberties, you know."

I nod. Liberty, as good a place to begin as any.

Author's Note

THE READER MIGHT BE INTERESTED in knowing what is and what is not historical in this novel. Abraham Lincoln did spend some time in Evanston, but that visit was earlier, in the spring of 1860, the year of his election. The afternoon reception at the White House which I have on Sunday, February 5, was really the day before. Lincoln's interest in science and his friendship with Joseph Henry (the first secretary of the Smithsonian) are genuine. That August Möbius traveled across the Atlantic to lecture at the Smithsonian is a fabrication, though Count Ferdinand Zeppelin was an observer with the Army of the Potomac. Asaph Hall and Asa Gray were in Washington in 1865; they were not, however, at City Point with Lincoln. John Hay, Lincoln's young secretary, later became Secretary of State under James McKinley and Theodore Roosevelt; he and John Nicolay were Lincoln's biographers, as well as co-editors of the works of Lincoln. As far as I know John Wilkes Booth did not dine at Willard's Hotel on the night the Lincolns saw *La Dame Blanche*. Abraham Lincoln did not die at Ford's Theater, but across Tenth Street at the house of William Petersen. Andrew Johnson did stay with Elizabeth Blair Lee until shortly before he became President. The young soldier from Pittsburgh that Lincoln directed to Secretary Stanton was not necessarily Jewish, nor presumably was his name Rosenthal (though my great-grandfather Morris Rosenthal, a native of Pittsburgh, did lie about his age to enlist in the army).

Lincoln did sign one letter, "Yours forever" (to Joshua F. Speed, October 5, 1842). For the balloon escape of Cyrus Harding from Richmond, I am indebted to my most beloved childhood story, Jules Verne's *The Mysterious Island*. Prentiss, Maine, is but a few miles from Lincoln, Maine. Joan Matcham also resides in the pages of Robert Louis Stevenson's *The Black Arrow*. For one "alternate" tale of Abraham Lincoln, I recommend Oscar Lewis, *The Lost Years: A Biographical Fantasy* (Alfred A. Knopf, 1951); and for another, Philip K. Dick, *We Can Build You* (DAW, 1972; initially published as "A. Lincoln, Simulacrum"). Lastly, on Christmas Eve of 1985, Robert Lincoln Beckwith died at the age of 81, Abraham Lincoln's last descendent outside this novel.

I WOULD ALSO LIKE TO MAKE small payment on the large debt I owe to more than a century of Lincoln scholarship. Given that Abraham Lincoln is the third most written about person in the history of humanity (after Jesus Christ and William Shakespeare), I will but mention the highlights of my reading over the last several years.

Jean H. Baker, *Mary Todd Lincoln: A Biography* (W. W. Norton & Company, 1987).

David Homer Bates, *Lincoln in the Telegraph Office* (The Century Co., 1907).

Alfred Hoyt Bill, *The Beleagured City: Richmond, 1861–65* (Alfred A. Knopf, 1946).

Adolphe de Chambrun, *Impressions of Lincoln and the Civil War: A Foreigner's Account,* trans. Adelbert de Chambrun (Random House, 1952).

Lord Charnwood (Godfrey Rathbone Benson, Baron), *Abraham Lincoln* (H. Holt & Co., 1916; Madison Books, 1996).

The Collected Works of Abraham Lincoln, ed. Roy P. Basler (Rutgers University Press, 1953; 8 vols., with index and 2 supplements).

David Donald, *Lincoln* (Simon & Schuster, 1995).

F. Stansbury Haydon, *Aeronautics in the Union and Confederate Armies* (The Johns Hopkins University Press, 1941; 2 vols.).

Harold Holzer, *Dear Mr. Lincoln: Letters to the President* (Addison Wesley, 1993).

Elizabeth Keckley, *Behind the Scenes, Or, Thirty Years a Slave, and Four Years in the White House* (Oxford University Press, 1968).

Lincoln and the Civil War in the Diaries and Letters of John Hay, ed. Tyler Dennett (Dodd, Mead & Co., 1939).

Lincoln Day by Day: A Chronology, 1809–1865, ed. Earl S. Meirs and others (Lincoln Sesquicentennial Commission, 1960; 3 vols.).

Emil Ludwig, *Lincoln* (trans. Eden and Cedar Paul, Little, Brown, & Co., 1930).

James M. McPherson, *Battle Cry of Freedom* (Oxford University Press, 1988).

Mine Eyes Have Seen the Glory: Combat Diaries of Union Sergeant Hamlin Alexander Coe, ed. David Coe (Fairleigh Dickinson University Press, 1975).

Mark E. Neely, Jr., *The Abraham Lincoln Encyclopedia* (McGraw-Hill, 1982).

Mark E. Neely, Jr., and R. Gerald McMurtry, *The Insanity File: The Case of Mary Todd Lincoln* (Southern Illinois University Press, 1986).

Stephen B. Oates, *With Malice Toward None: The Life of Abraham Lincoln* (Harper & Row, 1977).

Phillip Shaw Paludan, *The Presidency of Abraham Lincoln* (University Press of Kansas, 1994).

J. G. Randall, *Lincoln the President* (Dodd, Mead & Co., 1945–1955; Da Capo Press, 1997; 2 vols.; the last of the 4 initial volumes completed by Richard N. Current).

Ida Tarbell, *The Life of Abraham Lincoln* (Lincoln Memorial Association, 1900; 2 vols.).

Benjamin P. Thomas, *Abraham Lincoln: A Biography* (Alfred A. Knopf, 1952).

Wartime Washington: The Civil War Letters of Elizabeth Blair Lee, ed. Virginia Jeans Laas (University of Illinois Press, 1991).

Notes on Historical Figures

Note: Names that appear in small capitals are also referenced in this list. The *Abraham Lincoln Encyclopedia* (McGraw-Hill, 1982 [also available in paperback from Da Capo Press]), by Mark E. Neely, Jr., is a valuable launching platform for further delving.

Baker, Edward Dickinson (1811–1861). Friend of Lincoln, elected to Congress in Illinois in 1844 and to the Senate in 1860 (having moved to Oregon in 1859) as the first Republican senator from the Pacific coast. At the outbreak of war he raised a military command known as the "California Regiment." Colonel Baker was killed at the Battle of Ball's Bluff in October 1861.

Bates, David Homer (1837?–1926). Cipher-operator at the War Department telegraph office and author of *Lincoln in the Telegraph Office* (1907; Bison Books, 1995). Bates points out that not only was the Civil War the first time the Morse telegraph was used to "direct widely separate armies and move them in unison," but that aside from the White House, Lincoln spent "more of his waking hours" at the nearby telegraph than any other place (there being no telegraph connection at the White House). The use of the telegraph and rifled guns, by both sides, distinguished the Civil War from all prior wars.

Beckwith, Samuel H. (1840–1916). General GRANT's cipher-operator. DAVID BATES points out that it was Sam Beckwith whose dispatch from Port Tobacco, Maryland, to General THOMAS ECKERT, Chief of the War Department telegraph staff, brought the first "authentic" news of the whereabouts of JOHN WILKES BOOTH.

Bedell, Grace (1848–1936). An ardent Republican from Westfield, New York. At the age of 11, Bedell wrote a letter on October 15, 1860, to her party's nominee, saying, "I have got 4 brother's and part of them will vote for you any way and if you will let your whiskers grow I will try and get the rest of them to vote for you[.] you would look a great deal better for your face is so thin. All the ladies like whiskers and they would tease their husband's to vote for you and you would be President." Lincoln replied, "As to the whiskers, never having worn any, do you not think people would call it a piece of silly affect[at]ion if I were to begin now?" By mid-November Lincoln's beard was growing.

Blair, Francis Preston (1791–1876). Adviser to the Lincoln administration. Earlier, as editor of the Democratic newspaper, the *Globe,* during the administration of Andrew Jackson, Blair was a member of Jackson's "Kitchen Cabinet." In December 1864, Blair received a pass from Lincoln allowing him to travel to Richmond, so he could urge a scheme upon JEFFERSON DAVIS whereby following a truce, a joint command of Union and Confederate troops could drive the French puppet Emperor Maximilian from Mexico. Davis thought reconciliation between North and South impossible because of vindictive feeling, especially on the part of the South, but he did not entirely rebuff Blair. These negotiations eventually led to the Hampton Roads Peace Conference in early February 1865. Lincoln never took the Mexican scheme seriously.

Blair, Francis ("Frank") Preston, Jr. (1821–1875). General, U.S. Army. Brother of MONTGOMERY BLAIR and ELIZABETH BLAIR LEE. Frank Blair was one of the best of the "political" generals (i.e., not a career officer trained at West Point).

Blair, Montgomery (1813–1883). Postmaster General in Lincoln's Cabinet. Son of FRANCIS PRESTON BLAIR and brother to FRANK BLAIR and ELIZABETH BLAIR LEE. As a former Democrat, and thanks to his family's prominence in the border states, Montgomery Blair filled a vital niche in Lincoln's diverse Cabinet. Ultimately he came to detest the Radical Republicans (CHASE and STANTON). The day after General FRÉMONT withdrew his third party candidacy (against Lincoln and MCCLELLAN), Lincoln asked Montgomery Blair to resign his Cabinet post, presumably to keep peace with Radicals and supporters of Frémont. In a meeting with Lincoln at the Soldiers' Home, Francis Preston Blair assured Lincoln "that he might rely on my sons to do all they could for him." He reported that Lincoln sadly had said, "He did not think it good policy to sacrifice a true friend to a false one or an avowed enemy." Lincoln reportedly said that "Montgomery had himself told him that he would cheerfully resign to conciliate the class of men who had made their war on the Blairs because they were his [Lincoln's] friends." In fact General Frank Blair did return from the front, "arresting the whole movement" to denounce Lincoln (reported by Elizabeth Blair Lee in her letter of October 4, 1864).

Booth, John Wilkes (1838–1865). Actor who assassinated Abraham Lincoln at Ford's Theater on April 14, 1865. For many Lincoln scholars, Booth is an unwelcome subject. James Garfield Randall's massive four-volume biography, *Lincoln the President,* ends early in the evening of April 14, 1865, with Lincoln anticipating the pleasure of seeing *Our American Cousin* at Ford's Theater. Mrs. Lincoln, with a headache, suggested they stay at home, but her husband insisted they go. "Otherwise," Randall indirectly quotes Lincoln as saying, "he would have to see visitors all evening as usual. And so they went." T. Harry Williams's *Lincoln and His Generals* ends similarly, on the 8th of April, a Saturday, with Lincoln at City Point boarding the *River Queen* and starting for home. Williams draws on the portrait of Lincoln as witnessed by the MARQUIS ADOLPHE DE CHAMBRUN, who describes Lincoln standing "a long while gazing at the hills, now dark and silent." Williams adds, "He may have been thinking of the weary years of defeat—of McCLELLAN, Burnside, Hooker—or of the hour of victory and GRANT and SHERMAN." These wistful words precede the icy irony of the last sentence of his book: "That day John Wilkes Booth registered at the National Hotel in Washington." James M. McPherson's *Battle Cry of Freedom* ends (aside from an epilogue) on April 11, 1865, with Lincoln delivering "from a White House balcony a carefully prepared speech on peace and reconstruction to a crowd celebrating Union victory." Lincoln is speaking of the reconstruction of Louisiana and his wish that it would "have enfranchised literate Negroes and black veterans." Then comes McPherson's short last paragraph: "At least one listener interpreted this speech as moving Lincoln closer to the radical Republicans. 'That means nigger citizenship,' snarled John Wilkes Booth to a companion. 'Now, by God, I'll put him through. That is the last speech he will ever make.'"

Two books have recently been published, both of which would have been impossible in the 19th century. One is *"Right or Wrong, God Judge Me": The Writings of John Wilkes Booth* (edited by John Rhodehamel and Louise Taper [University of Illinois Press, 1997]). The other is Asia Wilkes Clarke's *John Wilkes Booth: A Sister's Memoir* (edited and with an introduction by Terry Alford [University Press of Mississippi, 1996]).

The latter was completed by John Wilkes Booth's sister Asia in 1874. Asia knew that publication was impossible in her lifetime. Not only was an "intimate portrayal of the most notorious murderer in American history" out of the question, but Asia's husband, comic actor John Sleeper Clarke, would have destroyed it rather than allow it to see the light of day. Instead, Asia Booth Clarke entrusted it to her friend B. L. Farjeon, a popular English writer, "to publish some time if he sees fit." Asia's daughter Dolly accordingly presented a black tin box containing the manuscript to Farjeon in 1888, but Farjeon discovered the time was still not fit. A generation later, Farjeon's daughter Eleanor took up the project, and in 1938 G. B. Putnam's Sons published it as *The Unlocked Book: A Memoir of John Wilkes Booth by His Sister Asia Booth Clarke*. The current edition, two generations later, situates the book for an audience unfamiliar with the history of the Booth family—for instance, that Edwin Booth, the brother of John Wilkes and Asia, was as famous in his time as any actor in ours.

Asia Booth Clarke's memoir reads strangely. She faults Lincoln for his "triumphant entry" into Richmond. Rather, the President should have "gone first to a place of worship or have remained at home on this jubilant occasion." She warns the murdered man that "conquerors cannot be too careful of themselves, as history has ever proved." Asia Booth Clarke's eyes see a theater so different from the one we see: "That fatal visit to the theater had no pity in it; it was jubilation over fields of unburied dead, over miles of desolated homes." Most of all, Lincoln's presence at the theater meant to her brother "the fall of the Republic, a dynasty of kings." She repeats her brother's last words, as he was dying at Garrett's farm on April 26: "Tell my mother—I died—for my country," and she adds, "He saved his country from a king." Her words echo her brother's cry from the stage of Ford's Theater: "Sic semper tyrannis" ("Thus always to tyrants," the motto of the state of Virginia). Boston Corbett (who fired the shot that killed Booth) she regards as "our deliverer, for by his shot he saved our beloved brother from an ignominious death." Little did she know of Corbett's insanity—he was a hatter most of his life (many hatters suffered from mercury poisoning, hence the phrase "mad as a hatter")—or that he castrated himself in 1858 to avoid the sinful temptations of women.

Appended to the memoir are various documents, the last of which is a transcript of the examination in New York City on May 12, 1865, of Joseph Adrian Booth, the youngest member of the family, upon his arrival in New York from Australia. Like so many tangents associated with Abraham Lincoln, the testimony becomes fascinating, thanks to the association with greatness, and tragedy.

A distant cousin to the Booth family was CHARLES WILKES, whose story is fascinating in its own right. Charles Wilkes' autobiography, written after the death of Lincoln, contains no record of his kinship to the Booths.

Bowers, Theodore S. (1832–1866). Colonel, U.S. Army. Trained as a printer, at the outbreak of war Bowers was editing the *Register* in Mount Carmel, Illinois. Following the first battle of Bull Run he raised a company of volunteers for the 48th Illinois infantry but went to the front as a private. After returning home on recruiting service, he became a clerical assistant to Brigadier-General GRANT. In December 1862, while Bowers was in charge of department headquarters at Holly Springs, Mississippi, the Confederates raided in the rear of the Federal advance. Bowers, with little warning, had the presence of mind to make a bonfire of all departmental records. He then refused parole, escaping that very evening. Bowers was commended for his service and was eventually with Grant in the field, serving on his personal staff until Appomattox, where he was among the Union officers present when the surrender was signed. Less than a year later, he was killed instantly while trying to board a moving train on the Hudson River railroad.

Browning, Orville Hickman (1806–1881). Friend and political associate of Lincoln. After the death of Senator STEPHEN DOUGLAS in June 1861, Governor Yates of Illinois appointed Browning to complete Douglas's term. In April 1862, Browning voted to emancipate slaves in the District of Columbia, but thereafter he reverted to a traditional conservative position regarding race. The Brownings remained personal friends of Lincoln, and Browning was one of Lincoln's pallbearers at the White House funeral service. He served as ANDREW JOHNSON's Secretary of the Interior, and in 1869 he became a Democrat. Early in 1865 Browning was the instrument of access to Lincoln for General JAMES SINGLETON, Senator EDWIN MORGAN, and others, for a scheme involving the purchase of cotton from the South, a "scheme [as Browning puts it in his diary] to make some money." Lincoln was always clear with GRANT to "Let nothing which is transpiring, change, hinder, or delay your Military movements, or plans" (February 1, 1865). On March 8, 1865,

Grant telegraphed STANTON regarding this questionable trade: "I would respectfully recommend that orders be sent to the Army and Navy everywhere, to stop supplies going to the interior and annulling all permits for such trade heretofore given." A second telegram was more specific: "I believe Genl Singleton should be ordered to return from Richmond and all permits he may have should be revoked. Our friends in Richmond . . . send word that Tobacco is being exchanged for Bacon, and they believe Singleton to be at the bottom of it." Grant requested the same regarding Judge Hughes, adding, "I believe there is a deep laid plan for making millions and they will sacrifice every interest of the country to succeed."

Buchanan, James (1791–1868). Democratic President of the United States, 1857–1861. He didn't consider secession a legal right, but at the same time he believed that the Constitution did not grant the federal government the power "to coerce a State into submission." While many Republicans blamed Buchanan for failing to take appropriate measures before the outbreak of war, it was Buchanan, of the five living ex-Presidents, who most firmly supported Lincoln's policies.

Campbell, John A. (1811–1889). Assistant Secretary of War, CSA; formerly a U.S. Supreme Court justice, appointed by Franklin Pierce in 1853.

Carpenter, Francis Bicknell (1830–1900). Artist who painted *First Reading of the Emancipation Proclamation of President Lincoln* and author of *Six Months at the White House with Abraham Lincoln.* Carpenter was at the White House from February through July 1864. The painting, presently hanging in the Capitol, was best known in the 19th century from Alexander Hay Ritchie's popular mezzotint engraving; nearly 30,000 prints were drawn before the plate was worn out. (For a photo of the engraving, see Merrill D. Peterson, *Lincoln in Memory* [Oxford University Press, 1994].)

Chase, Catherine ("Kate") Jane, II (1840–1899). Beautiful daughter of SALMON CHASE who acted as hostess for her father at their townhouse at Sixth and E Streets. Regarded by some as the "Toast of Washington." In November of 1863 she was married to William Sprague, senator from Rhode Island (formerly governor of Rhode Island), a man termed "unworthy and dissolute" by her father's biographer, John Niven (*Salmon P. Chase: A Biography* [Oxford University Press, 1995]).

Chase, Salmon Portland (1808–1873). Secretary of the Treasury under Lincoln. Appointed Chief Justice of the Supreme Court in 1864, replacing ROGER B. TANEY. Chase was a Radical Republican and a rival for the presidency in 1860. John Niven, Chase's biographer, said of Chase: from his days as a young lawyer in Cincinnati when the "plight of slaves stirred [him] to the depths of his being," Chase "never wavered in this dedication." This moral sense, however, was balanced by an "insidious ambition," which Lincoln described as that "maggot" in Chase's brain. Niven judged Chase capable in his office as Secretary of the Treasury, finding the funds to sustain "a million well-equipped troops in the field," as well as a navy second only to Great Britain's, all this managed without "drastic inflation or government controls."

Davis, David (1815–1886). Old friend of Lincoln, legal associate, and his campaign manager in 1860. Davis was an ally of Thurlow Weed, both opponents of SALMON P. CHASE and the radical wing of the Republican Party. Davis urged that Lincoln modify the Emancipation Proclamation when the Illinois legislature was apparently on the verge of passing a resolution calling for either the rescinding of the Proclamation or the cessation of the war. To Davis's surprise, Lincoln appointed him to the Supreme Court. After Lincoln's death, he was executor of the estate at the request of MARY TODD LINCOLN and ROBERT TODD LINCOLN. In 1877 he was elected to the Senate but served with neither party's caucus.

Davis, Jefferson (1808–1889). President, CSA; graduate of West Point, 1828; elected to Congress for Mississippi in 1845; in 1846 resigned his seat in the House to become colonel of the 1st Mississippi volunteer rifles. Davis fought heroically at Buena Vista in "Mr. Polk's War." Severely wounded, he remained in the saddle to the end of the battle, earning compliments for coolness and gallantry in the commander-in-chief's dispatch of March 5, 1847. Appointed to the Senate in 1847; then became Secretary of War under Franklin Pierce (1853–1857), reentering the Senate in 1857. Davis withdrew from the Senate in January 1861, after Mississippi seceded from the Union. In February 1861 Davis took office as President of the Confederate States of America. Not long afterward, he took up residence in Richmond at what had been the home of James A. Seddon (later his Secretary of War), the capital having moved from Montgomery, Alabama. In his last message to his Congress, March 13, 1865, with Appomattox less than a month away, Davis asserted that means to meet the emergency were ample. A month after the evacuation of Richmond in April 1865, the presidential party was captured near Irwinsville, Georgia. Davis was taken to Fort Monroe and kept in confinement for two years. In 1866 Davis was indicted for treason by a grand jury for the district of Virginia; in May 1867 he was released under bail of $100,000, the first name on his bail bond being that of HORACE GREELEY. Never brought to trial, he was included in the general amnesty of December 1868. In 1876 when a bill was introduced to remove all political disabilities which had been imposed on those who took part in the late insurrection, James G. Blaine offered an amendment excepting Jefferson Davis, accusing Davis as being "the author of the gigantic murders and crimes at Andersonville."

Davis, Varina Howell (1826–1906). Wife of JEFFERSON DAVIS and daughter of Zachary Taylor, then a colonel in the army. After the death of her husband, Varina Davis moved to New York City, where she supported herself writing articles for newspapers and periodicals. One of Varina Davis's last letters was written to DAVID BATES, who in September 1906 sent a picture of Little Jeff, "thinking it might be a pleasure, after so many years, to look once more upon the form of her old horse." Little Jeff had been captured early in 1863 at Grand Gulf, Mississippi. Bates tells the story of the horse, how it became one of GRANT's favorite mounts—another was Cincinnati Grant. Little Jeff was Grant's choice when he rode through the Appomattox campaign; whereas Cincinnati Grant was Lincoln's horse while Lincoln was at the front. It was one of SAMUEL BECKWITH's duties at City Point to exercise Grant's horses, and Beckwith noted that Little Jeff's gait was so smooth he "could have threaded a needle" riding it. When Grant became president, the two horses were kept at the White House stables. Varina Davis replied to Bates' letter on September 19, thanking him for the picture. Her letter went on to describe the breed, "a cross of a noted Canadian racing pacer called Oliver, with several blooded American and English mares." Shortly after writing her letter Varina Davis became ill; she died on October 16.

Marquis de Chambrun, Charles Adolphe Pineton (1831–1891). Author of *Impressions of Lincoln and the Civil War: A Foreigner's Account* (trans. Adelbert de Chambrun [Random House, 1952]). De Chambrun was a personal friend of Senator CHARLES SUMNER, thanks to his friendship with Alexis de Tocqueville. He met Lincoln at a White House reception in February 1861, where he expressed his interest in "Northern victories [which] concerned in the highest degree all nations who enjoyed liberty, or who aspired to possess it."

Donn, Alfonso. Coachman and doorkeeper at the White House. Initially assigned to the White House as a Metropolitan Police guard, Donn was promoted to doorkeeper. On the night of the assassination, Donn spent the evening with TAD LINCOLN. In 1924 the family of Alfonso Donn put up for auction a frock coat which they asserted Lincoln had worn at Ford's Theater the night he was shot. The coat did not reach the minimum bid and was returned to the Donn heirs.

Douglas, Stephen Arnold (1813–1861). Democratic senator from Illinois and rival of Lincoln. Known as the "Little Giant" (he was only five feet, four inches tall). Instrumental in 1854 in the repeal of the Missouri Compromise (which had limited the expansion of slavery into the Territories) when he engineered legislation that allowed the states of Kansas and Nebraska to decide for themselves whether to permit slavery. Lincoln's decision to run against Douglas for the Senate in 1858 resulted in the famous Lincoln-Douglas debates. Douglas ran for president with the Democratic Party, though Southern delegates split from the party and nominated John C. Breckinridge. Contrary to custom, Douglas campaigned actively, pleading in the South for union more than for his own election. Ultimately over 87 percent of his votes came from free states; he received electoral votes only from Missouri and part of New Jersey. At the inaugural when Lincoln was about to speak and was looking about for a place to put his top hat, it was Senator Douglas who offered to hold it.

Douglass, Frederick (1817–1895). Abolitionist editor and speaker, formerly a slave. Author of *The Life and Times of Frederick Douglass*. In 1865, after hearing Lincoln's second Inaugural Address, he appeared at the post-inaugural reception at the White House. When two policemen tried to bar his entry on the basis that no blacks were allowed, Lincoln made sure that "my friend Douglass" was admitted, and Douglass passed through the receiving line without incident.

Eckert, Thomas Thompson (1825–1910). Major, U.S. Army, and Chief of the War Department telegraph office for the better part of the Civil War. Eckert's office was located in the old library room, immediately next to Secretary of War STANTON's office, the proximity a sign of the telegraph's importance in the prosecution of the war. Prior to the Hampton Roads Peace Conference in February 1865, Lincoln sent Eckert to meet with the Confederate commissioners. Eckert was one of several people who were invited by Lincoln to accompany him to Ford's Theater on the night of April 14, 1865. Stanton, however, said he couldn't spare Eckert, wishing to discourage the appearance of the President in such a crowded theater. In 1900, Eckert became chairman of the board of Western Union. It was in Eckert's office that Lincoln initially drafted the Emancipation Proclamation.

Ellsworth, Elmer Ephraim (1837–1861). Personal friend of Lincoln and the first commissioned officer to die in the Civil War. In 1861 Ellsworth organized the Fire Zouaves with volunteers among the New York firemen.

Everett, Edward (1794–1865). Famed orator and former president of Harvard, whose two-hour speech preceded Lincoln's two-minute address at Gettysburg on November 19, 1863. The day after the famed speeches, Everett wrote to the President, expressing his admiration for Lincoln's "simplicity & appropriateness, at the consecration of the cemetery." He said, "I should be glad, if I came as near to the central idea of the occasion, in two hours, as you did in two minutes." Lincoln replied, also on November 20, that "in our respective parts yesterday, you could not have been excused with a shorter address, nor I a long one. I am pleased to know that, in your judgment, the little I did say was not entirely a failure."

Fessenden, William Pitt (1806–1869). Elected senator from Maine in 1854. Appointed Secretary of the Treasury in 1864, replacing SALMON P. CHASE.

Field, Cyrus West (1819–1892). Having made a fortune in the paper business, Field, though not a scientist, devoted himself to the laying of a transatlantic cable. Field relied on the research of Matthew Fontaine Maury, an American oceanographer, who in 1850 had charted the ocean depths (the shallow region in the mid-Atlantic Maury termed the "Teleraphic Plateau"). Maury, a Virginian, became the head of coast, harbor, and river defenses for the CSA. Field went on to lose another fortune in building New York's elevated railways, and he died poor.

Frémont, John Charles (1813–1890). General, U.S. Army. A southerner of French origin, Frémont earned fame as the "Pathfinder" and played a strong role in securing California for the U.S. He ran for the presidency in 1856 as a Republican. He was appointed in July as commander in the Department of the West (i.e., Missouri), but very soon after lost credibility with Lincoln. Lord Charnwood in his biography of Lincoln describes Frémont as "one of those men who make brilliant and romantic figures in their earlier career, and later appear to have lost all solid qualities." Military ineptitude was compounded by Frémont's declaring martial law throughout Missouri in August of 1861 and threatening to court-martial and execute citizens found with arms in hand. Additionally he ordered confiscation of property and the freeing of slaves who belonged to enemies of the Union.

Grant, Ulysses Simpson (1822–1885). General-in-chief, U.S. Army, by the end of the Civil War. Grant grew up in Georgetown, Ohio, a "far-off western village" about fifty miles from Pittsburgh. In his *Personal Memoirs* (1886) Grant spoke of "the line between the Rebel and Union element in Georgetown" as so marked that even the churches expressed their division, some regularly preaching treason. He wrote that he "did not like to work; but did as much of it, while young, as grown men can be hired to do in these days, and attended school at the same time." In 1843 he graduated from West Point, even though the "military life had no charms for me." Mathematics came easily to him; not so French, where his standing was "very low," so low that "had the class been turned the other end foremost, [he] should have been near head." What he was devoted to, he confessed, were novels, not "the trashy sort," but those of Edward Bulwer-Lytton, Fenimore Cooper, Washington Irving, Thomas Marryat, Sir Walter Scott, and others. He fought in the Mexican War, serving with officers who afterward "became conspicuous in the rebellion," including "General Lee," who he knew "was mortal," he wrote, adding, "it was just as well that I felt this." In 1852 he was regimental quartermaster during the construction of the Panama railroad; a year later he was in the Oregon Territory along the lower Columbia where the Indians, "as far as the Cascades and on the lower Willamette, died off very fast" from measles and smallpox. A year later he was in San Francisco, and all the while his wife and two children remained in the East. He resigned his commission as of July 1854. When the war broke out, Grant was working in his father's leather-goods store in Galena, Illinois.

Grant's attitude toward secession is revealing: up to the ratification of the Constitution, the original thirteen states might withdraw from the "experiment," but thereafter any such right ceased. And certainly so for states like Florida or those west of the Mississippi, which were purchased thanks to "the treasury of the entire nation." Ultimately, Grant felt, "secession was illogical as well as impracticable"; not only that, "it was revolution." Grant admitted he "was no clerk," but army forms were familiar to him. Eventually he was commissioned colonel of the

21 Illinois Volunteers, and by August he was a brigadier general. In February 1862, Grant's capture of Forts Henry and Donelson gave the North its first major victory and brought Grant to Lincoln's attention. In July 1863, under Grant's command, Vicksburg on the lower Mississippi fell, and Lincoln wrote Grant a letter of thanks. Finally, in February 1864, Grant, bearing the revived rank of lieutenant general, became Lincoln's general-in-chief.

T. Harry Williams, whose *Lincoln and His Generals* (1952) is still widely read by historians, describes Grant as "the first of the great moderns." Comparing him with ROBERT E. LEE, Williams writes that Lee "looked to the past in war as the Confederacy did in spirit," whereas Grant understood that war "was becoming total and that the destruction of the enemy's economic resources was as effective and legitimate a form of warfare as the destruction of his armies." Put simply, Lee refused to view the war "for what it had become—a struggle between societies." Williams concludes: "What was realism to Grant was barbarism to Lee." (Small wonder Mary Todd Lincoln called Grant "the butcher.")

Following the war and his two terms as President, Grant settled in New York City. In 1881 Mark Twain urged him to write his memoirs, but Grant saw himself as out of the army, out of office, and out of favor. Then in 1884, the Wall Street investment firm in which his son, Ulysses, Jr., was a partner, collapsed. Grant had all his money in the firm, and now he was debt-ridden. No more than a few months later, he was suffering from cancer of the throat. He then agreed to write four articles on his Civil War experience for *Century Magazine,* which in turn led to the magazine's offer to publish his memoirs, if he would write them. Hearing of this, Twain, who had been the first to suggest to Grant that he write his story, rushed back from a lecture tour and told Grant that his small firm should be the publisher. Grant agreed, but instead of accepting the customary royalties, he accepted Twain's offer of 70% of the publisher's profits—should the book fail, Grant would have nothing. Were it to succeed, his wife, Julia Dent Grant, would be secure.

In spring of 1885, ten thousand subscription agents, clothed in their uniforms of Union blue, wearing whatever medals they had won, scoured the country, knocking on doors. Chords were struck, soldier to soldier. The memoirs were no ordinary book—General Grant was engaged in his final battle. Then the leather-bound subscription book would emerge, the pen, the small bottle of ink, and the soldier-at-home would sign his name, agreeing to pay one dollar now, and upon delivery of the two volumes, the balance of $2.50.

In 1885, less than a week after he had completed work on the proofs, Grant died at Mount McGregor in the Adirondacks. *Personal Memoirs* was issued posthumously. It sold 300,000 copies and earned $450,000 in royalties for his widow.

Gray, Asa (1810–1888). "The Father of American Botany" and Charles Darwin's earliest supporter in the U.S. Appointed botanist of the U.S. Exploring Expedition under CHARLES WILKES in 1836 but resigned in 1838 shortly before the expedition sailed. Later, as Professor of Botany, Gray was the first faculty member at the University of Michigan. From 1842 until his death he was Professor of Natural History at Harvard (though he retired from teaching in 1873).

Greeley, Horace (1811–1872). Editor of the *New York Tribune* during the presidency of Lincoln. A Republican, Greeley had strange notions regarding secession; sometimes he urged an all-out effort on the Union part, at others he perceived defeat and urged "peace with the Rebels at once and on their terms." In the summer of 1864, Greeley urged negotiation with Confederate agents across the border in Canada. Lincoln surprised Greeley by naming Greeley himself to meet with the agents if they had official credentials and would agree to "the restoration of the Union and the abandonment of slavery."

Hall, Asaph (1829–1907). Astronomer at the Naval Observatory in 1862. Hall was an acquaintance of Lincoln, who in 1864 commissioned him as Professor of Mathematics. In August 1877, using the observatory's 26-inch refracting telescope (at the time the largest of its kind in the world), Hall discovered the two moons of Mars. Hall had begun his search for a Martian satellite on August 10, working his way systematically inward to Mars' surface. By the 11th he was so close that the planetary glare interfered with observations, and he decided to give up the search. He went home and announced his decision to his wife, who replied, "Try it just one more night." He did, and saw a tiny moving object near Mars. The next evening clouds rolled in, and not till the 16th did Hall confirm that the faint object first seen on the 11th was traveling with the planet. On the next night he discovered a second satellite orbiting the planet. He named the two moons Phobos ("fear") and Deimos ("terror"), after the two sons of Ares, the Greek god of war. Phobos is only 15 miles in diameter, and Deimos half that.

Halleck, Henry W. (1815–1872). General, U.S. Army. Appointed general-in-chief in July 1862. Lord Charnworth wrote that Halleck was well qualified to "take a broad view of the war as a whole," but, as Lincoln soon found, "Halleck lacked energy of will"; and worse, "his judgment was not very good." JOHN HAY in his diary quotes Lincoln: "We appointed him [general-in-chief] & all went well enough until after Pope's defeat [at the second battle of Bull Run, August 30, 1862], when he broke down—nerve and pluck all gone—and has ever since evaded all possible responsibility—[his usefulness] little more since that of a first rate clerk" (entry of April 28, 1864). General GRANT remarked that "it was very much easier for him to refuse a favor than to grant one." When Grant was promoted to lieutenant general on March 1, 1864, he replaced Halleck in his role of general-in-chief. Halleck then became the army's chief of staff, but he refused to take any active responsibility for most military decisions.

Harding, Cyrus. Captain, U.S. Army. Fictional character (thanks to Jules Verne in *The Mysterious Island* [1875]).

Harlan, James (1820–1899). Republican senator from Iowa, later appointed Secretary of the Interior by Lincoln; father-in-law to ROBERT TODD LINCOLN.

Harlan, Mary Eunice (1846–1937). Daughter of Senator JAMES HARLAN; in 1865 escorted to the inaugural ball by ROBERT TODD LINCOLN and married to him in 1868.

Harris, Clara (1845–1883). Daughter of Senator Ira Harris from New York. With her fiancé, Major HENRY RATHBONE, she was in the presidential box at Ford's Theater on April 14, 1865. Major Rathbone proved unsound, shot his wife, and himself died in an asylum in 1911. Harris and Rathbone are the subject of Thomas Mallon's novel, *Henry and Clara* (Ticknor & Fields, 1994).

Hay, John Milton (1835–1905). Private secretary to President Lincoln and in later years Lincoln's biographer. Hay was Ambassador to the Court of St. James and Secretary of State under Presidents William McKinley and Theodore Roosevelt. Hay's diaries and letters are, in the words of Mark E. Neely, Jr., "a crucial source for the history of the Lincoln administration."

Henry, Joseph (1797–1878). Physicist, who was an early experimenter in electricity and an American parallel of Michael Faraday. Elected First Secretary of the newly established Smithsonian Institution, Henry communicated with scientists worldwide. He was interested in meteorology and thanks to the telegraph obtained weather reports from all over the nation. During the Civil War, Henry headed the nation's scientific mobilization, recommending the construction of ironclads.

Hunter, Robert M. T. (1809–1887). Speaker of the House, 1839–1841; senator from Virginia, 1847–1861. Hunter served as Secretary of State for the Confederacy, 1861–1862. His portrait was on the Confederate $10 note between 1861 and 1864.

Jackson, Thomas J. ("Stonewall") (1824–1863). General, CSA. Jackson graduated from West Point in 1846; served in the Mexican War; afterward was a professor at Virginia Military Institute. Jackson was a devout Presbyterian who thanked the Lord for his victories and viewed Yankees as the very devil. He earned his nickname in July 1861, at the first battle of Manassas (Bull Run). General Bernard Bee of South Carolina, rallying his men, shouted, "There is Jackson standing like a stone wall!" Whether he meant that Jackson was a model of fortitude or was angry that Jackson didn't move will never be known—Bee was killed not long after. But Jackson's brigade did stop the Union advance, and ever after he was known as "Stonewall."

Jackson's rule of strategy was "always mystify, mislead, and surprise the enemy," a rule which also seemed to apply to his own officers, who considered him crazy and called him "Old Tom Fool." Before long, however, it was clear he was crazy like a fox. In the Shenandoah Valley, operating with interior lines and having studied maps of the region, Jackson moved his small army swiftly from point to point, aided in part by his own genius, but also thanks to information from Confederate spies and from Valley residents. As James M. McPherson writes in *Battle Cry of Freedom,* it was "a war of people as well as armies."

At Chancellorsville in May 1863, with the Yankees on the run, the battle continued in one of the rare night actions of the war. Determined to press the attack, Jackson rode ahead of the Confederate lines to survey the field. As he was returning at a trot, his own men mistook Jackson and his officers for Union men and fired upon them. Jackson's left arm was struck with two bullets and had to be amputated. Eight days later Jackson died of pneumonia—his loss a major tragedy for the Confederacy.

Johnson, Andrew (1808–1875). Vice President during Lincoln's second term and twice governor of Tennessee. He was elected senator in 1857, and of all the senators from states that seceded, he was the only one to retain his seat.

Johnston, Joseph (1807–1891). General, CSA, often compared to ROBERT E. LEE. Johnston was the highest ranking U.S. Army officer to resign and join the Confederacy. After Braxton Bragg's defeat at Chattanooga,

Johnston took command of the Army of Tennessee and directed a delaying campaign against SHERMAN's advance on Atlanta. His continued withdrawals angered JEFFERSON DAVIS, who replaced him with General John Bell Hood after the fall of Atlanta. Bell's reckless tactics in Georgia and the Carolinas led the Confederate Congress to force Davis to reappoint Johnston. Johnston's hope was to link up with General Lee, but Lee surrendered before the plan could succeed. On April 26, 1865, Johnston surrendered to Sherman at Bennett Court House, North Carolina. After the war Johnston was elected to Congress and wrote his *Narrative of Military Operations,* which was highly critical of Davis. Johnston died of a cold caught while serving as pallbearer at the funeral of General Sherman.

Keckley, Elizabeth (1818?–1907). MARY TODD LINCOLN's dressmaker ("modiste") and confidante. Keckley was born a slave in Dinwiddie Courthouse, Virginia. Still a slave, she became a seamstress in St. Louis. In 1855 with $1200 supplied by her customers, she bought freedom for herself and her son, Alexander Kirkland. In 1860 she established herself in Washington, D.C., where VARINA DAVIS, among others, was her customer. When the Lincolns came to Washington, Mary Todd Lincoln too became her customer. In 1868 *Behind the Scene. Or, Thirty Years a Slave, and Four Years in the White House* was published; unfortunately for Mary Todd Lincoln it included extravagant letters from Mrs. Lincoln, published without her permission. It also described Mrs. Lincoln's extraordinary debts to cloth and clothing merchants in New York (over $27,000). (See entry for ALEXANDER STEWART.)

King, Preston (1806–1865). Republican senator from New York (1857–1863).

Lamon, Ward Hill (1828–1893). Lawyer and friend of Lincoln (who called him "Hill"), and occasionally his personal bodyguard. Appointed Marshall of the District of Columbia, April 1861. On election night, November 1, 1864, Lamon slept outside Lincoln's door, wrapped in blankets and armed with a brace of pistols and knives. On April 11, 1865, Lincoln sent Lamon to Richmond to investigate conditions for reconstruction, so he was not with Lincoln at Ford's Theater the night of the assassination (earlier he had chided Lincoln for going "unattended" to the theater with no one present who could defend against assault). Though a Republican, Lamon enforced the Fugitive Slave Act in the District of Columbia. In 1872 *The Life of Abraham Lincoln* appeared under Lamon's name, though it was written by a Democrat, Chauncey

Black; the book was an unflattering portrait, questioning Lincoln's piety. ROBERT TODD LINCOLN refused to read the book, and in 1883, as the Secretary of War, he blocked Lamon's appointment as Postmaster for Denver.

Lee, Elizabeth Blair (1818–1906). Daughter of FRANCIS PRESTON BLAIR. In 1843 Elizabeth Blair married Samuel Phillips Lee, and together they had one child, a son, Francis Preston Blair Lee (known as Blair), who many years later became the first popularly elected senator from Maryland.

Lee, Robert E. (1807–1870). Citizen of Virginia and General, CSA. The son of Lighthorse Harry Lee, a famed Revolutionary War hero, Lee graduated from West Point in 1829, second in his class. He served in the Mexican War and thereafter in various capacities (which included the command, with J. E. B. Stuart, of a company of U.S. Marines which put an end to John Brown's raid at Harper's Ferry in 1859). In April 1861 General Winfield Scott, a Virginian like Lee, urged Lincoln to offer the field command of the U.S. Army to Lee. On the very day Virginia seceded, Lee received the offer of the Union command. As he said to a northern friend, he must "side either with or against my section." His choice was perhaps inevitable: "I cannot raise my hand against my birthplace, my home, my children." This, despite his considering slavery "a moral and political evil."

At the Battle of Seven Pines in 1862, after serious injury to General JOE JOHNSTON, Lee took over command of the Army of Northern Virginia and succeeded in keeping General McCLELLAN from entering Richmond. Thereafter Lee's generalship became legendary, perhaps too much so. Wisely, he fought defensively, knowing that the South could never defeat the North with its vast resources. Yet if the South could hold out long enough, the North might grow sick of the war and call for an armistice. His decision to take the offensive led him to Gettysburg in July 1863, a defeat which could have cost him his army had not General Meade allowed him to slip back across the Potomac, to the consternation of President Lincoln. Once GRANT took command of the Army of the Potomac, Lee fought tenaciously against Grant's much larger force, culminating in the siege of Petersburg and the surrender at Appomattox.

Following his parole, Lee lived quietly, accepting the presidency of Washington College (now Washington and Lee). He died in 1870 of the heart disease that had plagued him for a dozen years. His application for restoration of citizenship was misplaced, and not until 1970 was it granted. (For an assessment of Lee's military philosophy, see the entry under GRANT.)

Lincoln, Mary Todd (1818–1882). Wife and then widow of Abraham Lincoln. In the pandemonium that followed the shooting of the President, Mary Todd Lincoln was heard to cry, "Oh, my God, and I have given my husband to die!"

The shock, of course, was extraordinary. Every room in the White House was laden with associations. Finally a small room for her use was found, and then began "the wails of a broken heart, the unearthly shrieks, the terrible convulsions," as ELIZABTEH KECKLEY described it. Mary Lincoln did not attend the funeral, nor did she leave the White House till May 23, at the precise hour that the veterans of the Army of the Potomac were marching by the reviewing stands on Pennsylvania Avenue.

Her destination was Chicago—Springfield was too rich in memories. With her went Tad, a boy of twelve and nearly illiterate (in a primer with a picture of an ape and the word "ape," even with his mother's hints, he read "monkey"). He also had speech problems, which in the years to follow were addressed with cruel (and fruitless) solutions.

Mary Lincoln was considered by some to be mentally unstable. When she was six her mother had died and her father had remarried. She didn't get along with her stepmother, and her marriage with Lincoln was reputedly stormy. Jean H. Baker, in *Mary Todd Lincoln, a Biography,* counters the contemporary diagnosis of instability with a current judgment of Mary Lincoln: she may have been "annoying, improper, and unnatural but dangerous neither to herself nor to society—and therefore not an instance of medical or legal insanity. She was always more bewildering than bewildered and more sickening (especially to her son [ROBERT LINCOLN]) than sick." If anything, Baker suggests, she suffered from narcissism, for which no one needs hospitalization. In Lincoln she had found someone to idolize, and then the man who gave meaning to her life was killed.

Lincoln died without a will, and the executor of the estate was Judge DAVID DAVIS, a massive man (weighing well over 300 pounds) and an old friend. He had been appointed to the Supreme Court by Lincoln, but was confined to bed for months at a time by a painful carbuncle. Besides, he was "slow"; or was it that he considered Mary Lincoln prodigal? Not until 1868 were the funds from Lincoln's estate distributed. In her words, she was "in a narrow place." In October 1868 she went to Europe, living in Frankfurt for two years. There, Tad attended school and was praised for his "progress," but never his "accomplishments." Mary Lincoln wrote letters and read books, discovering the spirit literature of Elizabeth Stuart Phelps—*The Gates Ajar,* a best-seller at home and abroad.

In 1870 Congress awarded her an annual pension of $3,000, which broadened her "narrow place" considerably. A year later she left Europe for New York City, but Tad was sick with what his mother called a cold but turned out to be pleurisy. He slept in a chair with a bar across his chest to keep him from falling to the floor. Eventually the water in his chest accumulated around his heart, and at the age of eighteen, Tad Lincoln died. Mary Lincoln divided her share of Tad's estate with her surviving son Robert, though she was entitled to two-thirds. "A squat figure in black crepe," she became "a recognizable eccentric in downtown Chicago," judged peculiar in her shopping habits, buying multiples of the same item, curtains, gloves, ribbon. She was estranged from her daughter-in-law, Mary Harlan Lincoln, Robert's wife, whose hidden secret was her alcoholism.

On the morning of May 19, 1875, she answered a knock at the door. It was Leonard Swett, a Chicago lawyer who had nominated Lincoln for the presidency. She was wanted at the courthouse, where a jury was waiting to judge her sanity; the charge was lunacy. She replied that she was fit to take care of herself, and asked where was her son Robert? Little did she know that Robert had sworn out the warrant for her arrest as a lunatic, "for her benefit and the safety of the community." It was Robert who had hired Pinkerton detectives to follow her. The man they had chosen as her counsel, Isaac Arnold, another old friend of Lincoln, had second thoughts, perhaps wanting nothing to do with the kangaroo court. But finally he agreed, though the testimony was rigged. Her shopping sprees were brought up; her migraines were mistaken for hallucinations; clerks argued that she drove down their prices. Late in the day came Robert's turn to testify: "I have no doubt my mother is insane. She has long been a source of great anxiety to me. She has no home and no reason to make these purchases." No witnesses were called for Mary Todd Lincoln. Ironically, her greatest extravagance had been on her son Robert's behalf, nearly $25,000. Her biographer Baker asks,

"If he [Robert] could squander money on real estate, why could she not buy curtains?" In a few minutes the all-male jury reached its decision: she was insane and should be confined in a state hospital.

She turned out to be a model patient, though she worked hard to smuggle out mail to obtain outside help. Robert was annoyed that she could be so rational. Fortunately, a friend, Myra Bradwell, came to her aid—both Bradwell and her husband were lawyers. (The link was not women's suffrage, but spiritualism.) Robert did his best to oppose her release, but he had been outmaneuvered, and his mother was again a free woman. Mary Lincoln took up residence with her sister Elizabeth, in Springfield, where she gave every evidence of sanity. In June 1876, in the same Chicago courthouse that had found her insane, she was declared "restored to reason and capable to manage and control her estate." By then her son was compiling what he named the "Insanity File," which included letters making demands he deemed unreasonable. The mother never forgave the son, and as Jean H. Baker writes, "so ended her life childless."

Mary Todd Lincoln spent the next several years quietly in Europe, in Pau, in southern France. Efforts by "Aunt Lizzie" failed to bring reconciliation, the son refusing to write the mother. By 1880 Mary Lincoln's health was failing. A cataract had formed in her right eye, and soon she would be nearly blind. A fall from a ladder injured her arthritic spine, so that now she complained of a broken back. It was time to return home, and she sailed from Le Havre on the *Amérique*, sharing passage with Sarah Bernhardt, who was on her way to her first American tour. According to Bernhardt, one morning "a wild billow dashed so violently against our boat that we were both thrown down." Mary Lincoln was in danger of sliding down a staircase, and the actress grabbed the widow's skirts. "You might have been killed," wrote Bernhardt in her memoirs, adding that the service she had done, she ought not to have done: "I had saved her from death," as though Mary Lincoln's tragic life were better cut short.

Living once more with her sister Lizzie, Mary Lincoln behaved normally. She visited spas, she petitioned Congress for an increase in her pension; and eventually she lived in a darkened room, her blindness nearly complete. On July 15, 1882, the anniversary of Tad's death, she collapsed. She had died of a stroke. Like her husband, she left no will, having destroyed several earlier ones. Two years later Robert inherited her estate and was richer by $84,035.™

Lincoln, Robert Todd (1843–1926). Eldest son of the Lincolns. After the death of his father, Robert T. Lincoln lived with his mother until shortly before his marriage to Mary Eunice Harlan in 1868. He found his mother a difficult woman, and embarrassing, especially when she tried to sell her clothing in 1867. He brought charges of insanity against her in 1875 and had her committed [see MARY TODD LINCOLN]. His mother thought he was after her money, but in that regard he was scrupulous.

He had three children: Jessie, Abraham ("Jack"), and Mary.

In 1881 he became Secretary of War to President Garfield. He was at the train station when Garfield was shot in Washington, spending his second night in a presidential deathwatch. He was heard to murmur, "How many hours of sorrow have I passed in this town?" He remained in office under President Arthur after Garfield's death. He resisted all calls for the presidency, which he termed "a gilded prison." In 1889 President Harrison appointed him minister to England, which office he held until 1893. After the death of his friend George Pullman in 1897, he became the temporary president of the Pullman Palace Car Company, and from 1901 to 1911 he served as its president. He retained control of his father's presidential papers, allowing only JOHN HAY and JOHN NICOLAY access to them, and reserving the right to approve their use. His papers he willed to the Library of Congress, stipulating that they not be opened until twenty-one years after his death. His wife was reclusive and probably an alcoholic.

Robert T. Lincoln enjoyed golf and amateur astronomy, as well as his summer home "Hildene," in Manchester, Vermont. He lived to attend the dedication of the Lincoln Memorial in Washington, D.C., in 1922. He died in his sleep at Hildene.

His son Jack died young, in 1890. His elder daughter Mary married Charles Bradley Isham in 1891; their son Lincoln Isham was born in 1892 and died in 1971 in Dorset, Vermont; he and his wife Leahalma Correa had no children. The younger daughter Jessie eloped with William Wallace Beckwith, an Iowa Wesleyan football player (the father disapproving of the daughter's choice). They had two children, Mary Lincoln Beckwith and Robert Lincoln Beckwith, before their divorce in 1907. In 1915 Jessie married Frank Edward Johnson, an explorer and geographer, a childless marriage that ended in divorce in 1925. The following year she married Robert J. Randolph, another childless marriage. Mary Lincoln Beckwith (1898–1975) never married. Robert Lincoln Beckwith was twice married, to Mrs Hazel Holland Wilson and to Annemarie Hoffman, but had no children with either wife. He died in 1985, the last living descendent of Abraham Lincoln and Mary Todd Lincoln.

Lincoln, Thomas ("Tad") (1853–1871). Youngest son of the Lincolns. [See MARY TODD LINCOLN.]

Lincoln, William ("Willie") Wallace (1850–1862). Third son of the Lincolns.

Lowe, Thaddeus Sobieski Constantine (1832–1913). Creator of the first air force in America; appointed chief of army aeronautics by Lincoln in 1861. Lowe made his first experiment with a kite bearing as passenger the family cat. He built his first balloon in 1858, and in 1859 constructed at Hoboken, New Jersey, *The City of New York,* intended for a trans-Atlantic flight. After a temporary failure, Lowe took his airship to Philadelphia, where it was renamed *Great Western.* Half an hour before the intended departure the balloon's envelope burst. Despite these failures, thanks to the support of JOSEPH HENRY, Secretary of the Smithsonian Institution, Lowe carried on. Henry recommended an initial test over land rather than water. Accordingly, Lowe sailed from Cincinnati in a smaller balloon named *Enterprise* on the morning of April 20, 1861. The prevailing winds carried *Enterprise* east and then south. Nine hours later he landed west of Unionville, South Carolina, having flown 900 to 1200 miles.

At the last moment Lowe had taken aboard the ship a sheaf of *Cincinnati Commercials,* the early morning edition, with the ink still wet. The timing was unfortunate: one week after the firing on Fort Sumter. Lowe, with his Abolition papers only nine hours old, was arrested and jailed. With the help of town citizens, including faculty members from South Carolina College, some of whom knew Joseph Henry, Lowe gained his freedom and eventually made his way back to the North. With the support of Henry and then President Lincoln, Lowe initiated the use of balloons for war service, which continued until late in 1863. By then the unpredictability of balloon flight, as well as the risks, was deemed to outweigh its utility. The Lowe Observatory in Pasadena, California, takes its name from Thaddeus Lowe.

Lyon, Nathaniel (1818–1861). Brigadier General, U.S. Army. Lyon graduated from West Point in 1841, and like many graduates of both North and South, fought in the Mexican War. In 1861 in Missouri, with a pro-Confederate governor, Claiborne F. Jackson, and a pro-Union legislature, Lyon became suspicious when Jackson called out the state militia.

Disguised as a farm woman, Lyon spied on the militia's camp, and, deciding the intent was to seize the federal arsenal, Lyon surrounded the camp with his own men and saved the arsenal—and perhaps Missouri as well. Jackson promptly declared for the Confederacy and called for outright insurrection. Lyon campaigned to drive Jackson from the state but was killed leading a charge at Wilson's Creek near Springfield.

McClellan, George Brinton (1826–1885). General, U.S. Army, and Democratic nominee for president in 1864. McClellan graduated second in his class from West Point in 1846 and served in the Mexican War the following year. In 1857 he became the chief engineer of the Illinois Central Railroad. The following year he met Lincoln. In 1858 he supported STEPHEN A. DOUGLAS for the Senate. After the Union defeat at Bull Run in 1861, upon the recommendations of Democrats and Republicans alike, Lincoln chose McClellan to replace Winfield Scott as general-in-chief. To his wife, McClellan said, "By some operation of magic, I seem to have become the power of the land." A famous episode recorded by Lincoln's secretary JOHN HAY in his diary (November 13, 1861) epitomizes the strained relationship between McClellan and Lincoln. Hay wrote:

> I wish here to record what I consider a portent of evil to come. The President, Governor SEWARD [Lincoln's Secretary of State], and I, went over to McClellan's house tonight. The servant at the door said the General was at the wedding of Col. Wheaton at General Buell's, and would soon return. We went in, and after we had waited about an hour, McC. came in and without paying any particular attention to the porter, who told him the President was waiting to see him, went up stairs, passing the room where the President and Secretary of State were seated. They waited about half-an-hour, and sent once more a servant to tell the General they were there, and the answer coolly came that the General had gone to bed.
>
> I merely record this unparalleled insolence of epaulettes without comment. . . .
>
> Coming home I spoke to the President about the matter, but he seemed not to have noticed it, specially, saying it was better at this time not to be making points of etiquette & personal dignity.

J. G. Randall in *Lincoln the President* [1946–1955] wonders "what refreshments were served . . . that night."

McClellan, who was the son of a successful Philadelphia doctor, had at best a low opinion of Lincoln, calling him "a rare bird" and later "the original Gorilla." Popular with his troops, McClellan was skilled at training his men but reluctant to take them into battle. War was bloody; soldiers died in battle. He was also given to over-estimating the forces opposing his. In October of 1862, after the battle of Antietam (where McClellan had accurate information about the size of Lee's army, thanks to a Union soldier's finding a set of Lee's orders), Lincoln urged McClellan to follow up on the victory, but McClellan wouldn't budge, complaining that he needed fresh horses. Lincoln's reply: "Will you pardon me for asking what the horses of your army have done since the battle of Antietam that fatigue anything?" Shortly after that Lincoln replaced McClellan with Ambrose Burnside, noting that McClellan had the "slows."

Ironically, McClellan's victory at Antietam (which he termed "complete") provided the momentum that Lincoln needed to issue the preliminary Emancipation Proclamation. While McClellan said nothing publicly, he wrote to his wife that he couldn't "make up his mind to fight for such a cursed doctrine as that of a servile insurrection." Yet despite Lincoln's fears, McClellan was a Unionist, viewing the alternative to suppressing the rebellion as "destruction of our nationality." In 1864 he ran as a Democrat for the presidency; Lincoln, convinced McClellan would win, could only hope that the war could be won before he took office. Otherwise peace would come without union. Precisely what McClellan would have done is unclear. ALEXANDER STEPHENS viewed the Democratic platform as "the first ray of light since the war began"; GEORGE TEMPLETON STRONG in his diaries saw it as "surrender and abasement." But following SHERMAN's capture of Atlanta, the question was moot. McClellan carried only his home state of New Jersey, plus Delaware and Kentucky.

On election day McClellan resigned his commission; from 1878 to 1881 he served as the Democratic governor of New Jersey.

McCullough, Lt. Colonel William (1811–1862). Friend of Lincoln and formerly the clerk of the McLean County Circuit Court in Bloomington, Illinois. In spite of poor vision and the loss of his right arm, he enlisted and was elected Lieutenant Colonel of the Fourth Illinois Cavalry. In December 1862, after McCullough was killed near Coffeeville, Mississippi, Lincoln wrote to his daughter Fanny McCullough, having heard that her sanity was threatened. Lincoln's letter was short and moving:

> It is with deep grief that I learn of the death of your kind and brave Father; and especially, that it is affecting your young heart beyond what is common in such cases. In this sad world of ours, sorrow comes to all; and, to the young, it comes with bitterest agony, because it takes them unawares. The older have learned to ever expect it. I am anxious to afford some alleviation of your present distress. Perfect relief is not possible, except with time. You can not now realize that you will ever feel better. Is not this so? And yet it is a mistake. You are sure to be happy again. To know this, which is certainly true, will make you some less miserable now. I have had experience enough to know what I say; and you need only to believe it, to feel better at once. The memory of your dear Father, instead of an agony, will be a sad sweet feeling in your heart, of a purer, and holier sort than you have known before.
>
> Please present my kind regards to your afflicted mother.
> Your sincere friend
> A. Lincoln.

Medill, Joseph Meharry (1823–1899). Editor of the *Chicago Tribune* and an early Republican and supporter of Lincoln for the presidency. Medill served as mayor of Chicago after the great fire of 1871.

Meigs, Montgomery C. (1816–1892). Graduated from West Point in 1836, entered the army's engineering corps. He oversaw the construction of the wings and dome of the national Capitol. In June 1861, Meigs was appointed Quartermaster General, U.S. Army, and was responsible for procurement and care of supplies. Secretary of State WILLIAM SEWARD said that without Meigs' service the "national cause might have been lost or deeply imperiled."

Mesmer, Franz Anton (1733–1815). Austrian physician and hypnotist whose name gave rise to the word "mesmerism."

Möbius, August Ferdinand (1790–1868). German mathematician and astronomer. In 1844 Möbius was appointed director of the Leipzig Observatory. A founder of the branch of mathematics known as topology, he gave his name to the Möbius strip.

Morgan, Edwin Denison (1811–1883). Republican governor and later senator from New York. Lincoln offered Morgan the position of Secretary of the Treasury in March 1865, but Morgan refused. (See entry under BROWNING.)

Nasby, Petroleum V. Pseudonym for David Ross Locke (1833–1888), journalist, author of satirical sketches, and one of Lincoln's favorite humorists. Nasby's letters supposedly came from a pastor of the New Dispensation whose sympathies were with the "Copperheads" (northerners who sympathized with the South). Nasby settled in "Confedrit X Roads," Kentucky, representing a northern view of southern Negro-hating ignorance.

Nicolay, John George (1832–1901). Like JOHN HAY, private secretary to President Lincoln and later Lincoln's biographer (with John Hay as co-author).

Offutt, Denton (ca. 1803/1807–ca. 1860). In 1831 Offutt hired Lincoln, along with John D. Johnston and John Hanks, to deliver a load of produce by flatboat from Beardstown, Illinois, to New Orleans. After the successful journey, Offutt put Lincoln in charge of a store and mill in New Salem. Lincoln biographer Benjamin P. Thomas calls Offutt "the discoverer of Lincoln." For more information on Offutt and Lincoln's New Salem days, see Benjamin P. Thomas, *Lincoln's New Salem* (1954, 1982).

Porter, David Dixon (1813–1891). Commissioned Lieutenant, U.S. Navy, 1841; ultimately rose to the rank of admiral. Porter served on the *Mississippi*; in 1864 he took command of the North Atlantic Blockading Squadron, replacing Samuel Phillips Lee, the husband of ELIZABETH BLAIR LEE.

Rathbone, Henry Riggs (1837–1911). Major in the Union army and fiancé of CLARA HARRIS (his stepsister). He and his fiancée were in the presidential box at Ford's Theater on April 14, 1865.

Seward, William Henry (1801–1872). Lincoln's Secretary of State and formerly governor of New York, 1838–1842. Seward had been the Republican frontrunner for the nomination in 1860. He was an important and optimistic advisor in many regards, not just foreign policy. On the night of April 14, 1865, several days after his return from the Hampton Roads Peace Conference, Seward lay in bed at his home in a full body cast, recovering from a carriage accident. There was a knock at the door, and JOHN WILKES BOOTH's accomplice, Lewis Thornton Powell, burst into the Seward house. Seward was seriously injured; his cast, blunting the blows of Powell's knife, may have saved his life.

Sheridan, Philip H. (1831–1888). General, U.S. Army. Graduated from West Point in 1853 and eventually found his niche as a cavalry officer after a year as a quartermaster captain; thereafter he was worth his "weight in gold"—an apt remark, given his small stature. When Lincoln finally met Sheridan at City Point in 1865, Lincoln said (as DAVID BATES reported), "I thought a cavalryman should be at least six feet four high; I have changed my mind—five feet four will do in a pinch," thereby robbing Sheridan of half an inch. Time after time Phil Sheridan's tenacity in battle had averted disaster and won victories—at Stone's River, in the Shenandoah Valley, and finally at Appomattox. After Jubal Early's unopposed cavalry raid in July 1864 to the outskirts of Washington and as far north as Chambersburg, Pennsylvania, GRANT put Sheridan at the head of the recently formed Army of the Shenandoah, instructing him to go after Early "and follow him to the death." On September 19, at the third battle of Winchester, Sheridan finally met the outnumbered Early and soundly defeated him. He then took on the Shenandoah Valley, a vital source of supply for the Army of Virginia. Grant's orders called for Sheridan to reduce the Valley to a "barren waste . . . so that crows flying over it for the balance of the season will have to carry their provender with them." This Sheridan did, burning barns by the thousand, destroying farm implements, killing stock. "The people must be left nothing," he said, "but their eyes to weep with over the war."

In October, while Sheridan was in Washington to confer on strategy, Early gathered up his forces for a surprise attack at Cedar Creek. The Union forces fell back in a panic that extended to the entire Army of the Shenandoah. But it was only ten in the morning, and Sheridan was on his way. In *Battle Cry of Freedom* (1988), James M. McPherson eloquently describes this "most notable personal battlefield leadership in the war": "Puzzled at breakfast [at Winchester] by the ominous rumbling of artillery off to the south, [Sheridan] saddled up and began his ride into legend. As Sheridan approached the battlefield, stragglers recognized him and began to cheer. 'God damn you, don't cheer me!' he shouted at them. 'If you love your country, come up to the front! . . . There's lots of fight in you men yet! Come up, god damn you! Come up!' By dozens and then hundreds they followed him." By afternoon Sheridan had reorganized his army and counterattacked, and Early's "victory" turned to disaster. Five months later, at Five Forks, shortly before LEE's surrender, Sheridan's men, now fighting on foot, achieved the most one-sided victory in a year—Sheridan "storming up and down the line cajoling and god-damning the infantry to move faster and hit harder" (McPherson). The stunning victory of Five Forks precipitated Grant's broad attack along the line which in turn led to the end of the war in Virginia.

After the war Sheridan headed the reconstruction governments of Texas and Louisiana but was dismissed within half a year for severity. In 1884 he was named the army's commander-in-chief, like Grant and SHERMAN before him. He also worked hard for the creation of Yellowstone Park, an act so opposite to his decimation of the Shenandoah Valley.

Sherman, William Tecumseh (1820–1891). General, U.S. Army. Sherman graduated from West Point in 1840, ranking sixth in his class. Like so many other Civil War generals, he served in the Mexican War, resigning his commission in 1853. In 1859 he became the superintendent of a military academy in Louisiana (presently Louisiana State University), but upon the secession of the state, he moved to St. Louis, where he was the head of a streetcar company. Once war broke out, he volunteered for the Union army. Eventually he served in the west under GRANT and soon became the commander that Grant "could not spare" (James M. McPherson, *Battle Cry of Freedom* [1988]).

Ultimately, Sherman and Grant were the two generals who applied the strategy that Lincoln had been urging since 1861, which (as T. Harry Williams writes in *Lincoln and His Generals* [1952]) was "to hammer continuously at the armies and resources of the enemy at every possible point." In the spring of 1864, with Grant now promoted to general-in-chief, Sherman took command of the western armies. From his base in Chattanooga, Sherman launched his famed march through Georgia against the Confederate army led by JOSEPH JOHNSTON, a campaign of feints and maneuvers with relatively little direct battle. The fall of Atlanta early in September was not only a major Union victory, but it doomed the hopes of General GEORGE MCCLELLAN to defeat Lincoln in his bid for reelection. By Christmas Savannah had fallen. Shortly after the surrender of ROBERT E. LEE at Appomattox, Sherman had received and replied to a request for a peaceful surrender from General Johnston. On his way to Greensborough, Sherman learned by telegraph of the assassination of President Lincoln. Swearing the telegraph operator to secrecy for fear of violent retribution from his army, Sherman then met privately with Johnston and told him of Lincoln's murder. "The perspiration came out in large drops on Johnston's forehead," wrote Sherman. Johnston called it a disgrace to his age. Sherman then assured him it was no doing of men like himself or General Lee, though he couldn't be sure of "Jefferson Davis and men of that stripe." In a few days the whole of Johnston's army peacefully laid down their arms.

Following the war, Sherman remained in the service, replacing Grant as commander-in-chief. Not until 1884 did he retire from the army. Throughout, Sherman was steadfast in refusing to become involved politically. Hence his famous words, "I will not accept if nominated, and will not serve if elected."

Singleton, James W. (1811–1892). General, U.S. Army. (See entry under BROWNING.)

Spalding, Margarita. Fictitious companion of MARY TODD LINCOLN.

Stanton, Edwin McMasters (1814–1869). Lincoln's Secretary of War, replacing Simon Cameron. A Democrat, Stanton had served as Attorney General in JAMES BUCHANAN's Cabinet during the last months of his administration, urging Buchanan not to surrender Fort Sumter. Initially, he considered Lincoln ill-suited to lead the North; yet as the war progressed his opinion changed. A pragmatist, he established order in the War Department. When Lincoln announced to the Cabinet his intention to issue a Proclamation of Emancipation, Stanton alone urged him to issue it at once. Because Stanton's charge was the management of the war, Lincoln worked more closely with Stanton than with any other member of the Cabinet. Stanton was also responsible for internal security, and after the assassination of the President, he led efforts to capture the killers. ROBERT TODD LINCOLN recalled that "for more than ten days after my father's death in Washington, [Stanton] called every morning on me in my room, and spent the first few minutes of his visits weeping without saying a word."

The short and famous sentence,"Now he belongs to the ages," spoken after Lincoln's last dying breath at William Petersen's home across the street from Ford's Theater, was uttered by Edwin Stanton.

Stephens, Alexander Hamilton (1812–1883). Vice President of the CSA. Stephens and Lincoln were both Whig members of the Thirtieth Congress (1847–1849), and both were outspoken in opposition to the Mexican War of 1847. Perhaps the sole fruit of the Hampton Roads Peace Conference (February 1865) was Lincoln's arranging the exchange of Stephens' nephew, Lieutenant John A. Stephens, from prison at Johnson's Island on Lake Erie for an "officer of the same rank, imprisoned at Richmond, whose physical condition most urgently requires his release" (Lincoln to the Honorable A. H. Stephens, February 10, 1865).

Stewart, Alexander (1835–1911). New York's most renowned dry-goods and clothing merchant. In a single day MARY TODD LINCOLN ordered $2,000 worth of rugs and curtains from Stewart. His emporium at Broadway and Chambers Street, according to Henry James, was "fatal to feminine nerves." To pacify Stewart regarding her unpaid bills, Mary Todd Lincoln went on to order a black camel's hair shawl for $1,000. As Jean H. Baker, her biographer, says, "the more Mary Lincoln owed, the more she had to buy in order (or so she believed) to prevent her informal loans being called."

Strong, George Templeton (1820–1875). New York lawyer who was instrumental in establishing the Sanitary Commission, forerunner to the Red Cross. Strong was also an early supporter of the ideas of Charles Darwin. His diaries provide a rich picture of the Civil War era in the North.

Sumner, Charles (1811–1874). Senator from Massachusetts during the Civil War, opposed to slavery. In 1856 Preston Brooks, congressman from South Carolina, entered the Senate and viciously attacked Sumner with his cane, a moment some called the first blow of the war.

Taney, Roger Brooke (1777–1864). Chief Justice of the U.S. Supreme Court (1836–1864), famed for his decision in Dred Scott v. Sandford (1857). He freed his own slaves in 1818, yet he felt that slavery was necessary so long as Negroes were in the U.S. Shortly after Lincoln's inauguration he told ex-President Franklin Pierce that "a peaceful separation, with free institutions in each section, is far better than the union of all the present states under a military government & a reign of terror—preceded too by a civil war with all its horrors, and which end as it may will prove ruinous to the victors as well as the vanquished." At Taney's death GEORGE TEMPLETON STRONG wrote succinctly, "Better late than never."

Vallandigham, Clement Laird (1820–1871). Ohio Democratic politician and famous opponent of Lincoln. In April 1863, Vallandigham, given his outspoken sympathy for the South, was arrested by General Ambrose Burnside as a traitor. Upon conviction, at Lincoln's suggestion, he was banished to the Confederacy.

Welles, Gideon (1802–1878). Lincoln's Secretary of the Navy. Only Welles and WILLIAM SEWARD were members of Lincoln's Cabinet for his entire term of office. Hence Welles' diary is an invaluable source of information, covering such topics as the genesis of the Emancipation Proclamation.

Wilkes, Charles (1798–1877). Son of John Deponthieu Wilkes, who emigrated to the U.S. during the Revolutionary War; great-nephew of John Wilkes, radical English politician and reformer. Commander of the U.S. Exploring Expedition, 1838–1842. In September 1861 as Captain of the U.S.S. *San Jacinto,* Wilkes removed Confederate commissioners James Mason and Charles Slidell from the *Trent,* a British mail packet, and thereby was briefly celebrated as a hero in the U.S. (Mason and Slidell had been on their way to Europe to press for recognition for the CSA.) War with England loomed on the horizon, but thanks to the collective wisdom of both Lincoln and Prince Albert, each subduing the tempers on his side of the ocean, the *Trent* affair fizzled out. In 1864 Wilkes was suspended from the navy for three years for insubordination and disobedience. In December 1864, Lincoln reduced the suspension to one year. From June 1863 Wilkes lived in Washington, D.C., and was not unknown to Lincoln. Charles Wilkes was also a distant cousin to JOHN WILKES BOOTH (both claiming descent from the famous 18th-century English radical John Wilkes), a relationship, after April 1865, that he must not have relished. There is no mention of John Wilkes Booth in Charles Wilkes' massive autobiography, finally published in 1978 by the Naval Historical Center.

Zeppelin, Ferdinand, Count (1838–1917). Having received a military education, Zeppelin served in the U.S. as observer of the Northern Army of the Potomac. While in the U.S., at St. Paul, Minnesota, he ascended in a balloon for the first time. At the close of his military service in the German army in 1891, he devoted his time and money to aeronautical experiment, conceiving the idea of confining the balloon within a cigar-shaped aluminum structure. On July 2, 1900, one of Zeppelin's vessels first took to the air. The dirigible ("directable") balloon was, in common speech, a "zeppelin."

Acknowledgments

OOLIGAN PRESS takes its name from a Native American word for the common smelt or candlefish, a source of wealth for millennia on the Northwest Coast and origin of the word "Oregon." Ooligan is a general trade press rooted in the rich literary life of Portland and the Pacific Northwest. Founded in 2001, it is also a teaching press in the Department of English at Portland State University. Besides publishing books that honor the cultural and natural diversity of the region, it is dedicated to teaching the art and craft of publishing. The press is staffed by students pursuing master's degrees in an apprenticeship program under the guidance of a core faculty of publishing professionals. By publishing real books in real markets, students combine theory with practice; the press and the classroom become one.

The following Portland State University students helped to edit, design, and market *Abraham Lincoln, a Novel Life.* Meg Storey served as senior project editor.

Bernadette Baker

Michael Bales

Leticia Barajas

Robert Barnett

David Benjamin

Brad Bond

Yvonne Buchanan

Maggie Casper

Pat Coleman

Tamera Curtis

Clarice Dankers

Beth Dillon

Ruth Elison

Tineke Ferris

Christopher Gniewosz

Michelle Hanley

Krystin Hawkins

Pat Heuser

Kim Hildenbrand

Janice Hussein

Deborah Jayne

Kenny Jones

Raquel Kern
Thomas Dean Lake
Kiersten Lawson
Peggy Lindquist
Petra Lundin
Michele Madore
Joseph Marx
Wes Miller
Alice Mitchell
Ryan Mitchell
Lynn Molter
Monaca Noble
Elizabeth Pagano
Amy Paul
Amy Peabody
Julie Pero
Kharim Poorman
Heather Reyes

Mary Ellen Haugh Rubick
Hilary Russell
Srinivasan Sampath
David Santen
Eric Sears
Adrianna Sloan
Brenda Smith
Megan Stark
Meg Storey
Summer Steele
Krista Venn
Kristina Wells
Julia Wexler
Lindsey Walter
Jamie Walton
Lamont Wilkins
Michelle Williams
Robyn Saunders Wilson

Author's Acknowledgments

I am grateful to my parents who gave a boy a book or two; to my teachers, in particular Carl Cochran and Lowell Innes; to colleagues (I'll name a few: Les Whipp, Shelley Reece, Kurt Kremer, and Carol Franks); to Virginia Kidd, whose faith in my little books sustained me; to Dennis Stovall, Karen Kirtley, and Susan Applegate of Ooligan Press; to the partner, Lindy Delf, an honest reader; to my daughter Jessica Wolk-Stanley for her illustrations; to the Truthful Duo; and to Libby Solomon, who one Friday morning said, "I have a surprise," which turned out to be the catapult that launched this book into daylight.

TONY WOLK
Portland, Oregon
December 2003